I0745315

BLADE
OF MAD
VISION

Titles By Danith McPherson

<u>Cassie Windom Mysteries</u>
Averted Vision
Not Her First Murder

<u>Speculative Fiction</u>
Monarch of Lightning
Lightning World Book One

Blade of Mad Vision

Roar at the Universe

BLADE OF MAD VISION

DANITH MCPHERSON

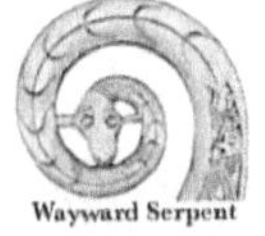

Wayward Serpent

This is a work of fiction. Names, characters, places, events, and dialogue are either the products of the author's imagination or used in a fictitious manner. Any resemblance to actual people, living or dead, or to actual events or dialogue is purely coincidental.

BLADE OF MAD VISION

Printed in the United States of America

Wayward Serpent first edition, April 2021

ISBN 978-1-950506-04-0 (print paperback)

ISBN 978-1-950506-07-1 (ebook)

Library of Congress Control Number 2021934641

Published by Wayward Serpent, Farwell

Up to no good but means well

For Matt and Aaron, the fencers in my life

CHAPTER I

The figure clothed in silver and white seemed to gaze past the dusty hard-packed dirt bordered by rocks toward the hazy mountains, but the vacant blue eyes saw only a distant nothing. Legs bent in perfect form, it moved silently. Advance and retreat, advance and retreat, the steps were precise and predictable. Advance. The gloved hand propelled the bright streak of a weapon into an attack.

Austin Swiftbrooke wielded his foil against it just as automatically. Parry, remise, parry-riposte. His sparring partner was a beginner's toy he had long outgrown, incapable of mimicking complex exchanges. He lunged and flicked his blade. The bright persona, like a reverse shadow, provided no resistance. Austin skewered a place in the air where a human heart would be, more irritated than pleased by the tinkling notes indicating he had scored a point. A pretend point in a pretend fencing bout with a pretend fencer.

He should head home. The planet Callister's soft sun would be low behind the mountains soon, washing the arena in dusk. The arena. His sister Skylar had called it that from the beginning. She and Austin had found the spot soon after moving to the remote planet. Skylar was a pudgy nine-year-old then, black hair always loose and chaotic. At twelve years old Austin was pale, skinny and impatient for a growth spurt he hoped would give him the long legs and arms he envied in other fencers.

Two stone jumbles, one at the north end of the oval and one at the south, formed crude archways. Wind, weather and time had shaped the natural rock, giving the illusion that the structures were intentional. The siblings had marched through them like champions. They'd saluted an imaginary crowd with their weapons then crossed blades to silent cheers. Although shorter, younger and less experienced, Skylar had a quick wrist and was fearless. Unlike the practice dummy, she had a flare for surprises and always gave her brother a good fight. Back then, the arena was their playground, a canvas for their dreams, a place where anything could happen.

Unblinking, the projection halted while the sequence reset. The young face glowed in the early dusk, yellow hair brushed to the side, blue eyes eternally fixed on somewhere else. As a joke Skylar had reprogrammed the dummy's image to look like Austin. She thought it was funny that he had to fence himself every time he used it. Austin didn't find it humorous. Not then. Definitely not now. Blank-faced and empty-eyed, the white-clad figure reflected too closely how he felt. Numb and without a future. He should switch it back to a generic avatar. He'd told himself that many times, but he hadn't even tried to get around his sister's security lock.

Austin twisted the control on the grip of his foil, cutting the weapon's power. The slim, elegant piece of engineering deserved a better opponent.

Moving through the light form, like passing through his own ghost, he picked up the capsule that cast it and switched it off. The figure dissolve around him. Why did he even bothered to keep up his skills? It was ridiculous. He only did it for the routine. The discipline. The old obsession that had become little more than a distraction. He prepared for something that wasn't going to happen. He would never leave Callister—not for a fencing tournament, not for anything. He wouldn't. He couldn't. He would grow old here. He would die here. He was here forever.

Dusk stretched out to him from the mountains as the sun sunk behind them. Taking his time, he stored his foil and the capsule in his pack. He knew his parents wouldn't scold him for being late. Two years of worrying and wondering about Skylar. Two years of trying to sustain hope. That's a long time. There wasn't much energy left for anything else. Certainly not for their son.

Austin leaned against the north arch, feeling the day's warmth radiating from it. He glanced around the graying arena, wishing, as he always did, that his sister would jump out from nowhere and shout *en garde*. He'd found her bag right here in the dust, as if she'd set it down a second ago; as if at any moment she would scoop it up, laugh at him for being so grumpy and challenge him to a race home.

He pushed himself away from the stone. Shouldering his pack, he turned away from the arena and headed for the path. Stupid to think there was anything special here. It was rocks and dirt, nothing more. Yet it had somehow taken his sister.

Barely an orange glow skimmed the sky as Callister's sun slid away for the night. Shadows lengthened across the abandoned oval of the arena and merged into darkness.

A blast of light, fractured as if reflected by a smashed mirror, filled the gap in the northern structure of weathered rocks. The glowing spider web crackled like shattering crystal and spit out a small figure. He staggered and collapsed, shedding water droplets. In the fresh darkness they plopped unseen into the dust. Slowly, shakily, he pushed himself to his knees. He stood, wide-legged for balance, and peered at the bit of landscape visible in the glare from the gap that had ejected him. He nodded with satisfaction, then he panicked. A damp breeze swept in from the place he had just left. Through the frame of the stone arch, thunder shattered the air. Blinding bursts flared across the sky. The storm still rolled loud and bright in that other world, but the rain that had provided safety no longer fell in heavy streaks.

The beasts could now follow. They must not enter here.

He sprinted away, seeking distance from the storm roaring in its stone frame. In response, the strobe vanished, leaving the soft sound of insects. Dry air whisked moisture from cloth and skin. Groping his way in the darkness, the figure stumbled against a ring of rocks. He slipped among them and settled into an uncomfortable crevice. He shivered, hoping sunrise would be soon.

CHAPTER 2

Far from Callister, the young artist Cabrill knelt on the rocky floor of Tarafalla, moon valley, a gash in the planet Saffrian. Obsessed with her task, she barely felt the jagged surface bruise her skin. Out of thin white bark stripped from a tree that grew miles away, she sliced a crescent, using a sharp flint shard. She made another, a mirror image of the first. Then she carved a large wedge.

Fissures hissed out hot gasses. Captured in hollows, liquid minerals glistened like slick pearls. Ashen light muted their jeweled hues to luminous grays. The girl knew the truth of their brilliant colors and worked from memory. She dipped a twig into amber and stroked it across the crescents. Her other sharpened sticks pierced jade, cinnabar, and indigo pools. She didn't know why she worked by the weak light. Somehow it was necessary for the art. The moon, round as a sea-washed pebble—so slight she could hold her arm at full length and cover it with her thumb—was part of the creation, part of the whole, as important to discovery as the mineral paint and the husk.

The barren stone basin reeked with whispered secrets. Sharp, acrid air smelled like lightning and held little that was breathable. Most living things avoided the poisonous stench. Some who had ventured in and stayed too long were now bones curled beside putrid ponds. She could not, would not, look at them, especially the ones of a human shape.

She felt the power that twisted upward through granite and shale, escaping from the planet's soul. Artists came to this place to inhale that energy and exhale its life into their work. The surrounding rocks glistened with their paintings. Some were the girl's own, made with silk-point brushes instead of the broken sticks collected on the journey here that she used now. The crudeness of the materials intensified the making. They were right. They were perfect. This was strong art, forceful art, that frightened her to her bones, but she could not stop. She would not stop. Never again. Never.

With indigo, she sketched a figure of a boy near her own age onto the dappled wedge. He stared with intense eyes, strained and determined. She had never met him, but her pack bulged with sheaves scarred by his image. Even when she set her mind to draw something else, the lines converged into his features. Often the landscape behind him was angular and stark, as alien to her as the clothing that hugged his body. Sometimes he was in local dress, backed by scenery she knew or knew of.

Always there was the sword of a style unknown on this planet. She stroked it into his hand. The metallic blue-gray shown leaden in the murky light. She waved a hand over the bark, encouraging the liquid mineral to dry. She creased the stiff skin back and forth, back and forth, folding the wedge into a fan. *My hands should be shaking,* she thought. But they were steady and precise.

The boy was not the only strange presence to invade her

work. On one of the crescents she sketched the dark-haired girl, pale in faded amber. In ebon and cinnabar, she stroked her own face onto the second, feeling that her art was true and her mind was sound. Using strands of her own long, black hair, she lashed casing and twigs together. She curved the twin crescents away from each other like the moon in partial phase reflected off polished rock. She lashed the fan between them, creases framing fingers of muted light.

Change had happened, was about to happen, was happening now. She raised the sculpture toward the lunar glow. In the gaseous heat she froze. She stood as a radiant statue in a deadly valley, rich air rising around her. She was more than creator; she was entwined within the twigs and bark. She was inside the change.

It was wrong to remain still when the world was shifting. She thrust her arms forward and released the painted structure, setting it free. In the pale hollow, steamy gases propelled it upward. It soared across whispering plumes, circling in quick swoops and slow glides. She pivoted to keep it in her sight.

The winged silhouette rose, as if detaching itself from its maker. In the uncertain light it seemed to duplicate itself. Two sculptures crossed the sky. The figures swirled and bobbed, reflections of one another. She heard the screech of a matac, a carrion bird, a meat hunter. Her art had been joined by a living creature.

The matac broke the pattern. Sharp beak extended, it dove at the fragile bark wings. She cried out at the inevitable destruction. Amazingly the sculpture slid to the side, as if at her warning. The bird missed its prey and shrieked in anger.

The structure spun, its crescents tilting as if alive. It climbed then plummeted toward the raptor, shearing a feather. The two creatures circled and dove in a frenzy. She watched the dangerous aerial dance, beautiful in its menace. They forced one another higher and higher in attacks and escapes, rising beyond her earth-bound vision. She stared at the sky, moonlight making her blind to the battle in the darkness. She waited, dazed from air strong with the valley's power.

A long primal screech crashed against the surrounding mountains and echoed into the distance. She could not tell if it was a wail of defeat or a shout of triumph.

CHAPTER 3

T he newly hatched Primbull Star caterpillars wriggled as if excited to be free of the cramped egg sac they had shared. They quickly sensed a familiar odor and hunted down runny globs dotting their transparent cage. Different in texture from the thick nurturing fluid they'd nestled in during incubation, it still smelled like food. Not that they were fussy. They furiously nudged one another aside to slurp up the puddles.

Appetite temporarily satisfied, one tucked in its head (or tail), curled its tail (or head) around itself and spun off through the bits of shredded leaves and the sudden explosion of feces. Black ridges along its yellow body acted like tire treads. It hit the container's vertical wall and flopped over. Undaunted, it straightened out and squirmed up the slick neo-glass, leaving a trail of sticky excretion. When it reached the junction with the cover, it continued the journey upside down, barely noticing the switch in gravity. Halfway across the lid it bumped into a mass of siblings traveling together from the opposite direction. Without pausing or turning around, it reversed course and became the leader of the flock.

Austin adjusted the vista-cam surrounding the specimen tank in the alcove of his room to remove a ripple in the three hundred and sixty degree recording of the hatchlings' movements. He hoped the fat crawlies would provide sufficient data for his report on Communal Habits of Primbull Star Caterpillars. Unfortunately, the adventurous one, who had discovered the rolling technique before its sac-mates, had already messed up the typical pattern. He hoped the rebellious youngster wouldn't ruin his graphs and charts.

He needed at least two hours of video before he could start tagging his subjects and mapping their movements. "Hey, the *Malacasoma callistrium* hatched," he said to the house memo board. "I'm out getting some exercise while they generate data for me. See you later." Planetary catalogers, his parents were off doing field work—in a real field—documenting the flora and fauna on a square of grassland. They'd probably never get the message. He was almost positive he'd return before they did.

He secured the house—not that there was any threat to secure it against—and walked toward the storage huts. Water trickled through the pebbly creek that snaked beside the path. Its high-pitched tinkling was a constant complaint about the dry air that kept it thin. The huts were tan half-bubbles against the rusty bark of massive, deep-rooted trees, leafless in their dormant stage this time of year. An error on the shipping manifest for the research complex had resulted in the second, bonus dome. Austin and Skylar had taken advantage of the mistake. Lines painted on the hardened foam floor defined a fencing strip. They had often used the space when bad weather kept them indoors, away from the arena.

Austin changed into his white fencing uniform. The torso

of the long-sleeved, padded jacket shimmered with silvery sensor threads that defined the target zone. He pulled on knickers, followed by socks to his knees. He shoved his feet into the almost indestructible, thick-soled shoes. The insulated high-tops protected him against a shock from a malfunctioning electrified blade. He tucked the similarly made glove into his pack. The only item he didn't bother with was the protective mask.

Wearing the formal clothing for practice had been Skylar's idea. Since they lived on a minor world, they were going to outgrow everything before they got a chance to wear them out in competition anyway, she had reasoned. They might as well get as much use out of them as they could. Not that catching a commercial ship to one of the heavily populated planets was impossible. They used to take family trips to tournaments. But that was before—when they were still a family. Austin continued to order new items as the old ones grew tight and short, even though he hadn't been off-planet in two years. He tucking the medallion he always wore inside the jacket, grabbed his pack and headed out.

The arena always seemed the same. Each brief rainy season scraped the area clean with flash floods. Each long dry season baked it tougher. The craggy rocks defining the oval stoically withstood the extremes, as if it were their duty to witness the passing of time. Austin's steps in the hardened dirt coughed up miniature dust swirls. He was hypersensitive here. The sameness was an illusion. A change had happened in this place. He held his bag by a strap, pulled out his foil then rummaged for the projection capsule. In the soft light he imagined one of the stones moved.

After Skye disappeared his parents declared the arena off limits. Austin couldn't pretend it didn't exist, that he and his sister hadn't spent most of their free time here, together. He never snuck away, exactly. He just often found himself in the oval almost by accident. Then his visits became as regular alone as they had been in Skye's company.

Already knowing the answer, his mom and dad never asked where he was during his absences. As time passed and they drifted further away into their own schedules, he wished they *would* ask so he could say he was where Skylar had been, so he could say his sister's name out loud in front of them. He would do so gently, hoping it would shatter the shell around them and let the pain out. But they never asked.

"Good afternoon, young sir," a stone said.

Austin jerked, popping his pack into the air. He fumbled to grab it but instead punched the bottom of the long, fabric bag, propelling the contents into flight. Arms seemingly disconnected from his brain, he tried to catch a glove and a towel and a water bottle. Each one, on a trajectory of its own, eluded him. He realized a talking stone, even a polite one, might be a threat. He forgot everything else and snatched up his foil from where it had plopped to the ground. Not as brave as he hoped he appeared, he pointed it toward the movement.

A small figure gracefully scrambled over the jumbled rocks to the smooth earth. It boldly approached Austin, unimpressed by the weapon. "Greetings I give to you from the many and significant relations of my family and also, most humbly, from myself as their ambassador." The adult voice sang with rich, bass notes. Keen, dark brown eyes met Austin's stare. Bristly white hair, little more than fuzz, topped the handsomely weathered face.

Austin didn't recognize the short-statured man. He wasn't with any of the research projects, and he certainly didn't dress like a local. His loose shirt and pants were of rough fabric but elegant in a way. Or maybe it was the cape and the man's broad-shoulders that gave a polished flair. A tourist? That seemed unlikely to impossible. Whoever he was, what was he doing way out here?

"Forgive my lack of extended courtesy, but my mission is significant and of timely consequence. Danger prowls the land, baring burning teeth and a-glitter with ember eyes." The man took a step closer, almost to the tip of the blade. "Is it so that you are Lord Austin of the Fast-flowing Water?" he asked as if conducting a friendly interrogation.

"What?" Austin was stuck on the gross image of burning teeth.

"If you are he, the Lady of the Zenith has need of your weapon and skill. She requires immediate action. She implores that you have speed. And action. Speed and action."

The stranger's statements seemed to be rehearsed lines combined with improvisation. Despite talk of danger and teeth, he didn't appear to be a threat. Austin put down his foil where he could still quickly grab it. "Who are you?" Embarrassed by his failed juggling act, he retrieved the things that had escaped his bag. He pulled on his glove and slid the projection capsule into a shoe so he wouldn't have to search for it later. The rest he stuffed back into his pack.

The man gave a low bow. "Grant me pardon that I do not announce my full ancestry. I will say simply with an impolite leap to privacy that I am Ko Lian Po, honored by the earned title of Master Translator. I am the lowest servant, by choice, of the Most High Lady. The Lady serves words, and so I am pleased to serve the Lady." He looked at Austin as if expecting an intelligent reply or some move to action. And speed. To speed and action.

Austin sorted through the cascade of words. There'd been something about fast flowing water. Flowing water, like a stream or a river or a brook. Fast, like quick or rapid. Or swift. Swift brook. Swiftbrooke, his last name!

Ko Lian Po watched him intently. "You are wise to be cautious, as I must be, as well. There can be no substitute. The Lady has given me a secret code, and you must respond appropriately. If you cannot, then you are not the champion of the Lady of the Great Azure Dome that I seek."

A cold tingle started in Austin's stomach and shivered through his body, raising the hairs on the back of his neck. This Ko Lian Po knew his name. And he was talking about another person, a female, who had something to do with the "great azure dome" and the "zenith." Both references to the sky.

Austin whispered, barely able to breathe. "Is this lady called Skylar? My sister Skylar?"

"Ahh, Skylar. A star, a song, a name to save and savor." Ko Lian Po seemed delighted that Austin was finally catching on. "This is how you will know that I truly come from her, and your answer is how I will truly know that you are Lord Austin of the Surging River." He took a stance, as if to strike Austin down if he gave the wrong reply. "I am to say to you—"

"No codes!" Austin snatched up his weapon and aimed it at the unexpected stranger with the three-part name. He couldn't be a messenger from Skylar. An extensive search had found nothing except an abandoned bag still holding his sister's fencing gear, and a few shoe prints the wind hadn't swept away. A scan of the entire planet had produced no trace of her bio-signature. She simply wasn't anywhere on Callister. This was a nasty, evil joke or a cruel scam.

Ko Lian Po ignored the metal shaft and stared up at Austin. "The Lady is in need of your assistance, *if* you are the sworder I seek. You are to provide the next word in this sequence." Very slowly he said, "Attack, parry-riposte, counter-riposte."

It was a standard series of moves describing an exchange between two fencers. Anyone would finish the sequence with remise, the action that would earn a point. That is, any fencer except Skylar or Austin.

The last competition the Swiftbrooke siblings participated in before moving to Callister was at an overly ornate complex on Metcalf's Haven that prided itself on having an authentic Earth theme. The mirrored lobby featured water plunging from fifty-two stories above into a huge crystal bowl. An engraved sign proclaimed it was a replica of a famous North American waterfall.

Surrounding the translucent basin, a marble moat calmly rippled with gliding ducks, swans, and geese. The genuine Earth waterfowl appeared bored with the subdued lighting and constant soft music of their insulated, comfortable lives on a foreign planet. One of the Mallards decided to act on his long-dormant, wild urges, and go on an adventure. Having lived in a building all his life, it didn't occur to him to charge through the air-pressure barrier separating the refined interior from the grimy city outside. Instead, he wove through flowered corridors. Startled by an equally shocked guest, he flew through an open doorway, soaring straight into the grand ballroom.

The brightly-lit cavernous space, marked off into multiple fencing strips, echoed with the organized chaos of simultaneous matches. Blades scraped blades. Buzzers announced the successful contact of foil tips against sensor-threaded jackets. Referees shouted instructions and awarded points. Eleven-year-old Austin was losing yet determined to beat his taller, more experienced opponent. The other boy initiated an attack with his long reach. Austin blocked it in a parry then pulled off his own attack, performing a riposte. The boy deflected Austin's foil and struck out with a counter-riposte.

Disoriented by the sudden harsh lights and sharp sounds, the duck hurtled through the room like a winged, green-headed bomb. Surprised fencers dodged and scrambled out of its way. Positioned so she could watch her brother get skewered by his opponent, eight-year-old Skylar suddenly saw the male Anas platyrhynchos speeding straight toward him. Austin had already started the forward momentum of a low lunge that would produce a perfect remise.

Skylar shouted a warning.

When your parents are biological catalogers, you would never say "duck."

<hr>

Now in the arena on Callister, Austin lowered his weapon. "Attack, parry-riposte, counter-riposte, *drake*." Drake, the term for a male duck. He and Skylar had reenacted the moment many times, always ending by laughing so hard they could barely stand. The word became their shorthand for the unexpected, for the crazy-weird you couldn't possibly predict. Skye's disappearance—drake to its core—had turned the meaning tragic.

Ko Lian Po grinned. "Excellent! The Lady described the event. Most amusing."

Austin could tell he didn't understand the story. But he knew it. Someone had told it to him. Austin hoped with his whole being that someone was Skylar. His satphone was in his bag amid his scrambled gear. He wanted to contact his parents immediately, but he needed to be sure. They were already battered and weary from a possibility here and a speculation there. Another failed lead would crush them. "Where is Skylar?"

Po twisted his lined face. "The where is significant. I believe I can explain the situation sufficiently. It concerns this." He grasped a cord around his neck and pulled it free from his woven shirt. A half circle of burnished gray dangled from it. The silky string looped through a sliced-out crescent that curved around a raised half sphere. Etchings swirled across the surface like vines growing through the metal.

Austin put a palm to his chest, pressing his own pendant against his heart. "That's Skylar's. Why didn't you just show it to me instead of asking me a riddle?"

"You might believe I had stolen it from the Azure Lady and was untruthful saying she had given it to me. You have a—an" —Po shook the cord— "one of these, as well."

Austin opened his jacket to show his own. The skewed parallelogram scored with angular symbols held a raised wavy strip flanked by cutouts of the same design. He and Skylar had discovered the unusual wafers during an early exploration of the arena. They looked modern, more like trinkets from a flash fad that had been left behind by surveyors than artifacts with historical value. Unable to pierce the strange metal, Skye had looped a cord through an existing cutout in each one, turning them into jewelry. She'd declared them welcome gifts from their new home.

"With all due responsibility and respect, I should like to examine—it." Po stamped his foot in the dirt. "I am embarrassed I cannot summon the word. You must think me a poor translator from a lesser family."

Austin hesitated then removed the ornament. He held it out for Po's inspection, cord firmly laced through his fingers. It was too precious to release to a stranger. "It's called a necklace." He had some sympathy for the man. Having lived on several planets where multiple languages were spoken, he had often struggled for the right word.

Ko Lian Po poked at the tilted rectangle. "Necklace. No. Not appropriate in this context." He strode to the southern arch and ran his hand over the stones, digging his fingers into one particular section. Then he stalked back to Austin. "You show the correct appearance, although I have no comparison on this world so I cannot say if your face, form, and costume are unique to you. I am persuaded that you know the drake, and I see you have the article. I accept that you are Lord Austin, sibling to the Lady Skylar, and the one I seek. Now we must go."

Austin followed as Po marched to the northern arch. "To find Skylar, right? We have to get my parents. And do we need help? Against the burning teeth?"

Master Po gently swung Skylar's necklace near a stone support. "*You* are the help required." The curved pendant eagerly danced toward the structure. Po slowly moved closer. The metal quivered and gently turned as if alive. With a soft clank it settled on its own into a depression that matched its shape.

Shattered white flashes crackled and hissed across the space between the stacked stones. Austin staggered back and raised a shielding arm against the sudden brightness. Creased and folded light pulsed violently then subsided into warm colors. Instead of the flat, arid ground of the arena, through the gap he saw soft grasses rippled by a lazy wind. He smelled a recent rain and new flowers. For a moment, the scene seemed like a vision of paradise.

Smoky knots rose up from among the waving stalks, as if awakened by the webbed strobes. Their growing bulks flattened the jade grass. Eyes like amber flames, they stared at Austin for only a blink. Then they sprang into the arena.

CHAPTER 4

Sunlight had cleared the horizon by the time Cabrill woke to its warmth. The night before she had climbed the jagged slope out of Tarafalla Valley by moon glow. Dizzy from the foul air, she had struggled high enough to take deep breaths of sweet wind from the west. Too exhausted to make a proper camp, she had wrapped herself in a cloak and curled up on a gritty ledge. She must have been dreaming about food. She could almost smell bread and cider.

"I've finished my breakfast," said a melodic voice. "You can have what's left."

Still groggy, Cabrill squinted at the fresh light. She pushed herself up to sit cross-legged, aware that her sword was more than an arm's length away. She recognized the voice, which increased her irritation at her own carelessness. "Mikol, it's been some time."

"You're the one who keeps slipping away." He handed her a doughy roll and a cup. "I can sympathize. I've been doing some hiding myself lately. The Guild wants to give me an appointment to Lady Tren Ne Seine's estate. Our honorable mentor Forliani is furious with me for going journeying instead. But then, that's her nature, as we both well know."

Cabrill sniffed the sweet-sour drink. She would not be reckless. Her throat was sore and her stomach growled for food, but she had endured thirst and hunger before. She detected no poison. No other cup was in sight. This was Mikol's own and should be safe. She took a sip. "I'm sure you declined gracefully. And I don't slip away. I simply have other places to be." She was not going to explain her actions to Mikol Wilsheem, especially if he was here to kill her.

Four years her senior, he had grown lean and towering. His long braids of midnight blue hair were gathered rakishly at the nape of his neck. He had nut-brown skin, handsome features and a flair for trouble. He slid his slate-gray eyes toward her in a sideways glance. "Are you still crazy?"

"Perhaps." He'd probably expected a definite yes or no. Let him think she was undecided about her own sanity.

He gave Cabrill's evasion a crooked smile. "I'm surprised the Guild hasn't scooped you up and carried you off to Seaba by force. Actually, there's a rumor that you *are* at the colony. That you'd gone there like a good little artist as you'd been told."

"They don't think I'm dangerous." Cabrill shoved bread into her mouth to cover the lie. She *had* obediently started the journey to Mount Wieldeld until the truth literally slammed into her. And agents of the Guild *had* come after her. Sometimes silently in darkness, sometimes shrewdly in daylight. Five times over the past years they had tracked her down. The first ones had meant to capture her, but the last had been an assassin. Her skill with a sword and her determination had kept her alive and free.

Curious. The Guild wanted her found, yet the marketplaces were not clogged with watchful apprentices. The search for her was a quiet one. Mikol lived on the fringe, more by his wits than commissions from his art. He preferred that whispered world and navigated it well. If he was not hunting her, he at least knew she was being hunted by others. "Why are you here at Tarafalla?" Cabrill asked. Perhaps he had not been sent to kill her, but to capture her in another manner than by force. Either way, he was more clever than the others. Was he the solitary shadow who appeared in the background of her drawings?

Her pack rested beside her sword. She was certain he'd pawed through it, examining the sheaves and sheaves of bark and parchment by firelight while she slept. Most of them were monochrome charcoals, sealed with chamapl milk to prevent smearing. The ones from last night, created before the bird sculpture, danced with the bright, natural paints provided by the valley. What did he see when he looked at her art? Who would he report to about the boy and the girl in her drawings?

Mikol prodded the fire, unnecessary now that the food was cooked and a rising sun warmed the ledge. "I'm here for my art, of course. Why else would anyone come to this stinking, desolate place, so far from a bath and a decent meal?"

How long have you been here? Cabrill wanted to ask. *Were you on a high crag last night standing beside the sand-colored moon? Did you watch two birds in savage battle? Did you hear the screech?*

Did you see which warrior won?

CHAPTER 5

Formed of smoke and air, six beasts prowled toward Austin and Master Ko Lian Po. Smoldering clouds set with burning eyes, they stalked like wolves. Behind them a patch of gentle, sunny meadow glowed like a portrait of paradise, contrasting sharply with the arid arena. The largest gray bulk tossed its head, as if signaling its companions. While the rest of the pack skulked to the left and the right, it boldly took a step toward its prey.

Ko Lian Po shouted. Austin didn't know the language, but he understood the panicked warning. Not that he needed it. The ghostly creatures seemed straight from a nightmare. He aimed his foil at the leader. The blade was meant for sport rather than actual defense. He usually kept it on a flexible setting. Deciding he might need more pressure, he thumbed the control to the most rigid position. The end was not a sharp point but a sensor, designed to send an electrical pulse to a scoring receiver when it struck an opponent's metallic jacket. Still, it was strong and could leave a bruise. He knew that from experience.

Forcefully he jabbed between the target's eyes, hoping a quick poke would encourage it to back away. The blade met no resistance, causing only a small dark wisp to swirl from the intangible body. Unharmed, the leader paused, as if judging the boy and his weapon. Its companions snarled from their flanking positions.

Ko Lian Po frantically tugged Austin backward. He sputtered in several different languages now, none of them English. Austin let the man guide him while he continued to threaten the main beast with his useless foil. How do you fight clumps of fog? The bright eyes came closer. The smoky wolf howled with a hot wind. Austin stumbled in terror and felt a hard pellet press against his ankle. He still clutched the medallion in his left hand. He had to let go, but he couldn't just drop it. Without taking his eyes off the beast, he shoved the necklace behind him at Ko Lian Po. "Take this." He felt the cord slide away. Hand now free, he crouched and shoved probing fingers into his high-top. The cool, slippery projection capsule slid away from his touch, burrowing deeper into his shoe. His head was dangerously at the same level as the terrifying eyes. He dug a finger under the cylinder, coaxing it against his thumb, and eased it into his palm.

He rose quickly. The beast raked a paw at him, blasting him with chocking heat. He squeezed the capsule and tossed it behind the dusky animal.

A white-clad image of Austin sprang up like a luminous ghost called to battle demons. The startled followers rushed from their strategic positions and swarmed around it. Their bodies grew thicker, more solid as they snarled, snapped and clawed at the specter saluting them with its foil. Ignoring the attackers, the false Austin extended his weapon and began a sequence of moves.

The leader twisted to see the spectacle. Austin scurried

backward as fast as Po could guide him. They must almost be at the south arch. A few steps beyond that, stones blocked them in. The path home was in the other direction, past the monsters. He couldn't outrun them, even if there was a place to run to, which there wasn't.

The leader was not fooled by the fake threat. Its ember eyes, definitely a-glitter as Po had warned, returned to the real Austin. It angrily churned like boiling ash, as if an insult had been given and a challenge had been slapped down at its feet. Austin knew it would charge. He knew it. There was no escape route, and he could think of no way to protect himself and the man in the cape.

A brilliant light flashed behind Austin, strobing his shadow before him, huge and menacing. Crackling and hissing filled the air, like wet marbles tossed into a sizzling pan. A blast of moisture pressed against his back. He didn't dare turn to look.

The beast didn't flinch at the light and the noise. It crouched then launched itself at Austin. In flight its swirling bulk grew to a dense mass. Instinctively Austin pierced it with his weapon. The beast passed through the silvery blade like a storm cloud. Its scorching paws slammed into Austin like a desert wind, knocked him off his feet. Hot, sulfur breath seared his face as he fell. He stared at hooked teeth that burned with an inner fire.

A cold geyser erupted around Austin. He crashed onto his back. The impact punched the breath out of him. Heavy, foul smelling liquid closed over his face, smothering him. He was suddenly shivering and submerged.

CHAPTER 6

Tarafalla Valley bubbled and hissed. From a ledge above it, Cabrill watched vapors rise and whorl then vanish. The rock slab under her trembled as if a sleeping giant beneath it stirred from a bad dream. Tremors were frequent here, where the restless land cracked and split, spilling its treasures. She should have left an hour ago, but she lingered over the last of the cider, like the soft light of autumn in her cup. Her eyes and throat still ached. At this elevation it took effort to pull the thin air deep into her sore lungs and expel last night's poison.

Mikol sat near her with his back against the mountain. He pierced seeds with a fine needle and eased them onto fishing line strung on a small loom, turning them into beads. Pale yellow, green, blue, black. Slowly the pattern formed.

Cabrill tried not to be lulled by the precise, rhythmic movements. "It's the same as your bracelet."

Mikol had skill with bronze. The cuff circling his wrist was etched with five ovals. Smaller circles thick with runes separated them. Pointed arcs of twisted braids bordered the curved figures, joining them with intricate filigree. The design was beautiful in burnished russet but more striking in the brilliant seeds.

"I'm not satisfied with the metal. The design seems to require color." Mikol poked through the kernels spread out on a bit of cloth for just the right one. "If I had a wealthy sponsor, I would use gold and gemstones. Fortunately, nature provides for those of us who choose to be independent."

Cabrill hid her irritation at his attempt to link the two of them together. *We are the same,* Mikol seemed to be saying, *kindred spirits who have freed ourselves of the controlling Guild.* She saw little of either choice or independence in her current circumstance. And he could pretend he'd removed himself from the influence of the union, but he'd never convince her he'd given up its protection and privileges.

Not that he hadn't experienced consequences for whatever his latest act of rebellion had been. Cabrill judged his lack of funds was somewhat recent. His shirt and trousers were of expertly woven cloth and had been tailored just for him, but the once bright hues were muted from harsh river washings. The fine, soft leather of his calf-length coat and tall boots had not been brushed in a while and were thick with the dust and grime of travel. It appeared the generous patron who had paid for the bronze circling his wrist was lost to him now. He was at the end of his purse. Had he bartered her life or her imprisonment in Seaba Colony for the position in Lady Tren Ne Seine's household he'd supposedly declined?

Cabrill's own shirt and loose pants were worn and mended. It had been a long time since she'd had coin for more than food and the expenses of her quest. She watched Mikol slowly duplicate the pattern on the bronze into the weaving, one seed at a time. "It reminds me of a merchant's mark, or a lord's, but more complex. Maybe it's the emblem of an alliance." She should stay quiet, but she missed being in the company of other artists, and talking about his art would reveal nothing of her own.

Mikol shrugged, but there was a tightness in what should have been an easy movement. "It's probably no more than a good luck trinket to sell at market."

"If that be, you would have created it once and been done with it. Since you felt compelled to repeat it and you came here to do so, it must be more." Cabrill resisted leaning forward to examine the details. That would put her too close to the slate eyes and slow smile. The circle of people she trusted had gotten very small, and he wasn't in it.

Mikol skewered a seed then halted as a tremor rippled under them. "It amuses me, nothing more. I came here for another project."

Despite his denial, Cabrill could see the prediction he crafted carried an importance. What that was, she had no right to say. Had he truly traveled to the remote valley to seek clarification of another design? If so, it seemed Tarafalla had no interest in what he wanted from it and had given him something else. Or more likely, he lied and had received the exact inspiration he was after. Perhaps she was too suspicious, thinking he was here because of her. He'd fed her filling biscuits and tartly sweet cider. She should stop worrying about the long reach to her sword and enjoy the rhythm of another artist's work.

Mikol coaxed a speck of grain into place. "I heard Lord Kriken broke with the Guild and illegally employed you. He's supposed to have you secreted away in Wasbiln Manor."

Cabrill emptied her cup slowly and calmed her suddenly pounding heart. "Did you hear it said, or did you see it—in your art?" It had been in her own. A ring of kidnappers, swords drawn, surrounding a dark-haired girl. The solitary watcher that invaded many of her sketches was there among the trees. She and her traveling companion, the friend who had saved her from Seaba, had evaded the soldiers for weeks. The time and energy it took had crippled Cabrill's ability to produce serious work.

"I heard a bit, snooped a bit, speculated a bit," Mikol said.

"Your information seems more specific than a bit here and a bit there."

Mikol shrugged. "I was in Rassaca. A farmer was asking about if anyone had seen his wayward dark-haired niece. That is, he was dressed as a farmer. He moved like a soldier. So did the others who were with him but pretended they weren't. A flash of a black and crimson tunic peeked out from one of their packs. Seemed to me Kriken had sent his agents to quietly, perhaps forcefully, offer you a shadow contract in his household. Later I heard you'd accepted."

Black and crimson just happen to peek out? With help from Mikol's nimble fingers no doubt. She suspected he'd twisted the story. Not that it mattered. He knew where she was rumored to be and that she wasn't there. The deception she had worked out would not hold for long. It might have already crumbled. "Obviously I am here and not at Wasbiln any more than I am at Seaba."

"Obviously."

Cabrill gathered her belongings. "Thank you for the meal and the company." She could not ask him if he'd watched the battle in the sky last night, if he'd witnessed the matac's screech. She could not ask if he knew that one of the warriors was not a natural bird but a creation of her hands and mind. That it flew by its own will.

Mikol gave a nod, elegant as a formal bow. "It was entirely my pleasure."

The ledge vibrated with the valley's unrest. Cabrill picked

up her sword last, keeping it in her hand rather than sliding it into the sheath on her belt. Fighting the tremors, she staggered to the path that wound over the mountain. It took strength not to turn around, not to check if he crept toward her to strike at her back, either to kidnap her for Kriken or assassinate her for the Guild. She listened for the crunch of gravel beneath worn boots. Only birdsong and a rustling breeze followed her. For the moment.

CHAPTER 7

Austin stared at churning gray and pulled in a sharp, terrified breath. He blinked, realizing he had been looking at the same thing for some time without being devoured. The shape wasn't really wolfish, more like an evil penguin or a scary sock puppet. Towering twisted branches draped with long jade scarves of filmy moss surrounded the dark patch. He realized he peered upward at storm clouds high overhead, not a smoke-beast standing on his chest. Slimy liquid surrounded him. His face barely cleared the murky stuff. He pushed himself up. His elbows sunk into inches of soft muck before finding enough support for his efforts to sit up. "Those things—"

Ko Lian Po's voice came from nearby. "Cannot tolerate water."

The air was rich with moisture, growth, and decay. Austin stood, shedding streams. His white and silver uniform hung soggy with brown and green patches. A fibrous tan growth clung to him like mutant cotton candy. The pattern reminded him of jungle camouflage. He coughed heavily and spat out foul water. "Yuk!"

"A swear word!" Ko Lian Po stood knee-deep in swamp. He wrung a waterfall from the hem of his shirt. "Not one the Great Lady of Words has taught me. Perhaps later you can explain the meaning. I could have used it while dragging you into shallow depths so you could again take in air."

"Please, just call my sister Skylar or Skye."

"Your sister also preferred a leap to informality. Since it is the custom of your people, I will conform. With no disrespect to the great family of Ko and the great family of Lian or to my earned position of master translator, you may address me as Po."

Austin wanted to wipe slime from his face, but his hands and sleeves were covered in stuff just as bad or worse. A soft clean towel was in his pack. But that was at the arena, and he was obviously somewhere else. "What happened?" His foil. Where was his foil? He scanned the swampy ground and thick foliage. Relieved, he spotted it safely in the crook of a tree, his dripping glove draped beside it. A sooty smudge and various earthy goos marred the metal.

"We are on the grand and beautiful world of Saffrian, made more splendid by the presence of your marvelous sister. Unfortunately, the crude beasts prevented us from entering into the serene meadow, as the Lady Skylar had when she arrived. We were forced to go through the other——." He rubbed his bristly hair in frustration. "Your sister Skylar has tried numerous English terms but none has satisfied her. In many languages we call it a *stiav*. You might think of it as a gateway, although it is far more complex than a simple entry from one place to another. It is fortunate you had the——" Po struggled as he had on Callister, still unable to find the appropriate word. "Charm, perhaps?"

Austin shook himself, producing an aura of soaring droplets. "We ended up here because I have a great personality?"

"Not charm-ing. Charm. Charm that is a physical object." Po held up the tilted parallelogram.

Austin grasped his medallion eagerly. It felt warmer than usual. He had often examined the cutouts and traced his fingers over the circular grooves, wondering if they meant something. He'd imagined the piece to be sheared from a larger sheet or to be part of a lost machine. Now he viewed it differently. There were legends about rifts that instantly transported you to other worlds. He'd read theoretical research explaining how they might exist. He never thought he'd actually travel through one! And his medallion had opened it, or activated it, or something like that. "So this is a key."

"Key!" Po said. "That is the exact word that escaped me. Your sister Skylar's *key* awoke one of the gateways, and your *key* awoke the other. It is unusual for two devices to be so close together." He paused for a moment, flustered. "No. I must correct the inaccuracy. It is *perhaps* unusual. Or perhaps it is not. No one would really know. Certainly not I, since there are no records from before the Separation."

Austin didn't know what the Separation was. Right now he didn't care. There were no stone formations here, no stones at all. The landscape was all trees, moss, ferny things, algae, and muddy water that rippled in an eerie way. The smoke-monster that came through with them was gone, but four more of the dangerous creatures were still on Callister, near his home and not far from the collection of shops that served as a town.

Po waded, thigh-deep in the water, and solemnly examined the trunks of two trees. They grew straight up for about seven feet then twisted together in a spire that soared at least another twenty.

"So that's this side of the wormhole or whatever it is we came through." Austin thrust his medallion at it. There were no lights, not even a spark. "How do I open it?"

"A key can function from one direction only. Two are needed to go both this way and that way." Po wiggled his fingers back and forth to illustrate. "To enter your world, I used a key gained on my own. To return through the same gateway, I have your sister Skylar's key. I did not anticipate we would be required to use another route. I apologize for my lack of preparedness for this scenario."

"We have to go back! I'll try Skylar's necklace." He held out his hand, expecting Po to give it to him. They'd found nothing else at the arena. Nothing that might unlock an opening from this side. If they had, his sister probably would have turned it into a brooch.

Po remained still. "I am of most certainty that it will not perform as you wish it to."

Austin shook his head. "Our medallions were both hidden near the arches. Maybe this key is close by too." He thrashed at some ferns, found a stick and poked at a mound of thick moss.

Po waded to Austin and put a hand on his arm to stop him. "If it's here at all, which it is most probably not, we will never find it. Nor should we search for it, since it is not ours to take." He lowered his voice. "The folk who dwell in this place do not share with strangers. Even with my considerable skills, I would never be able to secure the second key for this gateway."

Austin had to make Po understand. "Those creatures are still back there. They'll attack people—my mom and dad!"

"Do not fear for those on your Callister," Po said. "The pendants are here with us, far from the stone doorways they control. The road between the two worlds is gone." He made a slicing motion. "Severed. The beasts did not return while they had the bright opportunity. Their substances do not continue without it. They exist no longer."

"When the connection broke, it killed them? They died?" Austin was relieved he only had to think about what was happening on one world at a time.

Po nervously scanned the algae adorned water. "Died is not appropriate in this context, but it is sufficient since I do not have a more accurate word."

Austin tossed away the stick, not understanding Po's cringe as it splashed. He grabbed his foil. The familiar grip gave him some comfort. He drained water from his glove and held it by a damp finger. "Where are we? How do we get to my sister?" Po had the key that would take them home. That is, Austin hoped he still did. He worried it had fallen out of a pocket on Callister or here with all this water. "Are we stuck here?"

Po took his cape from the branch where he had draped it to dry. The limp fabric dripped discouragingly. "All good questions that I will answer in order: in a swamp where we are not invited guests and our impoliteness has been noticed; we will travel to your sister, although it is a considerably longer journey from here than it would have been if those beasts had not prevented us from passing through the other gateway; and mired but not stuck." Po folded the cape over an arm. "Since you are revived, we no longer have an acceptable reason to remain here. I suggest you carry your blade in a tranquil manner." He turned and sloshed away.

Austin followed, slogging through knee-deep, foul-smelling water. He glanced around warily, wondering who or what was keeping track of acceptable and unacceptable reasons for the presence of uninvited guests. His shoes squished into muck with each step. Insects, which he was sure meant him no good, buzzed at his face. Did Master Po really know where he was going, or had he picked a direction at random?

Overhead, gray clouds rolled into swells. Rain pelted down in angry drops. Lightning cracked open the sky in blinding bolts. Austin feared being electrocuted. The swamp trees thinned. Gigantic stalks topped in feathery plumes took their place. The ground became firm under foot, but the water depth increased until the brownish liquid reached Austin's waist. Po fastened his cape around his neck and swam, pushing his arms wide and giving scissor-like kicks.

Ripples not caused by the storm kept pace with them on both sides but did not come close or bar their path. Austin held his sword above his head, hoping that looked friendly but not too friendly. He was glad the muddy water made it impossible to peer below the surface so he couldn't see what their escorts looked like.

The storm passed, taking the downpour and fireworks with it and leaving an eerie stillness. They reached high ground. Austin scrambled onto the shore after Po, and hugged the wet grass. Then he bolted to his feet, suddenly wondering if creatures slithered onto the land after them. Nothing seemed to be snaking toward him. He studied the swamp. Rounded welts speckled the water, pushing up the liquid without breaking through the surface.

"Do I want to know what followed us?" Austin asked.

"You most excruciatingly do not." Po crawled on his hands and knees back to the shoreline. He took a deep breath and stuck his face into the dirty fluid. Austin winced, a warning caught in his throat. Bubbles gurgled around Po's submerged head. They slowed, then stopped. Austin crept toward the man. Were the creatures holding him under? Austin reached to pull him out, scared he was rescuing a headless body.

Po raised his head with a great gasp. He pushed himself

back from the edge and wiped at his face with a dripping sleeve. Across the water the welts erupted into foamy splashes as far as Austin could see. They disappeared, leaving the surface suddenly smooth except for a few last plops of rain.

"It is not wise to be here after dark," Po said. "More precisely, it is not wise to be here at all." Wearily, he pushed himself to his feet and set off across a soggy field of swaying reddish stalks.

Exhausted and overwhelmed, Austin watched the short man disappear into the taller vegetation. The only connection to his sister became a ribbon of swishing sedge moving farther and farther away. He forced himself to follow the wavy trail without a clue where he was going.

CHAPTER 8

Thick as ten hefty men, the tree had fallen long ago, ripping from soil saturated by a heavy rain. The trunk was angled toward the ground but did not touch it. A wheel of massive roots tangled about boulders they had clutched in the struggle to remain anchored supported one end. The tree's own branches braced the other. Small animals had worn a path under it to reach a nearby stream. Each year the trunk sank lower toward the ground as it suffered from gravity and decay. Bark flaked off, exposing the wood to worms and insects. They burrowed deep into the rings, advancing back in time, devouring history in reverse. Eventually the aged sentinel would split, exposing a rotted core where its youth had already crumbled.

Skylar Swiftbrooke sat on the ancient giant and thought it should be a poem. She swung her feet, wishing Po was here to help her pick which language to use. It looked like the tree in Cabrill's drawing. So did others she'd passed in the forest on her long walk to wherever it was she was pretending to go. It was too early for the evening meal, but she needed a reason to stop. She took a chunk of bread from the pocket of her cloak, unwrapped it and took a nibble, hoping this was the place, and she wouldn't have to build a fire later to cook just for herself. Crumbs collected in the cloth. Carefully she shook the fabric onto a bed of needle-like leaves below her. The shower of food caused a gleeful scurrying. Tiny multi-legged insects quickly carried off the unexpected bounty.

Fox-like things ran through the gap under the log. She chewed slowly and counted them. One. Two. At the moment she was bored, but that would change soon because Saffrian was so much more exciting than anywhere else she had ever lived. A new planet was always interesting. But just at first. On Callister and the worlds before it, she'd quickly settled into the same regular kid things—fencing and studying, and stuff with Austin and her parents and her friends. Saffrian was not the same old routine. It was sometimes scary—like now when she was doing this thing for Cabrill—and often uncertain—like now when she didn't know if she was in the right place at the right time. Mostly it was wonderful.

Except like now when she had to wait. Then it was boring.

More foxies. Ten. Eleven. She examined the way her dusty boots looked when she wiggled her toes. She folded knife pleats into a leg of her loose-fitting pants just below the knee to see what that would look like. Perhaps she'd start a new style. Perhaps pleated pant legs were already common in one of the many cultures here. Or maybe they'd bloomed into fashion centuries ago when the tree was a sapling then faded and were now laughed at as a curious costume.

"Here I am. All alone." She wasn't sure that was true. There was no rustling in the shrubbery and no sudden movement at the corner of her eye, but she felt she was being watched by more than the foxies. Whoever, whatever, it was, it was not what she was expecting. This was something that belonged here under the canopy of boughs in the leaf-filtered light. Something calm and quiet. Unlike herself, something infinitely patient.

"Hello, Spirit of the Forest," she said softly. "I come in peace. Do you?"

Skylar rewrapped the rest of the bread and tucked it away. She patted the tree trunk like an old friend and swung her legs. Her hair was braided. The sword borrowed from a stranger rested on the gray wood near her hand. She was ready, and she'd waited long enough.

CHAPTER 9

"Master Jomaray! Master Jomaray!" The servant boy newly assigned to the guild master's cottage at Seaba Colony started calling long before he charged through the open doorway into the study. Although he had been given boots along with fresh clothing, the child was barefoot. It was the way in his village, a hardened community to the east of the colony and at a much higher elevation. The practical residents there saw no reason to use valuable animal hide to cover their feet outdoors when there was no snow, and certainly not indoors.

"Such screeching is unacceptable." Jomaray Ganje rolled up another crisp sheet and bound it with cord. Golden skinned, golden haired, golden eyed, he was pure Cloosoo. He'd been raised in ornate, luxury-filled cities where proper manners were valued and practiced. Despite his constant reminders and superior example, the local folk seemed willfully determined to adhere to their own rough ways.

Today the items to be packed were mostly parchments. They were much easier to bundle than the abundance of woodcarvings last month. Bulkier and heavier than usual, that load had required one of the colony's chamapls to carry the sacks in addition to the goaddig the courier rode, leaving the kitchen short of milk and low in cheese production. The rider who arrived for the current packages had not brought the chamapl back with her, nor could she say where the shaggy animal was at present. Thinking about the loss increased Jomaray's irritation at his task.

For almost three years he'd been sending parcels to the Guild's prime colony at Bogoboln on direct orders from Grand Master Liaty Nobian himself. Jomaray's initial excitement at the attention, after being ignored by the hierarchy for over a decade, had soon morphed into resentment. If the works of insane artists on Wieldeld were of such importance, then you'd think just once Liaty would visit the colony. But no. The man could not be inconvenienced by a trip into the mountains even when the weather was fair.

What would next month's bundle be? Weavings, block prints, embroidery perhaps? The mad occupants of the two cottages in the complex swarmed from one medium to another like busy insects, producing similar images as if of a single mind—or a shared delusion.

"You must practice using a softer voice, boy." Jomaray couldn't recall the child's name. He would find out and remember it so he could instruct the grimy creature in appropriate behavior. There would be no running, screaming or bare feet in his home as if it were a common street.

The boy nodded as if he understood then shouted enthusiastically. "It's Tranquility."

For the past four days chaos had been slowly blooming at the locked residence, like an unfolding stink flower. No doubt the servant shifting from filthy foot to filthy foot on Jomaray's scrubbed floor brought news of another crisis at the optimistically named manor house.

"The inmates have gone crazy again," the boy yelled with glee. "One started painting with lamp oil. Others thought it a good idea and did the same. Some added candle wax. Might be a fire, Master Rom says."

Jomaray grit his teeth at the volume. The boy seemed fascinated with the many oddities in his new life, and perhaps hoped there *would* be a fire. "You are not to refer to the residents of Tranquility as inmates or as crazy. They are master artists, brothers and sisters in the Guild. And you will refer to Master Romielnsaokr as Master Romielnsaokr."

The boy shrugged. His eyes seemed especially large and dark in the round, ruddy face topped with freshly cropped black hair. "The other masters call her Rom."

"You are not an adult and not an artist. You are a child and a servant." Jomaray lamented he had no one competent to assign to this matter and would have to manage it himself. Aged guilders who came here to retire, and a few local hires barely kept the cottages stuffed with needy artists functioning. He should have a staff of keepers to manage the buildings and grounds. Instead, he had one who wouldn't even use a proper title. "Alert the Keep to haul barrels of water to Tranquility in case it needs a dousing. Next, you are to take ten buckets of water to Cook for boiling. Then tell Master Romielnsaokr we'll distribute the special tea, large quantities of it, with honey. She's to make sure every resident drinks, but none of the staff are to take so much as a sip. I'll bring it to her and supervise the brewing. Can you remember to do all of those things?"

"Keep, Cook, Master Romielnsaokr. Just as so, Master." The boy ran off to his tasks without being formally dismissed.

Jomaray took a chest from the locked cabinet. He found the correct key among the many others on the sturdy chains at his waist, pressed it into the indentation on the coffer's lid, and gave a twist. A pungent, almost painful fragrance invaded the room even before he fully opened the box. He took out three spheres of compressed tea leaves, thought a moment, and scooped up another. Designed for no more than eight artists, Tranquility held fifteen who were so severely mad they had been exiled here by the Guild.

That is, there were supposed to be fifteen. Master Calbran Coriadler had escaped from the locked building almost six weeks ago. So far, searchers had found only marks and symbols on rocks painted in what seemed to be ground-up minerals mixed with urine. Jomaray groaned. Another party was out today, leaving the colony with few clear-thinking adults if a cottage burst into flames.

He crumbled one of the balls into a pile of arid leaves on a parchment waiting to be packed. The delicate curls covered slashing, manic strokes that showed two figures engaged in swording. Common folk called the game nicks and jabs. He put a hand to the braids twined through his long yellow hair, feeling the crossed locks that recorded the victories of his youth. He lamented the sport was forbidden within the colony but he fully supported the rule. He certainly did not want those in his care running about with weapons.

He folded the paper so it firmly held the tea and slipped the pouch into a covered urn painted with people fleeing from a mud slide that destroyed an entire village two years after the pottery was created. His instructions were to send every single work to Bogoboln, but the grand master would not miss one small painting he didn't know about. And why should the special tea be only for those incapable of appreciating its calming properties?

Jomaray should have advanced to master at Bogoboln at the hub of the Guild by now. With his family connections and his ambition, he hadn't imagined anything else. But, as he approached his sixtieth lifeday, he presided over crazy people so far from civilized company it would turn anyone mad. Those with the power to make him Grand Master Liaty Nobian's successor barely knew he existed. The embarrassment to himself and his family was like a rash that constantly burned. His art should have warned him, should have shown him another path, but it had failed him.

The leaves' sharp, spicy perfume clung to his clothes and fingers. No one would think it unusual if the odor was with him for the rest of the day. He locked the chest and placed it back in the cabinet. With a dignified stride, he hurried to Cook, tea globes weighty in his hands.

CHAPTER 10

Ko Lian Po stood on the hard floor, ignoring the beautifully carved, well-cushioned chair. He did not presume to sit, since that courtesy had not been offered by the aged woman with blinding white drifts of hair piled on top of her head who sat behind the massive desk. The pattern on her gown duplicated a centuries-old painting foretelling the rise in wealth of a Lian ancestor. It had been stitched by a local with great needle skills but no predicting ability of his own, so he was not a true artist. The historic design suited the woman. At the moment she was not his Gram Shu, bringer of gifts and stories. She was Lian Sunang Shu, revered matriarch of the clan, earned master in many areas, shrewd manager of the vast family businesses.

By right of First Name, Po could have sat comfortably, with or without an invitation. He was, after all, *Ko* Lian Po. True, he had chosen alliance with his Second Name, thereby accepting Lian Sunang Shu's authority; but the Ko family had superior ancestry. Gram Shu knew that of course. Po suspected the chair, so near but not granted to him, was a test of his respect, his obedience, and the strength of his loyalty. Or perhaps it was an evaluation of his ability to deal with difficult people.

"He doesn't look like much, this foreigner." Shu didn't look up from the page she reviewed. Stacks of fine paper and rolled parchment obscured the polished surface of burgundy wood that separated great-great grandchild from great-great grandmother.

"I believe him to be necessary." Po had sent a message tactfully saying he was bringing Austin to Astlia, but he had not exactly asked for permission. She had not sent a reply. Did she know about the boy's appearance from others or had she secretly spied on him herself?

Shu skimmed the document into a bin. Po noted the faded ink and knew the matriarch, her eyesight fading, had only pretended to read it. The fresh eyes and careful hands of one of her great-great-great grandchildren would create a new, more legible, copy to replace it.

"This project of yours has turned us into thieves," Shu said. "We will *not* be thieves. I will return the item myself. I am the only one who can sufficiently apologize for such a rude violation."

A more ambitious offspring, hoping to gain favor, would praise her wisdom. Po merely nodded. This was more than just a project, and it had never been exclusively his. He, too, regretted there had been no way to borrow, purchase, or barter for the stiav key. Removing it without permission from the Yeawoche had been the only way to gain its use. Replacing it in the same manner would be a double insult. Acknowledgement of the act was the most sensible course.

Po eased the distorted circle from a pocket in his cape. Warm. It was always warm, as if it sucked heat from the air. The metal was ajrief. He had seen items forged from it in the family archives, but he had never touched it until he'd held the sliver Lady Skylar treated as an ornament. And now he'd had two more in his possession: this bit in his hand that he'd shamefully stolen, and Lord Austin's key that had saved their lives. Rare on Saffrian, the raw ore must exist in larger quantity elsewhere. The location was probably marked on a map or described in a document stored in one of the many rooms filled with the records his ancestors had collected.

He dared not place the ajrief's slight weight on the fragile parchments littering his gram's massive desk. He had learned early that each manuscript was of great value and must be treated as such. Reluctantly, he rested the sculpted metal on a tray holding a bowl of cold soup, but he did not let go. Once released, it would be gone—returned to its custodians, this time hidden beyond the ability to be found. The stiav in the meadow would become as unusable as the one in the swamp.

According to the research Gram Shu had directed him to study before he'd gone to fetch Austin, no other gates linked Saffrian and Callister. He would drown trying to get the key from the water people. Without the one still in his grasp, Austin and the wonderful Skylar would be stranded here. Perhaps that was meant to be, part of the prediction Cabrill continued to illuminate with every new work, but Po felt no less responsible. He remembered his lonely night in the alien desert waiting for the boy. He'd been too anxious to sleep, worrying the stiav would lapse back into the dormant state it had held for centuries, severing him from home. He'd feared he would be exiled in a world he did not know, and where he did not belong.

Po lifted the metal wafer, rubbing his fingers across the warm surface. With one quick move it would be back in his pocket.

"I will be glad to have this settled," Shu said. "Not just to repair our relationship with the Yeawoche. If the item's disappearance became public and connected to the family, our clients would no longer trust us. We would be ruined. Once skin is torn, a skilled healer and time might mend it, but there will always be a scar."

Po knew she was right. His family's future pressed against his palm. He lowered the deformed circle to the tray and released it silently. If he, Austin, and Skylar survived the ordeal that was sure to come, he would have to find another way to get them home. "With your permission, I'm taking the boy with me to Saffshier. I must find some distraction to keep him occupied while Cabrill sorts this out."

"This Cabrill Shistayia. Advanced to master before she was sword age! Whatever the girl's talent, it makes me question the Guild's standards and the wisdom of its leaders. I've examined every piece you've sent me. The artistry is fine enough but the works are repetitive. And she inserts herself into her own drawings, which is not to be done, yet she does it. The works all seem on the edge of an event she is incapable of showing."

"She continues to seek clarity," Po said.

"Artwork is the same as any report that comes to me," Shu said. "Some sources are more reliable than others. All information should be viewed in a larger context and acted on cautiously. I would have classified Cabrill Shistayia's efforts as a minor foretelling except that the strange girl she's drawn surrounded by the landscape of another world is now here."

"And the boy, as well," Po said.

"The girl came here by her own doing. The boy did not."

Po smiled. It was an old philosophical exercise. Did an artwork truly predict a future event? Or did the scene in a drawing, painting, needlework or beading become real because people like he and Gram Shu took actions that made them happen. He gave a standard reply to the debate. "He is here and so it is."

"And so it is," Shu said. "But I fear we are headed not toward fulfilling a foretelling but toward preventing it. Like the floods, famines, wars, diseases, and fires in the most famous works of our many cultures, this future your artist struggles to clarify is likely to be one we must change. Are you certain she can provide the guidance we need?"

"She is extraordinary." Po would not say what he had seen in Cabrill's art that it seemed Gram Shu had not. Or perhaps she had seen it. Perhaps she had looked at a drawing and watched the lines of Skylar's hair ripple as if moved by a wind. She would not admit it any more than he would. "Her talent is beyond words."

"It's good you're taking the boy with you. He's too big to stay here. The family can provide you with adequate supplies but limited currency."

Po was tempted to remind Gram Shu of the danger she herself had hinted at that went beyond the strangeness of active stiavs and misty beasts he'd described in his report. Something was terribly askew and out of balance. He would have known it even if he'd never become entangled in the entrails of it through Cabrill. A wrongness infected the air. It felt like an ancient predator returning to reclaim its prey. The family should devote all of its resources to making sure no one got eaten. Instead, he was getting "adequate supplies" and "limited currency." Not much, considering the wealth tucked away in the family vaults.

Po stood straight. He banished such self-indulgent thoughts. He was not the only one working on this puzzle. The old matriarch had a web of Lians constantly carrying messages and gathering information. He could only guess at the scope of the network and what it cost. He had a valuable profession and considerable intelligence. He would find a way to finance the enterprise himself. Perhaps that was Gran Shu's thinking. Perhaps it showed her confidence in him.

Or perhaps she was just a miserly, prickly old lady who took pleasure in challenging her offspring. Po gave an adequate and limited bow. "That is most generous."

Shu placed a gnarled hand on a stack of documents. Unlike the others, they were neatly squared to the corner of her desk. "Study these. Show them to no one. Return them to your cousin Maoinge tomorrow morning—that's Maoinge the younger, not the elder. The elder has grown too inquisitive. You'll find you're not the first to encounter intangible beasts with ember eyes."

Po dutifully picked up the bundle. It would take him all night just to give the age-stained pages a quick read. "Histories from before the Separation?" It was an unnecessary question, since nothing more recent could possibly be useful. And it was bold; but it seemed around his great-great grandmother, he always had to stick his hand in the fire, at least a little bit.

Matriarch Lian Sunang Shu gave him a piercing stare. "No written records survived the Separation."

The lie was widely told, especially by those who possessed the supposedly non-existent documents. Po had repeated it many times himself. "Forgive my error. I will not make it again."

"Journey well. I'll expect frequent reports."

Dismissed, Po cradled his overnight assignment. As he left, he gave the carved chair a glance and wondered if anyone had ever been allowed to sit upon the soft cushion.

CHAPTER 11

Lian Sunang Shu waited until the door closed behind her great-great grandson before she massaged her knotted knee through a heavy robe thick with beaded embroidery. Each year the pain burrowed deeper into her bones. The stinking, acrid salve she'd used for decades could no longer reach the root of the ache. She had come to rely on a bitter soup simmered by a great niece and quietly delivered to her daily.

Ko Lian Po had grown from an energetic, curious boy into an energetic, curious man. Although respected in the family, he had yet to distinguish himself in her eyes. Without his knowledge she arranged for opportunities to be placed before him, ones with the potential to advance his growth and shape his character, if he handled them adequately. He rarely followed the paths she so clearly marked out for him, but he had done well enough. And there was time, she wanted to think, for him to become the scholar the family needed and the advisor she wanted near her for the uncertain future.

Po had taken on Cabrill Shistayia's search to understand

her art on his own, without Shu's selecting the task for him. He seemed to think the boy's very existence proved the importance of the drawings he'd sent her. Shu recognized the strength in them, but Cabrill was not the only artist following the same thread. Her agents had found others. A lesser mind would not connect them, but she saw them linked, like the individual stitches in the embroidery on her gown. Even combined, they were only a scrap of a larger pattern she still couldn't see.

Her own lack of insight worried her. She'd prowled through the archives to retrieve scrolls and loose pages she remembered from when she was a girl assigned to copy fading text. Her handwriting had been fluid and precise then. Now her stiff fingers struggled to form understandable characters. She knew she could trust the documents, no matter how often they'd been re-penned. Other cultures passed along history as if it were myth, allowing variations to creep in. Only Astlians and the Yeawoche guarded details like treasure. Astlians kept vaults of manuscripts. The Yeawoche? Shu wasn't sure. They had no writing. Perhaps the spoken tales were memorized with care generation after generation. Or perhaps blood carried the stories, and all newborns came into the world babbling the experiences of their ancestors.

But history was more than words, written or spoken. Art from long ago that had predicted events now almost forgotten provided a foundation for what was to come. She had searched the inventory of paintings and tapestries sealed in special cases to preserve the precious items that could not be as easily copied as a document. She had reviewed the halls crammed with artifacts from before her birth, finding more riddles than revelations.

Shu leaned back in her chair. Through a soft sleeve, she clutched the band she'd taken from the cluttered drawer of a massive cabinet in a double-locked room. Meant to be worn on the wrist of someone belonging to one of the larger peoples, the cuff circled her upper arm like an ornate shackle. Made of blue-gray ajrief, it had rested among small statues depicting the horrors that preceded the Separation. The ancient rune for the Engineers Guild was stamped into the surface. To the right and left, smaller icons indicated members of an alliance or an association of some sort. She recognized only one of them: the original mark of the Lian clan. To leave behind the shame of that time, the symbol had been abandoned by the family after the Separation and never used again.

She felt the significance of the design but didn't understand it. Had the Lians been allied with the Engineers or had they fought against them? And what had "with" or "against" meant in that chaos? Now, in supporting this uncertain mission driven by her great-great-grandson and a mad artist, she might be continuing a plot that had begun in her clan's past, or she might be making up for harm her family had done. Which was it? She didn't know.

The cuff had grown warmer against her skin than when she'd first clamped it to her arm. It troubled her mind but eased the pain in her shoulder. She plucked the stiav key from the soup tray. It held the same comforting heat. She pulled up the hem of her gown and pressed the metal against her aching knee. Officially, studying the years before the Separation was forbidden, as if that era never existed, leaving a hole in history. She needed to consult with someone who, like herself, did not feel bound by that restriction. There was no one in the family. But there was someone. And the journey was already planned.

CHAPTER 12

"Master Jomaray! Master Jomaray!" The boy's cries from the courtyard wound through the cottage and invaded the guild master's study, shattering his solitude. The boy soon followed his own echoes. "Master Jomaray, the searchers who went out with Keep's second oldest daughter are back."

Jomaray frowned at the boy's disheveled clothes sprouting bits of straw. The child had been in the barn again, playing with the animals. Jomaray closed his thoughts to what might have entered his house on the bare feet. Cook had often reminded him the boy's name was Cheche, a ridiculous repetition of sound. "Your enthusiasm tells me that Master Calbran has been found."

"Not so he could be captured and dragged back," Cheche said.

Tolerance, tolerance, Jomaray silently chanted to himself. The day was going poorly. A fire had broken out at Tranquility while the servants had been scraping up wax and sopping up lamp oil from the earlier excitement. By then the residents had slurped down all the calming tea Jomaray had provided and were too content to take the order to evacuate seriously. Fortunately, the flames were quickly smothered, although there had been some damage. The next shipment of artwork to Bogoboln would be lighter than usual and a bit charred.

Jomaray had been about to brew his own tea. The pungent fragrance filled his study. He glanced at the urn that held the leaves and inhaled deeply. "We are not *capturing* Master Calbran, and we certainly are not *dragging* him. He is lost and we fear for his safety. We want to escort him home where we can care for him." If only the boy understood how fortunate he was to have a respectable position at the colony, tending to artists rather than scrambling across the mountains after his uncle's flock.

"Just as so, Master. You know Hopro Leap." Cheche shifted from foot to foot, excitedly slapping his soles on the slab floor.

"I have seen it." Jomaray closed his eyes against the dizzying memory of the local landmark.

"Mad Calbran's been at it."

"You will not refer to Master Calbran Coriadler, or any of the residents here, as mad." The artists at Seaba might be incoherent idiots for the rest of their lives, but Jomaray would always insist they be spoken of with dignity. "And how, exactly, has Master Calbran 'been at' Hopro Leap?"

The boy gave a mischievous grin. "The place be a bit different now. Decorated, might be. Keep's second oldest daughter says you'll want to see for yourself."

Jomaray took a deep breath. He absolutely did not want to see for himself how mad Calbran had defaced the world-famous cliff.

CHAPTER 13

From the crest of a hill Austin gazed down at an expanse of water that reflected the tangled feathers of wispy clouds floating overhead, and sparkled as if stitched with sequins. The far shore blurred with the haze of distance. The near shore bowed in, creating a harbor adorned with oared boats and slack-sailed ships. Strips of docks and walkways crisscrossing the rim. Shops and houses rambled inland. Their rooftops glistened with azure tiles, so it seemed the bay floated up the surrounding hills across submerged buildings.

"Saffshier," Master Ko Lian Po said. "Your sister compared it to the blaze confined within a crystal from your home world."

"A sapphire." Austin had immediately thought of the jewel too. After the long trip he was excited and a little anxious. They were meeting Skylar here. Maybe she was already waiting for them. Or maybe not. Po was suspiciously vague about the details. Would he recognize his own sister after such a long time? Would she recognize him?

Austin pawed at his hair. It had grown into a messy mop, and his effort to trim it had been disastrous. His laundered fencing uniform, polished foil, and camping gear were stored in a long sack, like a closed sling, that bounced against his back when he walked. Dressed in the local style, he wore a loose shirt and wide-legged pants tucked into soft boots, like leathery socks. Held in place with laces and drawstrings, each piece was faded to a different shade of brown.

"It must be a beautiful gem indeed," Po said. "The Lady Skylar came to call the entire world by its name. She's very clever, choosing a sight comparison that is also close in sound. Saffshier the city, Saffrian the world, and sapphire the jewel. Alas—alas, that's a grand word. It was a gift from the Lady. Alas, I shall probably never see a sapphire. But it's joyful to have a sound so delicious."

The city seemed like a maze of tight streets leading to open plazas. Set into hills, most buildings held one establishment on the lower level and another stacked above it that opened onto the next street. Po rented a room over the Stormy Wave Tavern and below the Calm Horizon Import Shop. It held two weary cots and a rough table flanked by scarred benches. Street noises swept in through an open window, along with odors of spice, people, and poor sanitation. A small fireplace promised to keep the occupants comfortable through damp nights. Austin guessed even such a cramped space was expensive in a crowded port town. Po said nothing, but Austin could tell he was worried about money.

Whatever the cost, Austin was relieved to have walls around him. During the long days on the road, he had watched the shadows for wolf creatures and tried unsuccessfully to think of ways he and Po could defend themselves against the misty beasts. Po assured him the ones left behind on Callister had evaporated forever. Austin doubted the disappearing thing applied to the one that had pushed him into the swamp. That one, the leader, had landed back on Saffrian. Unlike its companions, it had returned to its homeland. It could still be prowling after them, wounded from the water and wanting revenge. And there might be others, a pack of wolf-beasts angry at having lost some of their own. He'd tried to discuss it with Po while they had visited his family to clean up and collect provisions, but the master translator had always redirected him to another topic.

After that, there wasn't a good time to drop it into the conversation. Not while they walked narrow paths with foliage close around them that could hide all sorts of dangers. And certainly not during their nightly language lessons, hunched over a fire with darkness and strange rustling noises less than a sword's length away. Austin was determined to bring it up again, but not just yet. For now, he wanted to enjoy the security of a room where he could see all the corners.

Po left him alone with the last bit of food they still carried. The single window framed a busy street and a slice of the harbor. "Good day" Austin heard people shout to one another in Lynawic. Other tongues flew about and could sometimes be matched to different types of dress—but not always. Just as he concluded that everyone wearing striped pants spoke a high-pitched dialect, two such people strolled by in an animated conversation of guttural sounds.

The adults were of varying heights, some as short in stature as Master Po and his family. Austin had felt like an awkward giant among the graceful, petite Astlians. He didn't know where they had managed to find clothes that fit him, or how they had washed the camo-slime out of his fencing uniform, making it more intensely white and shiny than from before the adventure in the swamp.

Po said that fortunately his home was on the most direct

route from the swamp portal to Saffshier. Austin had no way to know if that was true. And he was still unsure if Astlia was a country, a territory, a province, a region, or a gigantic estate. Po's relatives had been reserved but attentive and kind. Austin had been fed excellent food, given an embarrassing bath, and constantly prompted for English words.

"Good day," Austin quietly replied to the street sounds outside his window, practicing the Lynawic Po had taught him while they traveled. "How is your health? Do you have any dybil eggs for sale?" He and Skylar had often done similar exercises together when learning a new language on yet another planet their parents had hauled them off to.

"Have you seen a lost girl dancing through the street?" Austin scanned the faces below, hoping one of them framed by long dark hair would look up, golden brown eyes shining, and shout his name. None did.

Po returned in good spirits. "A vessel arrived from Diggion with cargo to sell. I offered my services and was employed to facilitate the deal with a Saffshier merchant. Both parties were well satisfied, and I humbly accepted an honest fee. Let's celebrate with some fine fare."

They descended the narrow, winding stairs to the common room. The meal being served to all patrons that day—and perhaps every day—was bread, fish, boiled vegetables, and fruit cider. Austin and Po sat across from one another on benches at a long table, elbow to elbow with other diners. If you wanted privacy and personal space, you had to go elsewhere.

"We'll eat then go find Skylar. Okay, Po?" At least four different languages were being spoken in the room. No one turned a head at Austin using English. Stomach-growling hungry, he dug into a chunk of hard-crusted, slightly sour bread. Mushy mystery vegetables of various colors and shapes filled the plate a server set before him. Po handed him a knife. Apparently, this was a bring-your-own-utensil establishment. Austin watched the people around him. Mimicking their eating style, he stabbed an orangey shape and shoved it into his mouth. Bland, overcooked, but good enough. He tried some other colors and quickly learned to be cautious of the thin green ones that sent a spicy heat through his mouth and made his eyes water.

"Patience is required." Po shoved several thin green veggies into his mouth and savored them as if they were candy.

"I haven't seen my sister in two years," Austin said. "I've been attacked by a strange beast, slogged through a swamp, and walked for days to get to where we are supposed to meet her. Patience is not appropriate in this context."

"Soon," Po said.

"Are we near the you-know-what that Skye came through?" Austin asked. Po had cautioned him to speak of it only in English. He wished he knew where Po kept the warped circle that would open the portal from this side. It must be tucked somewhere in the man's cloak. He definitely didn't want Skylar's medallion back. Let it stay here so it wouldn't snatch away his sister again. But he needed the other key to get home.

Po dug into the beige wedges in the vegetable medley as if they were the best he'd ever tasted. "I understand your meaning, although your phrasing is confusing. The great Azure Lady and I had many conversations about the you-know-what. It is more than a doorway or link or tunnel or portal. The word for it in some languages equates to guardian. I believe the most accurate term in English is lock. The kind that is a structure on a river, which alters water depths for boats. The you-know-what takes two locations and adjusts them so they are on a pathway of the same level, making it easily traveled.

Also, it is a security lock, requiring keys. Your Marvelous Sister of the Zenith described it as a lock with a lock. That is very clever."

"Skylar," Austin said. "Just Skylar."

Po straightened his shoulders. "I am a master translator. I can converse with anyone likely to enter this room and some most unlikely to appear. *Skylar* gave me a language that, since you have arrived, only three of us on this world can speak and understand. That is rare beyond rare, and a delight for me. I cherish the gift and the giver. I only wish to honor her. My apologies if that is contrary to your culture."

A large, muscular man to Austin's left wagged a fish bone at him. Reddish hair bound in braids of different thicknesses and lengths covered his head and draped across his neck like gnarled tree bark. "You've seen the rough side of a wager." His voice rumbled like tumbling boulders. "Must have been a great tourney to be so shorn. And I wonder, how one barely sword age had so many plaits to lose. And I wonder, how could such a competition be unknown to me?"

Austin didn't understand most of what the rusty-haired man said in Lynawic. Something about a sword. Neither he nor Po carried one, but it certainly was the style here. Many of the adults wore full scabbards belted to their waists or slung across their backs.

Po smiled at the man. "My client has had experience beyond his years."

"Must be from far since he needs a wordsmith."

"Far beyond far," Po said.

The man looked at Austin. "Why travel to Saffshier?"

In English Po said to Austin, "He wants to know why you came here? Turn to him and say your own words. I will translate."

"What should I say?" Austin thought about Po's surprising

appearance in the arena, wispy wolves, and transporting arches.

"The truth, as simply as you can," Po said. "Within the limits we discussed."

Austin looked what seemed like a long way up into the man's sunburned face. Round and bumpy as a gourd, it held heavy brows, weather-chaffed cheeks and a chin like withered fruit. "I'm here to find my sister."

Po gave the man a steady, pleasant gaze. "I am searching for my sister," he said as if he were Austin himself. "She came here on family business but did not return home on the expected day."

"And I wonder what that business be." the man said to Austin.

"What business is your family in?" Po translated.

Austin wished he could reply in Lynawic but he didn't have all the terms and he lacked the confidence. "They're scientists. My mother studies animals and my father studies plants."

Po said, "We are collectors and traders in exotic beasts and boughs. But as you have keenly noticed, my interest is competition. Perhaps we could have a friendly bout of nicks and jabs."

The man raised his thick eyebrows in shock and, Austin thought, in admiration. Scientists must be well respected here.

The man looked Austin up and down. "No braids to wager but I'm always hungry. We could go a short one, platter to a point. I'm curious how a younger has gained then lost so much to end up with ragged hair."

All Austin got out of it was that the man wanted to take a local dish and sharpen it. Maybe he was a chef who wanted to cook for them. That didn't seem right. Austin looked to Po, completely lost in the foreign tongue and suddenly worried he would never learn it well enough to survive here.

Po asked Austin, "Do you fence as well as your sister?"

"That's your question, not his," Austin said.

Po leaned forward. "This gentleman proposes a swording contest. You'll find it very like competition on your world. Three hits to win. With a bit of braid, you'd look less like an outsider."

Austin didn't know what braids had to do with fencing.

"Ehh," the very big man said, "you be more than translating, Master Wordsmith. Seems such is against your duties."

Po nodded. "In ordinary, you would be correct. However, I am a cultural guide as well as a translator. Since my client is from very far away, I am obligated to explain your words and their implications."

The man twitched his jaw in thought. "Fine then."

Austin evaluated the man. His great long arms could easily reach an opponent, but a heavy fencer was not as quick as a lighter one. "Has my sister fenced here?"

"And won," Po said. "She would have earned many plaits except that she's not yet sword age."

Austin was still confused, even by some of the things Po had said in English, but he could see no reason to turn down the offer. "I suppose I could use the practice."

Po smiled widely. "You will find it more than that, my friend."

CHAPTER 14

"It would be a stronger prophecy if it were in gold and jewels, of course." Hunched over, head bumping the roof of the carriage, Master Artist Mikol Wilsheem presented his latest work to the famous Lian Sunang Shu as if it *were* made of precious materials instead of common fishing line and seeds.

Shu ignored his discomfort and probably detested the way he hovered over her in the cramped enclosure. He was a Floriklian, one of the large peoples, a bigger. To her, he was awkward and inefficient, requiring double the food, fabric and space of a compact Astlian.

"I suspect it's expensive enough already, Master Artist."

Mikol had been amazed when the matriarch of the powerful Lian family had responded to his written inquiry with a commitment to purchase the bracelet. The plan had been to meet at a busy way station frequented by travelers more interested in their own affairs than in those of others. He'd still been two-days walk from it when the elegant carriage coming from the opposite direction surprised him.

Now he found himself conducting business squeezed into a tight black box on wheels in the middle of a road, instead of relaxing in a proper inn where he would have coaxed a meal out of the old crone.

"You're purchasing more than art." Mikol's stealth and silence cost extra. Her eagerness added to the sum. She understood that, but had rushed to meet him anyway. Her haste reinforced Mikol's belief that the pattern of linked ovals he'd described in his letter meant something to her and carried a significant prediction.

Bundled in a heavy cloak despite the warm day, Lian Sunang Shu shifted the design to catch light slanting through the carriage window. She ran a finger over the bumps and crevices, feeling the border from one kind of seed to the next. Ovals of red, green and velvety brown shone like polished lacquer. Another, dull as sand, seemed out of place in comparison. The blue was also unique. Intense as the sky when viewed from one direction, it faded to flat shale when tilted in another. "You couldn't create the same effect with gems."

Mikol silently agreed. Nor with bronze. Variations in the seeds brought out details lost in jewels or in the monotony of metal. He was careful to keep the cuff on his own wrist hidden. It would taint the transaction if his patron discovered she was not buying the only version of the design. There were three in fact—one in seeds and two in bronze. The twin to the one he wore had been financed by a special patron who also seemed to understand the pattern and who thought she had purchased the only one. As much as Mikol ached to recreate it in richer, more sparkling materials, his soul told him the seed bracelet was exactly as it should be. Perhaps poverty enhanced his art. He still preferred money in his pocket.

Bent over, chin almost touched his knees, he graced Lian Sunang Shu with a charming smile. "Shall we discuss my fee?"

He had a generous amount in mind that included compensation for the lack of dignity in his present position. It would be enough for new clothes and boots, and for that fine meal he felt cheated out of. But those luxuries would have to wait. The Grand Lady Shu's payment must get him to his destination—and quickly. He had set certain events in motion. They had become twisted and he must realign them before damage was done.

Mikol named his hefty price for the elaborate bracelet of simple materials. In his heart he knew he would gladly give up a portion of it to learn exactly what the Lian matriarch knew about his design and why this prediction was so important to her. But such information would never be shared from one such as her to one such as him. And so he smiled his most seductive smile and graciously accepted the heavy bag of clinking coins.

CHAPTER 15

Paved with uneven stones, the courtyard near the tavern was little more than a wide spot in the street. The buildings that lined it pressed into a natural indentation in the hill, providing the space. Austin and the large red-haired man watched others cross swords while waiting for their turn. Competitors circled and darted like birds, avoiding a hit, making a hit. Austin was surprised by the graceful way the rivals wielded their heavy weapons. Much thicker than an elegant foil, the swords had flat blades, more like sabers. They were meant for cutting, rather than stabbing; but they were still effective when used in a pointy fashion. A casing of bark or animal hide was strapped over each blade. A special reinforcement covered the end, decreasing the possibility that blood would be spilled, accidentally or otherwise.

There were no silvery uniforms here, no padded jackets, helmets, and gloves for protection. Austin figured the only sensor-embedded fabric on this world was tucked away in his bag. Dressed in his uniform, he would have looked strange among the earth-toned clothing, like a patch of snow in a grain field. There were no electronic scoring devices here to register a hit with a blare and a flashing light. Instead, three volunteer referees watched from different angles and awarded points. Austin was fine with that. He and Skylar had never used hit boxes for practice. They'd relied on one another's honesty in declaring a touch. This must be how his sister fenced now. She didn't have her foil with her when she disappeared so she'd be using one of these large swords.

Po explained nicks and jabs, street fencing that often erupted spontaneously. It lacked the organization of the formal tournaments that were popular entertainment throughout Saffrian, but the casual gaming was well respected and provided experience. As in the kind of competition Austin was used to, the target area was the torso. You scored a point by touching the tip of the weapon to your opponent between the shoulders and the hips. Striking the arms or legs might cause pain, but it didn't earn a point. Slashing was not allowed. Even with the protective sheath, it could result in serious injury, taking the event beyond a friendly sport.

The big man tapped his chest with a calloused thumb. "Ryster Brimbren."

"Austin Swiftbrooke." Austin wished he could use some of his newly acquired Lynawic, but they were in an entirely different territory than "good day, how is your health."

Ryster Brimbren examined Austin's weapon and offered his own in return. Austin wasn't sure how his opponent would react to the foil. Still set to its most rigid form from the smoke wolf attack, the end retained a bit of flexibility. Made of a substance this planet might never develop, it was far from the local design.

Ryster grunted at the thin blade, curved guard that

sheltered the hand, and hilt molded for a solid grip. He tapped the tiny sensor on the tip and roared with surprise. "Could barely skewer a beetle with it. Seen many but never this. Don't know the metal or process. Too wobbly for a proper sticker. And I wonder how you'd get a cut with it. No need for a skin, as I can see. You've got me curious, Austin Swiftbrooke."

Po did some diplomatic translating, but Austin knew what he was leaving out. His blade didn't have to be covered by a "skin" because Ryster thought it silly. He was glad the big man hadn't discovered the power switch. Austin didn't know how he would have explained a glowing light on the end of the grip or the electrical charge when the sensor came in contact with anything metallic.

Thick handled, Ryster's weapon felt bulky and rigid but well balanced. The edges were keenly honed, the end tapered to a sharp point. Austin shuddered. He knew the people around him had real swords, blades, weapons in their hands and strapped to their belts. But he hadn't understood until this moment that they were *real* swords, blades, weapons, carried not just in case a fencing tournament suddenly popped up. These were serious tools for work and self-defense. And they were dangerous.

Austin's foil was strictly non-lethal and meant only for gaming. It was a toy in this world. A tightness crept into his stomach as he watched the current pair of battlers circle, turn and twist. The skillful movements fed his growing panic. The weight of Ryster's sword made it worse. This wasn't the sport he knew, the one he had practiced for years, the one he excelled at. It appeared similar, but it was completely different.

A motherly looking woman scored her third point on a disappointed young man. The crowd made appreciative murmurs. The area cleared. Ryster Brimbren took back his weapon. He pressed the foil into Austin's shaking hand with a laugh.

Austin couldn't move. "This isn't exactly how we fence where I come from," he tried to tell Po.

The little man gave him an encouraging shove into the oval. "I'm confident you will do well."

CHAPTER 16

Lian Sunang Shu stood and waited. The day was slipping away. Giant trees blocked the low sun, washing her in early twilight. Their heavy trunks were four times as thick as her small frame and fifty times taller. A wave of wind rushed through the lacy leaves, spreading a tinkling melody. On a map the sprawling Gregen Forest meandered through most of the provinces. In various places it was marked as legally owned by municipalities, lords, ladies, and families, including the Lian clan. But everyone respected it as the domain of the Yeawoche and only the Yeawoche. All others were guests, no matter what property rights were stated in official documents.

Returning home from her meeting with Master Artist Mikol Wilsheem, Shu had traveled the public road beside it for miles. As soon as the carriage crossed into Astlian land, she had signaled a stop. Without providing an explanation, she had walked into the woods alone. Her driver, a granddaughter skillful at handling the swift, spirited small-breed goaddig that pulled the vehicle, knew better than to question the strange order—or any order from Gram Shu.

Not used to waiting for anything, Shu waited. This part of the Gregen was called the Grove of Chimes. A large stone would have made a passable chair, but she didn't sit because no chair had been offered. An evening chill crept out of lengthening blue shadows, causing shivers in her old bones, but she didn't build a fire. That would be like barging into the home of a long-time acquaintance and setting a painting alight.

Shu waited. A melodic tinkling rippled overhead. It circled her then faded into the distance. The tune returned with vigor as a breeze ruffled the hanging leaves. Then all became still.

Shu sensed the figure before he silently stepped into view. Recognizing him, she gave the bow granted to an equal. Since he already knew her lineage, she spoke a shortened Astlian greeting. "Success and wellbeing to you and your family."

He replied in the tradition of the Yeawoche. "Your presence brings the joy of soft rain." Slightly taller than Shu, he wore a simple short tunic. Tattoos that mimicked tree bark but were also something else covered the lean, muscular body. His calm, angular face appeared deeply lined, as if eroded by rivulets of time. She knew all his names but would not be so impolite as to speak them. While Astlians honored their ancestors by presenting their lineage and family affiliations, Yeawoche guarded theirs as sacred.

"I apologize for the inconvenience of my visit. I very much need your interpretation." Shu held out the beaded bracelet, knowing he would disapprove. Seeds fed birds and animals. They produced fresh plants that replaced the old, the worn out, the withered. They meant life and renewal. Weaving them into an ornament, even one for prediction, was blasphemous.

He didn't take it from her. "The Astlian people have advisors of great reputation."

"It is wise to gather many views," Shu said. "Your perspective has great value." She had outlived the elders who used to council her. She had outlived all those before her, all of her siblings, all of her peers. She was eldest of the elders by more than a decade, and that wasn't nearly old enough for this. She had only children around her now. Their certainty and over confidence were tiresome. She had done the hard research herself and was not ignorant of the pattern in her hand. Before she turned her speculations into conclusions, she wanted verification from the only people on the planet with a longer history than her own.

"We rarely interact with others."

And so the negotiations begin, Shu thought. "A certain key has gone missing."

"A certain key has been stolen. It is a thing that must be carried. Therefore, it is a burden. We accepted it into our care, the responsibility heavier than the weight. We have been concerned for its safety."

"It could be returned," Shu said.

"That would bring joy." The Yeawo stepped forward and took the bracelet from Shu, not betraying his repulsion at the misuse of life.

Too much of Shu's patience had already been spent. She was recklessly eager. "Does it represent the five worlds?"

"There is no value in asking if you already know."

"Sometimes there is."

"Once fire could be made to dance in the air. It gave light, heat and comfort while consuming no wood."

"There are moments when that would be appreciated." Shu knew the stories from before the Separation. If a thing could be thought of, it could be done—by some but not by all.

"Fire was also fashioned into demons that burned what they touched," the Yeawo said. He folded the colorful strip to show only the muted yellow oval. "One world, bright as the others. Scorched and charred into death."

"Is that the past or the future?"

"It was the tragedy that cleansed minds and brought about the Separation."

A world destroyed. Shu had found nothing of it in the archives. The documented crimes were numerous—forced poverty and unearned wealth, murder, frivolous games that damaged people and property, disputes that ripped the land and the innocent unlucky enough to be in the way. But an entire planet—

He folded the beading differently, showing the blue oval as brilliant and beautiful. "It may again happen." He shifted the angle. In the declining light the shiny azure transformed to dull gray.

Shu pulled her cloak tighter about her. Once five lands had been united in friendship. Connected by the stiav guardians, they'd enriched one another with commerce and culture. The old records used a specific gemstone, or rather, a specific color to identify each. The identities of four had crumbled into obscurity along with the parchments that documented their existence. Only the world represented by blue was known to her.

Saffrian.

He handed her the bracelet. "The guardians had a different title before the Separation. Their new one gives false comfort."

Shu tucked the beadwork into her cloak. The stiavs provided protection only as long as they were dormant—she didn't need Yeawoche wisdom to tell her that. Now they were active, drawing power from an unknown source. The girl had passed through. And her great-great grandson Po. And the boy. The Separation was broken. That made all keys dangerous. She removed the metal wafer from her deepest pocket and presented it to him with both hands. "Allow me to return what is missing. Know that I do so with great respect and humility."

"Before accepting, I request an inconvenience."

"There is no inconvenience between friends." Shu had been bargaining from a tenuous position, using an item her opponent knew had been stolen from his care. He could ask anything and she would do it to repair the discord the theft created. Although he was unlikely to request property, she was prepared to sign over ownership to the Grove of Chimes.

"You wear an ajrief artifact," the Yeawo said.

Hidden by her robe and gown, the blue-gray band circling Shu's arm provided the only warmth in the fading day. She could almost feel the ancient Lian symbol etched close to that of the infamous Engineers Guild. The artifact could be used by an enemy, or an angry ally, to damage her clan's reputation. She should not have taken it from the security of the archive, and she should never give it to anyone who was not blood.

When she'd ordered Po to take the key, she'd known the cost would be high. The forest folk, aware of every movement in their tree-filled home, had allowed it be stolen. Or perhaps not allowed exactly, but they had not prevented it, as they easily could have.

It was still theft. And the Lian were not thieves.

She nodded agreement. A thing broken must be mended. Trust can only be repaired through trust. There was no other way. She would surrender the dangerous ornament into the hands of the Yeawoche, hoping they would keep it hidden in the forest for eternity, or at least as long as the Lian clan existed.

"As a sign of continued friendship between our peoples,"

the Yeawo said, "give the artifact to the girl who has brought you to this place in your journey."

Shu's heart clenched. "I do so with joy," she forced herself to say. Trust was a difficult beast to ride.

The Yeawo accepted the key from her outstretched hands. "A convenient courier is known to you." He bowed, showing great respect. Shu did the same. Then he was gone. The forest rang with rich chimes as she trudged back to her carriage.

CHAPTER 17

Austin advanced. He had a good reach with his long weapon, but Ryster gave a great stretch with his giant arm and heavy sword, deflecting the blow. Austin retreated. He made more attempts at getting past the heavy blade. Moving in a straight line, he worked his way forward and back, forward and back, just as he did with the practice dummy. He'd watched the previous sworders, but he'd been too nervous worrying about his own upcoming bout to notice strategy. Ryster mostly stood in one spot, as if studying Austin's movements.

Taking a chance, Austin took quick steps toward Ryster and attacked. The tip of his foil connected with the man's chest. The referee declared a point and the crowd whooped.

Austin made his next approach. Ryster gave a sly smile and took a wide step to the right. Startled, Austin pulled back. He adjusted his position and went in for another attack. Again the big man moved sideways. Soon Ryster had Austin spinning in a circle. Constantly realigning himself, Austin could do little more than block Ryster's strikes. Used to the narrow rectangle of a regulation fencing strip, his training was almost worthless in an open space against a foe practiced at dodging in any direction.

Ryster stabbed. Austin felt the tip slam hard into his chest. That would leave a bruise. One-one.

This time, ready for the sidestep, Austin rebuffed the next attack and prepared for his own charge. The big man made a motion to the right, as if to perform his usual shift. He suddenly stepped left. The feint caught Austin off balance. He felt the pressure of Ryster's blade in his ribs. Two-one.

Austin deflected attack after attack, not finding his own rhythm. Ryster was good. He was *very* good. It would be no disgrace to lose to him. Austin wanted the bout to be over so he'd have a chance to analyze this kind of competition, but giving up would be dishonorable and an insult to his adversary. And he hadn't slogged his way through a swamp just to quit when things got out of his comfort zone. Actually, he'd left known territory the moment Skylar disappeared. Nothing was normal after that. Only one thing could repair the damage. He was going to get Skylar back, even if he had to fight every Ryster here.

Forehead slick with sweat, Austin tried some circling of his own. He barely defended himself with a parry and a riposte against Ryster's next assault. He had to react faster, but it was hard to respond quickly to the unfamiliar style. Accustomed to the automated fencing dummy, he'd become slow and used to a pattern. His mental muscles had gotten flabby from inactivity. That wouldn't have happened if he'd had his inventive sister to spar with.

Ryster started toward the right. Austin prepared his attack for the real shift to the left and managed a strike below the collar bone. Score! Ryster grinned, as if to say "You're learning, boy." Two-two.

For all his footwork, Ryster's attacks were always a simple jab. Perhaps it was the rigidness of his weapon or just the style here. Austin was worn out from the awkward moves he had to make. He needed to think through his opponent's strategy and find an opening. Ryster bobbed back and forth, threatening to go one direction and then the other. Austin pretended to match the movements, but he kept his weight centered. Ryster leaned to the left then suddenly swung to the right, thrusting out his sword. Austin twisted and dropped into a lunge below Ryster's aim. He flicked his wrist. The flexible blade whipped into Ryster's side.

Point number three! Austin plopped to the ground, flush with a hard-fought victory. Ryster rushed toward him. Austin didn't want to be on the receiving end of that serious weapon when it was no longer a game. He scrambled to his feet, not sure he could convince his tired legs to run away.

Ryster faced Austin. He dropped his sword and pulled a knife from his belt. He grasped one of the many braids sprouting from his head and sawed it off. Laughing he thrust the bundle at Austin. "Well met!" he cried. "Take the whole skein. You deserve it and I've still plenty left."

Austin wasn't sure what Ryster had said, but he could tell he was supposed to accept the greasy chunk of hair as if it were a trophy. He took it, not knowing what he should do with the hank that was bound on one end with twine, and that smelled of sweat and campfires.

Twice as many people surrounded them now as when they'd started. Standing with the spectators, Po made a fist with his thumb pointing upward. Austin gave him a weak smile and returned the thumbs up with the chunk of hair dangling from his grip. He wondering if it was a local gesture or if Skylar had taught it to him. Po flattened out his hand and waved it back and forth as if to cancel the previous action. He grabbed a bit of his own stubby white hair and tugged it upward. Austin feared he would pull it from his scalp with his enthusiasm. Then Po jerked his fist upward and gave it a shake.

Austin got it. He raised the thick braid above his head while the crowd roared, excited by the unexpected outcome. Exhausted, he dragged himself out of the courtyard, muscles and mind aching. It had been a long time since he'd worked that hard for only three points.

Po whisked the woven hair away from him and quickly tied a length of string around the loose end—the end that had, until a moment ago, been attached to Ryster Brimbren's head. They went back to the tavern and climbed the steep stairs to their room. Po wagged the chopped off hair at him. "Six plaits and two crosses. An outstanding beginning. You must put them in your hair immediately."

"I don't want that thing anywhere near me." Austin stowed away his foil and flopped onto a cot. "It stinks."

Po went into what Austin thought of as his "patient-uncle mode" that he used whenever he had to explain something he thought Austin should have figured out on his own. "Did you notice all of Master Ryster's braids?"

Austin wondered what he'd missed. Many people in the tavern, on the street and in the crowd watching the bouts wore some woven hair, but not all. "So, they're in fashion here. Sometimes they are where I live too. And sometimes they're not." Ryster had a lot more than the others. Maybe he was an especially stylish guy.

"It's more than fashion," Po said. "Here you *earn* braids."

"Earn by fencing?" Austin said in English. Then he repeated it in Lynawic. "Earn by swording?"

"By *winning*. And you surrender them when you lose."

Austin thought of the large man's gnarled hair. There were no stubby wisps, no sign of a section having been cropped until Ryster sliced off the chunk after losing to him. His stomach had just begun to recover. Now he felt as if he'd swallowed a stone. His first match here and he had faced a man who had not lost in as long as it takes to grow a full head of long hair.

Po held out the braid as if Austin should examine it. "Master Ryster is an expert sworder, and you beat him. The wager was for a plait, that's three cross overs, but he awarded you twenty crosses because he was impressed by your ability. Now you're entitled to weave that same number into your own hair. More accurately, you're obligated to do so. Ryster would be offended if you rejected his generous reward."

Austin figured it would be a bad thing to have the large man as an enemy. He'd done some braiding—rope, yarn for a school project, string. He'd watched Skylar effortlessly weave her long tresses without even looking in a mirror. "I understand the process, but I don't know how to begin."

"I will instruct you." Po rubbed a hand across his own bristly head. "It is a skill every learned person must have in order to prosper in this world, even if, such as myself, one is not a sworder and does not personally require it."

The clamor and odors of the street below tumbled in through the window. Austin sat on the rough timber floor so Po could easily reach his head. Patiently, Po explained how to divide his pale hair just so and how to cross one tress over the other.

In his room on Callister Austin had medals hanging from ribbons. He had polished crystals etched with his name, and tournament holographs reliving his winning points. No one but his family ever saw the awards he'd won for his physical ability and his mental game. On Saffrian every day you *wore* your victories—and your defeats. Ryster now had a stubby spot that showed his recent loss. Of course, his hair would grow out. He wouldn't have to live with the failure forever. No one should have to do that.

When Po finished, Austin shook his head, feeling the clumped weight of his new trophy. He couldn't wait to show Skye.

"Your swording technique is unusual," Po said. "As was the Great Skylar's when she first arrived. I now wish I had discussed it with her in detail." He sat on the bench and folded his hands in his lap like an attentive student. "Tell me about fencing where you come from."

CHAPTER 18

The next day with the sun overhead Austin followed Master Po along curved avenues slanting up from the harbor to a rock face in a steep hill. Frothy water bubbled from a crevice in the wall and swirled into a half-moon basin. The captured liquid cascaded over the rim, slipping between stones that paved the plaza. In the streets they'd passed through to get here, people hurried about, always going somewhere else. But this fountain was a destination at the hub of many lanes. Neighbors visited while children chased one another and played games with colored pebbles.

Austin used cupped hands to slurp a frigid drink. "I'm guessing the water comes from snow higher up, maybe glaciers. Where does it go after it sinks below ground?"

Po paced, scanning the crowd. "Into cave places perhaps. I haven't studied such things."

Austin dried his hands on the tail of his loose shirt. "Caverns. That makes sense. Flowing water can do a lot over time. It probably cut a path underground to the harbor."

"Caverns. Hmm."

Austin didn't care that even a terrific word only mildly distracted Po from being upset that he had insisted on coming along. He enjoyed being out in public with his new braids. Before, he had noticed people's clothing, language, and gestures. Now he focused on their hair. Many of the adults had both woven patches and gaps where hanks had been clipped off. Mostly he searched the faces for Skylar. "My sister is supposed to be here, right? This is where we're meeting her?"

He helped a great-grandfatherly man lift a sloshing animal skin tote out of the basin. When the man said thank you, Austin comfortably responded with the local equivalent of "you're welcome." Literally it meant "there is no obligation." He felt great. He could speak Lynawic—at least a little. He had fenced. He had earned a wearable trophy! "Po, how come you don't have braids?"

"It is not our custom. Not all peoples are of swords."

A language slip again. It slapped Austin like the icy spray from the cascading water. The master translator was more than upset at Austin; he was deeply worried. "Is something wrong?" Austin asked.

"Do not disease me with your curious," the little man said flatly without so much as a glance.

Austin knew he should respect Po's need for quiet, but he didn't like being dismissed like a child dissolved his good mood. He was sixteen years old. That made him sword age, as Po called it. Old enough to compete at nicks and jabs. Old enough to wear braids. Old enough to make some demands of his own. "If I don't see my sister very, very soon, I'm going home—even if I have to slog through that horrible swamp again." He sincerely hoped that wouldn't be necessary. And he wasn't going to do it anyway. He wouldn't leave here without Skye.

Po sighed and shifted his attention to Austin. "It would not be wise to attempt another passage through the Droombians' territory."

"Droombians?"

"I am embarrassed to say it is how air-breathers refer to them. Their name for themselves can only be accurately pronounced under water. They surrounded us during most of the journey. Usually they just drown intruders." He looked around at the busy plaza. "Our unexpected arrival probably confused them and they needed to consult their oracle for guidance. That gave us time to reach land, where I thanked their ancestral Egg Mothers for safe passage. I could not speak directly to them. That would have been even more impolite than trespassing on their sacred territory, since we had not been formally introduced and exchanged water-bug gifts."

Austin barely heard the explanation. A woman filled a large pouch, slung it onto her shoulder and strolled toward one of the branching streets. Multiple honey-colored braids hung down her back. Two children laughed and skipped beside her. They probably hadn't lived—and would never live—anywhere but here. They came to this vibrant plaza every day to collect the sparkling water, greet neighbors, listen to the flute player, sell a length of weaving, buy a sweet. This was their home. Austin wondered what that felt like.

A figure coming from the other direction stepped aside to let the trio pass. Dust and the weariness of travel clung to her cloak, but she strode with the confident step and balance of an accomplished fencer. Despite the fair weather, she wore a hood shadowing her features. A rope of dark braided hair hung forward over a shoulder and swung to her waist. She saw Po and subtly raised a hand in greeting, as if unsure she should approach.

Over and over Austin had envisioned this moment,

planning clever remarks that would melt away the absent years. He could think of none of them now. He rushed to her and wrapped his arms around her. He picked her up as he had often done. She had grown taller and much thinner, feather light. Sometimes it seemed she was a phantom, an imaginary girl he had created like other children invented pretend friends. Now her name gushed from him like water flowing from the rock. "Skylar! Skye!" He'd found her. He'd found his sister.

CHAPTER 19

Master Jomaray Ganje spent most of the ride to Hopro Leap with his eyes closed. The untrustworthy boy walked ahead of him, leading his goaddig. He would have preferred being guided by the Keep, or the woman in charge of livestock (Was that Keep's second oldest daughter or third oldest?), or even Cook. But everyone not searching for Calbran Coriadler had more important work to do than tending to their acrophobic master.

The plodding beast swayed with a steady gait as they climbed. Of the high country, the animal was shorter, slower and less elegant than its flatland cousin, but more sure-footed on rough terrain. Jomaray should have found the regular clop, clop, clop of its hooves reassuring. Instead, he tensed with each beat, afraid the next sound would be the scraping of a stumble. Queasiness churned through him. He told himself it would subside if he opened his eyes and found something stationary to fix on. Then he would realize that he was actually quite stable, despite the jostling. Unfortunately, if he wasn't careful, he might also see that the path he rode on was only a hand's width away from the edge. The hurtling fall alone would definitely kill him. He was sure his heart would explode from terror long before his body smashed onto the boulders far below.

Jomaray forced himself to open an eye. He kept his head tilted back so he saw the mountains rising around him and not the split in the earth below him. The Leap was at a significantly higher elevation than the colony. To his left spindly trees snaked their roots into cracks, hugging the stone as they pushed themselves upward. How could they grow here? He wanted to embrace the rock as they did, cling to it with all his strength. He would have put out a hand to touch the rough wall for comfort, but he was unable to release the saddle horn. A jolt of surprise caused him to clutch tighter. The scene, he realized, was not what he had expected. "Boy, you've taken the wrong route. We're on the opposite side of the gorge from the Hopro."

Cheche held the reins slack, allowing the goaddig to make its own way. "As we should be to see what we came to see. It's not far now. There be the steps."

Ahead and to his right, what seemed like a long way across the dividing crevasse, the first horizontal slate slabs stuck out in profile. Stacked like giant stairs scaling the cliff, they should have been somber slats, muted and lifeless, but they flamed gold, amber, and crimson. Both eyes wide open now, Jomaray was in no danger of looking down. A plunging, horrifying death as close as a single wrong move could not pull his attention from the vivid colors.

As the goaddig's slow progression caused more of the landmark to become visible, the first bulges appeared to retreat. Instead of fading into dullness, they were absorbed into a larger fiery explosion. New protrusions, similarly painted, showed for a time then melted into the mural that grew with each barefoot step of the boy and plodding hoof of the beast. Section after section joined the piece until they reached the place directly opposite it that revealed the whole.

The boy stopped. The bored animal saw no reason to keep walking.

Viewed straight on, the mountainside glowed. Sparkling blue-grays bubbled and flowed like a river but were not a river. They burned with streaks of yellow, scarlet, wine, and smoke. The riotous colors floated in a frame of wavering mist.

"Seems you'd be mad to paint a cliff," Cheche said.

The gigantic scene loomed before Master Jomaray. He should reprimand the boy for his reference to Master Calbran's unfortunate condition, but it was hard to contradict the obvious. "He is truly mad."

Jomaray thought of the next shipment of artwork he must prepare. A mountain could not be rolled up and stuffed into a pouch. It could not be shoved into a box and strapped to a pack animal for transport. A chuckle loosened his tense chest. It rolled into a laugh then escaped in great guffaws, bouncing against the stone walls and echoing until it could have been a dozen men sharing a great joke.

This time his colleagues would have to leave their comfortable manor at Bogoboln and come to him. With luck, a storm or two would accompany their trip, punishing them for their past neglect. He would send them a message immediately, and he would demand that they bring the chamapl back with them.

CHAPTER 20

Clear, lustrous water chimed from the rocks into the plaza's fountain, then gurgled over the cracked edge to the cobble-covered ground and silently vanished. People came and went, came and stayed to enjoy the cool breeze from the bay below. Babies and young children laughed or wailed while the adults who tended them filled urns, pots, gourds and hide pouches. Loud conversations and serious whispers spread the latest news of daily life.

Irritated that he'd been ordered to stay by the overflowing basin, Austin gazed down the irregularly tiled street where his sister and Po argued with hushed voices and tight gestures. He had expected a cheerful, and tearful, reunion. Skylar had sent Po to get him and here he was—ready to rescue her! He had imagined himself the hero, her champion, sword in hand. Instead, Skylar had greeted him with shock, even dread, as if a grave catastrophe shadowed him.

Two years was a long time, he reminded himself—two important years in growing up. Skylar was easily four inches taller and more long-limbed than when she had disappeared.

Before, she had only been graceful when fencing or performing gymnastics. The rest of the time she'd boldly charged into physical activities with an awkwardness that often resulted in bruises and injuries. Now her every move seemed balanced, as if synchronized with the gravity of this world. Her childhood pudginess was gone. To Austin's shock, she had developed a mature figure for thirteen. He didn't want to think about the boys here noticing how curvy and pretty she was.

He must seem different too. He was inches taller himself, and he thought he'd gained some muscle. His baby cheeks had hollowed, giving him a more adult face. Probably. Maybe. He saw his reflection everyday so it was hard for him to judge how much he had changed.

Could her memory have been affected by the ordeal of trying to survive here? Did she have some other brother, enhanced by time and distorted by trauma, pictured in her mind? Was the boy she remembered in her dreams smarter, better looking, stronger, wiser than the real one who had suddenly appeared too late, years too late?

There was definitely something different about Skye that went deeper than growing up. Something in her eyes. What had she lived through here, alone and only eleven years old? He could not imagine his fearless sister frightened of this place. There were dangers, such as the creature-people living below the surface of the swamp and the smoke wolves. But with their parents' highly mobile careers, he and Skylar were used to being plopped onto new worlds. Of course, this wasn't exactly the same thing. He and Skylar had always had their parents to prepare them, to teach them, to protect them, and to provide the basics. How had Skylar found food? Where had she slept on frigid nights? Had people been kind, or had they mistreated her? There was so much he wanted to ask her.

He wouldn't have had to question the old Skylar. Without

the slightest urging, she would have relayed the entire two years to him by now. Instead, she kept her distance and energetically spoke to Po. No, she spoke *at* Po. Scowling and stomping back and forth, sending up dusty puffs from the paving stones. She looked as if she shouted, but she used a low voice so Austin couldn't hear. Po gestured, trying to explain or convince her of something. Then he seemed to be accusing her of some misdeed.

Austin wanted to be an understanding brother, but it hurt to be so obviously excluded. He had to get Skye out of here so she could be normal again, and so she'd stop treating him like a stranger. "Hey, what am I, a virus?" he called.

Po and the girl froze, as if they'd been caught plotting to rob a jewelry store and leave him in the vault to take the blame. The people in the plaza gave them glances then went back to their own affairs. Tired of being banished, Austin walked to his sister and stretched out his hand. He wanted to feel hers wrapped in his own, to know she was solid, real, and not an illusion. "Skye, let's go back to Callister right now. Let's go home."

The girl tucked her braid under her cloak and did not extend a hand to meet his. Stiffly, she gave Po a nudge.

"Austin," Po started and then stopped. He tried again. "Lord Austin of the Surging River and the great estate of Texas, my friend—"

"Texas?" Austin had never been to the North American Earth country. And he wasn't named after its capital city.

"You can't leave." Skylar's voice was deeper than Austin remembered. Her English had the same twist he'd noticed in Po's pronunciations, only hers was stronger. Other than instructing the master translator, she wouldn't have spoken or heard her native language since she'd arrived here. It was understandable that teacher and pupil now sounded alike—wasn't it?

Po said, "You and your sister cannot leave our lovely world, just at this moment, because—I am most ashamed to admit that I lost the key in the Droombian swamp."

"I saw you tuck it somewhere into your cape when we were at your aunt and uncle's house." Austin had been watching, but he still couldn't tell where Po's many hidden pockets were located.

Po scratched at his stubby white hair. "Yes, yes, I forgot. I thought I'd lost it but then I found it."

"Po, you just tried to lie to me," Austin said.

"I did. Yes, I did. And I feel gigantically badly about such deplorably behavior. That's because the truth is a very hard thing. A stone. A boulder." Po seemed to be struggling with a decision, the effort affecting his English.

"There is a man named Kriken," his sister said softly.

Po interrupted, glancing about to see who might be close enough to hear. "There is indeed the eminent Lord Kriken, protector of the Kriken Estate, who dwells in the glorious Wasbiln Manor."

Austin stopped listening to Po. He stared at the dark-haired girl, at his sister who had been lost and was now found. He fought down a grim thought that hadn't quite risen to the surface. He wanted to stay exactly at that instant, to live in it as it seemed to be. He could be happy for a little while longer if he just accepted without question—for now, for another second and another after that. But his mind would not be still.

"Skylar." Austin could barely chock out the words. "Attack, parry-riposte, counter-riposte."

The girl's eyes, flecked with gold and green, were so familiar and yet unknown. They held a touch of sympathy but remained guarded. She spoke softly. "I know the story. I could say the word, but I will not. It was never my intent to trick you. *You* are the one who named me sister, but I am not your Skylar."

CHAPTER 21

In Wasbiln Manor stretched three levels to the building's roof. Skylar tried to take in every detail. Central fire pit Double staircases leading to balconies along all sides of the second floor with a matching set stacked above on the third. Banners of varying lengths streaming from the highest walkway, some almost brushing the main floor. *Nice place for parties*, she thought. But it was more than that. People scurried about like busy insects—carrying, delivering, fetching. This was the core of the house, crisscrossed hundreds of times a day by those who lived and worked here. If someone wanted to be a pain in the ass and disrupt Lord Kriken's privileged life, this was the place to do it.

Cabrill had given her only a few instructions, leaving her free to improvise. During the long, tedious trip, Skylar had developed her own ideas about how to handle the mission. It was the guards' fault that her mind had focused on mischief. There were ten of them. Ten sent to capture one person! It promised fireworks and drama. Instead, they barely spoke to her. She was treated like a thing they'd picked up along the side of the road. Something someone else had accidentally dropped and, when they'd discovered it was missing, not bothered to go back for it.

Being kidnapped had left her limp with boredom. To keep from falling off the dingy goaddig, shuffling along just as dull as she felt, she'd spent the time devising strategies and plans and contingencies for all sorts of situations she'd played through in her head.

Lord Kriken had kidnapped her. Okay, he would have to deal with the consequences—lots of consequences.

Skylar was to be imprisoned on the third floor. She'd seen the windows from the outside. The two guards escorting her from the stable talked freely about their orders, as if she wasn't even there. They behaved as if all guests were brought to Wasbiln against their wills to be locked in their rooms. She didn't like being ignored. Even worse, she didn't like being treated like a routine duty. Well, that was going to change.

Skylar stopped beside the curved hearth and slapped a hand to her head. She pulled in a sharp breath and stared upward.

"She's going to spew," one of the guards said, taking a step back.

The other one shook a fist at her. They both had their swords drawn, but they carried them low, unconcerned that she might try to escape. "None of that. You wait until you're someone else's problem."

Skylar pointed to the longest pennant, a narrow flutter of fabric cascading from a top railing to barely a foot from the ground-level floorboards. The length caused folks bustling through the great room to elbow it aside or nudge it out of the way with their baskets. Scarlet lizards crawled through leaves within a swirling double border of gold thread. Definitely overdone. "That one." The room itself gasped. The scurrying people became statues. They knew who she was, or rather, who she was supposed to be. They stared, as if expected her to fashion a prophecy on the spot. "I need that one." She pointed to the next longest streamer. "And that one." She selected six in all. "Have them brought to my room!"

A woman was suddenly before her without seeming to have rushed into the position. From face to hair to clothing, she was stern, crisp, and disciplined. "You are causing a commotion. The loyalty banners of His Lordship's supporters will remain where they are."

"I need a stout pole this thick." Skylar made a circle with both hands. "And this long." She jerked out the sword arm of the tallest guard and indicated the length from wrist to shoulder. The startled man instinctively tried to recover control of his weapon. Skylar snatched it from him. "Swords." Everyone in the room who was carrying drew theirs and aimed them at her, prepared to defend the manor. "Yes," she said as if they acted at her command. "Lots of swords, *all* of them. Put them by the fire pit. I'll need them later."

Skylar tossed the guard's blade on the floor to indicate where she wanted the pile. It pained her to release the hilt. As herself, she was too young to go about with a weapon on her belt. As Cabrill, she was sword age. Unfortunately, the real master artist had needed to keep her own. To help with the impersonation, Cabrill had given Skylar a battered relic borrowed from a friend. It had hurt Skylar to let her captors take it from her.

No one came forward to place more metal on the floor beside the guard's sword. She wasn't worried. They'd be following her orders soon enough. Although a prisoner, she planned on running this place.

Dull brown hair smoothed back and tucked into a net bag at the nape of her neck, the rigid woman scowled at Skylar. She visibly struggled to fit the chaos she had just witnessed into her organized mind. "I am Ishty, the hearth keeper. I am in charge of His Lordship's household."

"I'd like to get settled in my room now, Ishty," Skylar said sweetly. "I have a great deal to do." As if she knew exactly where she was going, she strolled to the nearest staircase and began climbing to the top floor. Her guards scrambled to get ahead of her and lead the way. Once the Ishty woman consulted with Lord Kriken and had things in the right mental bins, Skylar knew the tasks she'd demanded would be done. The railing under her hand was solid and reassuring. At the moment she liked being the kidnapped Cabrill Shistayia, Sword-age Master Artist, rather than plain Skylar Swiftbrooke.

CHAPTER 22

Guild Master Jomaray Ganje had hoped the narrow trail, a whisper away from a fatal plunge, would make an impact on the distinguished visitors to the Deld Mountains. At least Grand Master Liaty Nobian was appropriately and logically terrified. Ashen-faced, he clung to his saddle and kept his head turned toward the solid land that rose close on the left. A year younger than his host, Liaty's once blue-black hair had turned white since taking on leadership of the Guild only eight years ago. Wrapped in a stylish but inadequate cloak for the mountain air, his usually straight form hunched over, trembling. His fame and advancement within the Guild were mostly due to a series of woodcarvings predicting a severe crop failure from a blight. The warning had spurred the storage of grains and prevented a major famine.

The boy led the grand master's goaddig. Jomaray had remembered the boy's name long enough to praise him as the most nimble of the guides; therefore, the one who should take charge of the honored leader of the Artists Guild. The lad's name had slipped from his mind since then. Patches of heavy, wet snow dotted the trail, remnants of the latest storm. Jomaray had the Keep lead his own mount. He felt more secure with the lean, muscular man in control of his goaddig than on the previous trip to Hopro Leap with a scrawny child holding the reins. Still, barely less terrified than Master Liaty, he struggled to appear even marginally at ease. He should be directing the beast himself. This was his territory, after all, his home for more than two decades.

"Which mountain is this? It isn't Wieldeld." Master Forliani Morokr heaped embarrassment upon him by declining a guide. She expertly steered her mount herself while gazing about as if she found it pleasant to ride along the edge of a deadly precipice. Fifteen years younger than Jomaray, she served as guild master to Bogoboln, the most influential of the colonies and the residence of the grand master.

Jomaray found her too tall. Her hair was excessively brown, as were her eyes. Her cheeks, blushed with cold, dominated an unpleasantly round face with a small chin. She was known for her works in textiles, gems and glass. Her most famous piece predicted the drowning of Lady Onopor. Unfortunately, the connection was not made between the art and the person until after the event.

"I'm not sure it has a name." Jomaray forced himself to smile. It seemed the exalted guild master expected him to be an expert on the terrain and to prance along the precarious path like one of the beasts native to the area. Which reminded him—despite his insistence, the colony's missing chamapl had not been a member of the party arriving from Bogoboln.

"Abijdeld," the boy called out. He pointed across the gorge toward the Leap. "That's Viepldeld."

Forliani nodded, obviously pleased to learn more useless information. "Thank you, Cheche." Jomaray grimaced. She remembered the boy's name after hearing it only once.

They reached the beginning of the giant ledges. Jomaray swallowed back vomit that threatened to burst forth. Voice trembling, he invited his guests to observe the array of vivid colors coming into view, and he explained the illusion of the local novelty. An artist could appreciate how protrusions jutting from the cliff face when viewed at an angle vanished when seen straight on, giving a flush appearance, as if the mountain had been sliced clean like a loaf of bread.

Grand Master Liaty forced himself periodically to squint across the abyss. Then he quickly returned to staring at the rock wall by his side. Master Forliani critically examined each new revelation of amber and crimson. "How was he able to procure the paint?"

Despite the chilled air, perspiration slicked Jomaray's skin. Recklessly he freed a hand from the saddle horn and wiped his forehead with a sleeve. "I analyzed it myself. The pigments are achieved by soaking various ground up minerals, which are found a short distance from here, in urine, presumably that of Master Calbran Coriadler himself. By adding more ground rock, one can form a substance the consistency of plaster or stucco." It was a partial truth. Thin shiny lines used sparingly amid the sweeping strokes were a mystery, but he was not going to admit his own ignorance. "The concoction adheres to the rock and is surprisingly durable." Several storms had pounded this area since he'd reported the existence of the mural. Unfortunately, only one, and a mild one at that, had circled Mount Wieldeld while the visitors had made their way to Seaba Colony.

As they plodded along, the canyon separating the side-by-side mountains widened, as if two chunks of a whole were pried apart. The split ran for miles. The jutting stairs in Hopro Leap performed their disappearing act, revealing the full scope of the mural. Jomaray was again awed by the difference a simple change in perspective produced.

The Keep stopped the procession at a relatively wide spot in the trail. He stepped around the side of the goaddig, giving it pats and soothing words. He spoke softly to Jomaray. "Master, this should be done quickly. The man is not well. Might be he suffers the high sickness, as well be you."

Jomaray nodded. He found satisfaction in Grand Master Liaty Nobian's discomfort. He did not want to hurry this, even for his own sake.

Liaty cupped shaking hands around his eyes, blocking everything from view except the painting. "How did Master Calbran manage something so gigantic?"

Forliani dismounted and draped the reins over a tree that was barely more than a stick. The action was tidy but unnecessary since her goaddig was unlikely to wander off. "Master Calbran must have used ropes for some of it."

"I was thinking more of the quantity of urine," Liaty said.

"What is it meant to show?" Forliani asked. "There's sunlight and," she shrugged, "more sunlight. I see no clear forms in it. Do you, Liaty?"

"It appears very random." The grand master slumped against his goaddig, hugging its thick neck. "Forgive me. I am suddenly fatigued and my head throbs."

"Deep breaths, Liaty," Forliani said. "The work is probably of no importance, but I suppose we should have an advisor or two review it. Are there other paintings?"

Jomaray was insulted but not surprised that neither of the eminent artists asked for *his* impression of the piece. "Small drawings scattered about. Nothing else of this scale." He resisted adding *that's been found*. Calbran continued to elude the searchers. Most likely he was nearby dangling from ropes, painting another cliff with his piss.

"I'll want to see them later." Forliani expertly turned her goaddig around on the narrow ledge and mounted. "Right now, we'd better get the grand master to a lower altitude."

Cheche found the strangers entertaining, but he didn't like them. After careful maneuvering, he and Keep headed the animals they led back toward Seaba. The man was a worse flatlander than Master Jomaray. The high sickness came upon him before they had ascended to the second plateau, long before the colony master was affected. Although he was leader of an entire guild, he let the other artist, who was of a lower rank according to Jomaray, tell him what to think.

The woman, unaffected by the altitude, knew how to ride a needle path and walk easily about a ledge. She moved well but with thought, showing more planned swagger than effortless skill. Cheche guessed some of her early years had been spent on cliffs and crags, but she had not grown up in mountains. The natural balance of a highland native, born and raised, was not in her gait.

Cheche didn't hold any of that against them. Not everyone was as lucky as he, to be of the Deld Mountains. What rubbed him raw was their behavior toward Master Jomaray and the workers at Seaba. They said all the right things, all polite and respectful, but the words were pretty fruit with no taste. The foreign masters looked directly at people and called each by name, which Master Jomaray rarely did, but one was the same as the next to them.

Mostly, Cheche was bewildered by their reactions to mad Calbran's creation. He found it far more exciting than the boring art Master Jomaray displayed in his cottage—

predictions of drought that happened generations ago, an influenza epidemic, the sinking of some ship. They were dull and stagnant, while the mural was alive with more shades of reds, yellows, blues, grays, and sparkles than he had ever seen together in his young life. The impact of the colors alone made it worthy of covering a mountainside. Cheche had expected masters Liaty and Forliani to be impressed, if not by the quality then at least by the size and brilliance. But after traveling so far for the single purpose of viewing it, they appeared indifferent.

More puzzling, they didn't seem to notice the picture in the paint. Cheche knew people didn't always agree on what they saw when they looked at the same thing. And art was about tricking you into seeing what wasn't really there. It was as much an illusion as the disappearing steps of the Leap.

To him, the scene was clear. Perhaps being around the unusual pieces the Tranquility crazies produced every day gave him a different eye. He was used to images that were looser, more free in shape and form, than the precise works in the Master's cottage. He especially liked the finger paintings done once with Cook's gravy and grits. Those pieces had not been included in that month's package to Bogoboln. Maybe other canvases hadn't left Seaba either, giving Cheche an advantage over the strangers.

What did Jomaray see when he looked at the wall? The Master hadn't said when Cheche was close enough to hear. Now he would probably only agree with the two visitors.

As they reached the switchback to the third plateau, Cheche closed his eyes. His naked feet knew the path better than his sight. In his mind he saw mad Calbran's masterpiece. An opening suspended in the sky spewed out a liquid road. Flames and gray splotches stalked the length. Even in memory, the road shimmered as if it flowed while the figures flared and swirled as if alive.

CHAPTER 23

T he walk from the plaza back to the tavern seemed endless. Feeling sick and beaten, Austin forced one foot in front of the other. He couldn't talk to Po and was glad the man who was definitely *not* his friend didn't try to offer an explanation or an excuse. He kept his gaze down, so he wouldn't accidentally glance at the nameless girl, face hidden in her hood, who was definitely *not* his sister. Instead of being mindlessly angry, a double loss filled every part of him, as if Skylar had appeared then vanished again.

He trudged up the stairs and into the room. Po bolted the door and leaned against it, as if to assure himself the barrier was strong. Obviously distressed, he spoke to the girl in Lynawic. Austin didn't try to translate in his head. He couldn't avoid looking at her now. She removed her cloak, hung it on a hook by the door and dropped her pack. Both were weathered smooth and faded like sun-bleached wood. Chin-forward, she boldly defended herself against Po's disapproval of something she'd done. She looked so very much like an older version of the Skylar he remembered. A braid, rich as twisted velvet, fell to her waist. Austin remembered catching a glimpse of it at the fountain. Subconsciously, he must have realized his sister wasn't allowed to wear her hair that way here because she was too young. Only those over swording age could earn and wear braids. But that wasn't how he had known, absolutely, that the girl was an imposter. It was much simpler than that.

Po and the girl tossed Skylar's name back and forth. Austin heard his own sprinkled in. He wanted to stay numb and ignore the argument in foreign words, but his sister was being discussed. He had a right to be involved, despite his limited vocabulary. He forced himself to follow along. What he could decipher in the fast-paced exchange ran a chill through his spine. "Skylar's been taken? Captured? By somebody's what?"

Po and the girl looked at him, as if they'd forgotten he was in the room. Po replied in English. "Your brilliant Lady Sister and Cabrill were both to join us at the fountain at midday as soon as they received my message through a dependable cousin that we were in Saffshier."

Austin had met many of Po's family. He suspected undependable cousins were not tolerated. "My sister and *who*?"

"I," the girl said sharply in English. "I am Master Artist Cabrill Shistayia. You are Austin Swiftbrooke, Master Swordsman, Lord of a great land on some other world, and brother of Skylar Swiftbrooke. Now we are introduced." She grabbed a pouch from her pack and pulled a thick roll from it. "Days passed without a message from you," she said to Po in Lynawic. "I needed to work at my art, but sketch after sketch showed Kriken's guards coming for me. I couldn't draw anything else. And then I did this." She peeled off curled sheets of tree bark and scattered them on the table. She selected one and shoved it at Po.

Shades of black and gray showed a girl with long dark hair

in a single braid that snaked across her shoulder. She stood in a forest, sword in hand. A mischievous, almost wicked smile curved her lips. Armed figures surrounded her, their uniforms marked with an insignia.

Austin felt a wave of nausea. "Skylar."

"Yes, definitely Skylar," Cabrill said.

"Is it she? Or is that what you want to see?" Po examined it. "An artist should not interpret her own work."

"That is what the Guild promotes. But experience has shown me otherwise, so I no longer believe it to be true. Besides, you know I couldn't take it to an advisor, even if I could find one I trusted." She shoved the drawing into Po's hands. "This was coming closer and you were silent. I feared you were having difficulty getting the key to take us to Skylar's world." She looked pointedly at Austin and then back to Po. "Apparently not."

Po adjusted his cloak uncomfortably. "It was a sensitive transaction, requiring more diplomacy than anticipated. Eventually I was successful."

"Po, we agreed. The three of us were supposed to go together to fetch the brother."

Po tried to soothe Cabrill. "It would have been a more enjoyable venture with you as company, but I was distressed by the considerable number of days that had gone by, and I felt the need for haste. Lord Austin was discovered near the stiav, as expected. It should have been a quick journey to this lovely city. Unfortunately, we were forced to take a long and strenuous detour. I am joyous you were spared the discomfort."

"Hey," Austin shouted, "important information here. My sister has been kidnapped!"

Po pounced on the opportunity to break out of the dispute with Cabrill. "Kidnapped! An excellent word. Yes, My

Lady of the Azure is the honored captive of the noble Lord Kriken."

"We have to notify the police." Austin wasn't happy about the girl saying he would be *fetched* or Po thinking being kidnapped somehow *honored* a person, but this was not the time to discuss word choice. "You have police here, don't you? People who arrest the bad guys and put them in jail? Kidnapping is against the law, isn't it?"

"We have local militia in each region," Po said. "On Lord Kriken's estate, which is extensive, his guards serve the function you describe. They are unlikely to arrest themselves and their employer."

Cabrill took her drawing from Po and offered it to Austin. "Look. It is as it is supposed to be."

Austin gave it a glance. "So you're a good artist."

"Yes!" Cabrill said, as if that explained everything.

"She is far beyond good," Po said. "She is extraordinary, exceptionally extraordinary."

Austin wanted to know about his sister, not discuss art. "Then I guess you earn a lot of gills sitting in the sunshine, selling pretty pictures."

"You think me so irresponsible?" Cabrill shouted. She looked to the open window as if afraid of the attention she might have attracted. She lowered her voice. "My art is too dangerous to peddle on a public road."

"Great Lord Austin of the Fast-flowing Water and the magnificent estate of Texas," Po said, "my friend. If you would indulge me by examining the drawings." He selected some from the heap on the worm-eaten table and presented them to Austin as if they were treasures.

Austin wanted to shout at Po that he'd never been to Texas and they were not friends, not anymore. He ignored the slices of bark. "Where does this Kriken guy live?"

Po carefully handed the sheaves to Cabrill, apparently disappointed that Austin had not seen their value. He calmly went to the window and leaned out, seemingly concerned with nothing beyond inhaling the pungent street air. Cabrill clutched her drawings as if injured. Some slipped to the floor, fluttering about her feet like tired moths. She knelt on the rough boards and gathered them back.

Austin sighed and went to the window, resigned that he would have to do this Po's way. "Why did Kriken kidnap Skylar? Does he want a ransom? You know, money or something in exchange for her?" Voices in a dozen languages sweetened and soured the breeze. A vendor strolled by in a nebula of veils, sending up scents of citrus and cinnamon.

"I don't believe 'ransom' is appropriate in this context, but it is not so very far from accurate. When My Lady of the Sky, came to this land, the very moment she delicately placed a dainty foot onto its dewy meadow, she was found by Cabrill Shistayia." Po gracefully indicated their dark-haired companion behind them. "Although only a little older than this child she'd discovered, Cabrill was already a master artist of considerable skill and reputation. She shared what little she had with The Lady of Wonderful Words and used her sword to keep her safe."

Austin knew the "delicate and dainty" part was all wrong, but he was relieved to hear his sister had not been wandering a strange planet alone.

In the street below a clot of golden-haired, golden-skinned people rudely pushed through the chaotic flow, their business more important than good manners. "Cloosoo," Po said sadly. "Avoid them if you can. Fortunately, I am rarely required to have dealings with them. Being polite is much better for commerce."

"I really don't want a lesson right now."

"Does your culture respect talent?" Po asked.

Austin forced himself to consider the question. He thought of people he knew and people he knew about who had done great things. Some of them were widely famous, like the fencer Solier, who had won more awards than anyone. Some were unknown outside of their fields, like his parents, but were well regarded by those familiar with their work. A friend of his could burp classical music, including the entire Pleiades Symphony. The reactions he got were far from signs of respect. Someone in the street banged on a drum. Austin hoped no one would encourage the musician with coins. "Sometimes. It depends on the talent."

Po nodded. "Often the owner of a large estate will employ a member of the Artists Guild to create work that focuses only on local concerns. Kriken's resident artist unfortunately became ill and died just at a difficult time. Because of Cabrill's great talent, His Lordship requested that she join his household."

"That could not happen," Cabrill said from behind them, pulling Austin's attention from the street. "I refused, so Kriken sent his guards to take me by force. The drawing you dismissed, shows they were coming and that they would take Skylar instead."

Austin wasn't following the timing. It sounded like Cabrill made the drawing before the kidnapping happened. "For a protector, you didn't do a very good job."

Drawings curled across the scarred wood like flower petals. A mixture of bark and heavy paper, they resisting Cabrill's efforts to organize them as if they didn't want to be bundled and shoved away in a knapsack. "You are no older than me, I think. But your experiences and mine are far different. How can I explain that an impossible meeting with a girl from another world changed the direction of my life? If it was within my power, I would never allow her to be hurt. Never."

Ashamed of his comment, Austin knelt next to Cabrill and held down the corners on the stack she was trying to construct. At the sight of the top parchment, his breath escaped him. Charcoal strokes curved across the creamy page. Set against a background of rocky crags he didn't recognize, a determined looking girl stared straight at him. Her dark hair billowed behind her as if she faced a gale. Although more sculpted and mature than he remembered, he knew the face, he knew the eyes, he especially knew the "Don't mess with me" expression. A distance behind her an almost duplicate image stood undisturbed by the wind. Austin examined the two faces closely. They were very much alike but not the same. Subtle differences suggested the person in the background had lived a harder life. He touched the cheek of the wind-blown girl. "Skylar."

Po stood at his shoulder. "Ahh, the intelligent Lady of the Azure Heavens. Be assured she will perform well and Lord Kriken will not dare harm her."

Austin's curiosity overwhelmed him. He pulled another sketch from the feathery pile. He found his own face gazing back at him, as if from a formal portrait. Dressed in his fencing uniform, he held his foil ready to salute an opponent. Rocks adorned the sparse landscape. Behind his image a tall pile formed a stone arch. The arena back on Callister! Cabrill hadn't met him until today. Skylar must have described him and the scene to her. Austin stared, amazed at the accurate detail. Po had not exaggerated the artist's talent.

Austin grabbed another. The drawing was strong and rich. In it he and his sister faced each other while something angry burned behind them. Braids, like the ones he wore now, twined through his unkempt hair. Skylar had never seen him in braids. Cabrill must have added that on her own. A gap between the siblings showed Skye's placid twin in the distance. To one side farther back, trees or figures were silhouetted by the fury—one short, one tall, the other taller still.

They're just drawings, Austin told himself. But they felt important, as if they carried a secret meaning, a code he didn't understand in a language he hadn't yet learned. He found another of his sister. And another. And more of himself. "Po, you said Skylar would perform well. Perform what?"

"A simple pretense requiring little effort," Po said. "Your honorable sister presents herself to His Lordship as Master Artist Cabrill."

Austin stared at Cabrill. "She's pretending to be you?"

Cabrill snatched the drawings from him. "I had tasks that needed to be done. Skylar and I are—connected—as sisters. She chose to be kidnapped in my place—to act as me, freely, of her own mind—so I could do my work."

Skylar chose? His sister was not a victim but a willing partner in some scheme. "If you were really her friend—her *sister*—you wouldn't have let her." Austin knew how stubborn Skye could be once she decided something, but *he* wouldn't have let her take *his* place. Guilt that had been living in him for a long time boiled into grief and jealousy. Skylar shouldn't have needed a pretend sister. *He* should have been here with her, not a stranger. *He should have been with her that day two years ago.*

Austin closed his eyes, remembering. They had both logged out of school for the afternoon. Skylar was bored with everything except fencing and eager to get to the arena. Sure he would never survive macrochemistry, Austin wanted to schedule an extra session with his remote tutor. Not understanding how important that single moment in time was, he told Skylar to go ahead and he would catch up with her. "You're just delaying getting beaten," she tossed at him. Thick braid swinging against her back, bag dangling from her hand, she rushed out the door. And disappeared.

Austin opened his eyes to see images of his sister vanish into Cabrill's hands. He swallowed down sobs. "If you'd stopped her, we could have been home by now."

Cabrill rolled the sheaves together and eased them into a pouch. "Understand this, if I had gone with the guards, you and your sister would not be back on your own world. You are meant to be here until this is done."

Austin made no sense of it. "This guy kidnapped Skylar, thinking she was you, because he wants a new painting to hang in his dining room. That's pretty extreme." He thought of his sister's previous artistic efforts. Would His Lordship appreciate a chunky unicorn jumping over a toothy toad?

"To one such as Lord Kriken," Po said, "who possesses considerable power and wealth, and who holds responsibility for vast land and those who dwell upon it, insight into the future is beyond measure. Devastation has been avoided because a painting depicted a brutal storm or a tapestry showed a flood and gave warning. Of course, not all art is useful. The quality of the prediction depends upon the skill of the artist. Master Cabrill's talent is unique."

The future? Austin remembered beadwork and jewelry he'd seen on display in the market. When he'd stopped to admire an ornate clasp for a cape, the shop owner had said, "This was made by my son. It is a small prophecy—perhaps meant for you." Austin had thought it strange, but at the time he wasn't sure he'd understood correctly. Did people here create art that told the future? He wanted to dismiss the idea as nonsense, but throughout the known planets there were documented cases of rare people with abilities that went far beyond what was considered normal.

Well, Austin didn't care about any fortune telling. He grabbed his pack and dug into it. "I'll tell you His Lordship's future. I'm going to go kick his Kriken ass and get Skylar back."

Cabrill gave Po a puzzled look and spoke in Lynawic. "I need a translation."

"So do I." Po spoke to Austin in English. "Perhaps you indicated we should travel to the beautiful and usually prosperous Wasbiln Estate and unkidnap, or nonkidnap your sister."

Austin took out his foil. "Not we. *Me*."

"Do not make haste with this," Po said.

"Oh, yes, haste will be made." Austin unwrapped the blade then rewrapped it more tightly. If only all conflicts were as direct as a fencing bout. He would need more than the mostly non-lethal weapon to free his sister. He'd figure that out later. "I'm going to *unkidnap* Skylar. Just point me in the right direction.

"We will do it together," Po said.

"The three of us," Cabrill said.

Austin wanted to rescue Skylar by himself, to rush in and snatch her away to safety. But it would be foolish to try on his own, especially since he didn't know where he was going or what he was going to do when he got there. Like it or not, he needed Po and Cabrill. He stared at the girl he had thought was his sister. Unflinching, she returned his gaze. He knew that determined, stubborn look very well. To her, the path was already set.

"Okay. Po, you're the one who figures out things. What's the plan?"

Po wore his confidence as easily as his well-tailored cloak. "It is a long way to Wasbiln Manor. Inspiration will travel with us. By the time we reach our goal, the strategy will be revealed."

Austin scowled. "That's your way of saying you don't have one, isn't it?"

The little man grinned at the boy who, still kneeling on the floor, met him eye-to-eye. "It will require some expense and my funds have almost expired. But I have determined a way to finance our journey. It involves your considerable skill with a sword. I believe you will find it invigorating."

Austin heard little of Po's enthusiastic explanation of some financial scheme. He could think of nothing but his sister. Kidnapped. Locked away in a stone-cold prison cell. Shivering. Alone. Hungry. Afraid. How she must be suffering!

CHAPTER 24

Thick tapestries softened the lacquered walls of the elegant bedroom. The richly embroidered banners Skylar had selected draped in elegant folds over an ornately carved chest. A pole the length of a guard's arm hung suspended from two tall iron stands meant to hold candles. Skylar reclined on a feather-filled mattress, sunk deep into an abundance of bolster pillows, each in a different intense color. She felt smothered by giant, well-meaning crayons. She had described the waxy sticks to Cabrill once, but the master artist hadn't understood. She guessed they didn't exist here.

She would have been more comfortable with crayons than with the charcoal Cabrill had included in the bundle of art supplies she'd given her. She propped the small easel against her knees and made a few cowardly strokes on the scary blank parchment. One was too crooked. The other was too straight. She tried to rub them away with a cloth. The cruel soot retained all of her indecision and failure in ugly smudges.

Fencing and other sports were exciting physical and

mental challenges. Math was a series of complex puzzles that she loved solving. Science was wonderfully logical and at the same time forever surprising. But art mystified her. Not art itself. She appreciated the intellectual and emotional impact that could spring out of line, shape, and shading. It was the making of art, the construction, the bones of it, that eluded her. Her attempts at traditional drawing and painting had always been disastrous. Landscapes never progressed beyond flat outlines. Animals and people seemed frozen in stiff, nightmare poses.

Her only hope was a three-dimensional structure she could actually build out of stuff that already existed. That approach had gotten her through more than one art course. Her stunt in the great room had already committed her to that path anyway. The household buzzed about her demand for swords. She needed a sketch of what the finished piece would look like to convince Kriken she wasn't just making it all up. Which she was, but he mustn't know that. She also had to show how the banners and pole fit in so no one would suspect their real purpose.

She bunched up a bright yellow pillow to support her elbow. Saffrian, another planet to add to her collection. She always thought of herself and her family as nomads, pitching their tent wherever they happened to be. Sometimes it was a real tent. She knew she wouldn't stay with her parents and her brother forever, that someday she would venture out on her own. She hadn't expected it to be by accident and so soon.

She thought she had the details of her sudden change in location figured out. She was on Callister at the arena, going through her warm-up routine while waiting for Austin. The cord holding her good luck charm got twisted. She straightened it out so it hung free. Bracing her hands against one of the arches, she leaned forward, stretching her hamstrings. Her medallion clanked against the stone. A flash blanked her vision. As if snow blind, she stumbled through the whiteness and slammed into—

Herself!

Together they rolled, not in the hard-packed dirt of the arena, but in swishing grass. When they stopped spinning, Skylar sat up slowly, dizzy and dazed. Her other self held her head in both hands, as if to steady her vision. Then she stared at Skylar with familiar green-gold eyes. "Are you real and not an illusion? Do I call you demon or friend?"

Skylar heard the words but made no sense of them. The older girl showed her drawings of the two of them together and expected her to understand something about them. The next days felt more like a very long, very detailed story her mind invented. They traveled to places that weren't anywhere she'd ever been before and ate food unfamiliar to her. She was often tired from walking. And hiding. They did a lot of both.

She went back and forth between thinking of her new situation as real, and thinking she must have been in a terrible accident that left her unconscious. In a dream. Or in a coma. The girl named Cabrill was a guide she'd conjured up so she wouldn't be alone. She had to admit it was an adventure unlike anything she'd ever experienced. If this was only in her addled head, she was impressed with her own imagination.

Communication was a moment-by-moment challenge. It improved once she learned some of Cabrill's language and taught the older girl a few English words. Things became more spirited when Po joined them. The Astlian absorbed English like a drought-stricken plant in a sudden rain. He begged Skylar for descriptive phrases and poetry he could memorize. When he spoke them back to her, they were beautiful and full of life.

Po demanded jokes and puns. A language was best understood through its humor, he said. Skylar always found that to be the most difficult part of comprehending a new tongue. She and Po struggled back and forth with funny stories and witty sayings in English and in Lynawic. Sometimes Po recognized why a punch line was funny. Mostly he didn't. Skylar rarely did. Perhaps that's why Cabrill seemed so serious to her. She simply didn't understand when the older girl was joking.

As Skylar's skills with Lynawic improved, it became easier for her to imagine that she'd always lived here. It was a strategy she'd used often as her parents finished an assignment then took on a new one, once again hauling her and Austin off to another remote world. That's how she'd been able to fit into a new environment right away, while Austin moped around.

With Cabrill and Po she pretended she was traveling with a cousin and a friend, that her family knew exactly where she was and were glad she was having a great time. It worked. Mostly. She missed Austin and her parents terribly. Were they worried about where she was and what had happened to her? Or were they sitting beside her comatose body hoping she would wake up?

One night by campfire light Skylar watched her companion, almost in a trance, transform blank canvas with swoops and swirls. A portrait emerged of herself and Cabrill, together yet apart under angry clouds. The lines moved and flowed across the page as if alive. They became a vision of two girls, so alike and yet different, each with an arm stretched to reach the other, fingers almost touching, yet gazing straight ahead as they walked into a storm.

Skylar understood the scene on a level she couldn't describe. It told her a truth as strongly and clearly as if she read words inscribed within the figures. From that moment, she accepted the world around her as real and not her own delusion. She had something important to do here. She was needed here. She belonged here.

Many times after that, Skylar watched images move in Cabrill's works. She saw motion in colorful smudges of paint. And in bones, feathers, and bits of metal joined with knotted thread. She saw life etched in sand; scrawled on rocks, bark, cloth; and hanging like wind chimes from branches. Together they formed a collection that was still unfinished.

Austin was in them, again and again in charcoal, paint, feathers, and sand. Beside her. With her and Cabrill. Alone, holding his sword like something sacred. He was on the rocks and the bark and the cloth. He was in the clattering music of suspended metal. She saw him and heard him and felt him in the art, and she knew he would join them soon.

Now, in Kriken's manor house, Skylar willed herself to concentrate. She had to pretend to be the master artist long enough for Cabrill to complete all the parts of her prediction. How strange they looked so much alike! She tried to think of a reasonable genetic explanation but came up with nothing better than random chance.

She stared at the smudged page and told herself the task was easy. All she needed was one fake drawing of one fake sculpture. She examined her prison for inspiration and found none in its soft bed and smothering pillows. She hoped Cabrill had been able to get a message to Po about this delay in their plans. He should have the key to Callister by now. She was eager to see her parents again, to assure them she was okay. And to assure herself that they were okay. Then she, Po and Cabrill would bring Austin back and set things right here on Saffrian.

She swiped a vertical line. The dark, straight mark sat in

the smeared background of her previous mistakes. Why was this so hard? Swords were the ultimate stick figures, after all.

She took a breath for courage. As if the paper were an opponent, she brandished the charcoal like a weapon, and attacked.

CHAPTER 25

Austin found himself standing on the end of a wobbly ramp tilted up to a plank stretched over a very smelly animal sty, complete with animals. The round beasts waddled about on short legs. Similar to hog-like creatures on Callister, the vibbys were uglier and smelled worse—sort of a blend of feces, urine and rotting eggs. This wasn't what Austin envisioned when Po said he had a way to finance their trip to rescue Skylar.

After the nicks and jabs bout with Ryster, Austin had complained to Po about the difficulty of facing an opponent experienced in moving around in any direction. Po had been fascinated by his description of a regulation fencing strip and the idea of restricting movement to a long, narrow rectangle. Much too fascinated, Austin realized. While he had spent a long uncomfortable time in the claustrophobic room with the girl who was not his sister, Po had been out arranging this strange competition.

The girl Cabrill had sat at the rough table, keeping her eyes on a bowl of fishy chowder she slurped with a wooden spoon. "Is Skylar okay?" he'd asked her.

Cabrill had not looked at him. "She is protected."

Protected. That didn't mean safe. And that wasn't the intent of the question. Austin was asking in a larger sense, across the chasm of two years. Was she healthy? Did she miss him and their parents? Did she think about him, talk about him? Had she gotten taller, fatter, thinner? Did she still crinkle her eyes shut when she laughed really hard? *Did* she laugh here? Or was she sad and homesick all the time? Austin made a few stumbling attempts to get the details he craved, but Cabrill's replies were short and unsatisfying.

Po broke the prickly silence, charging in excited as a child by his new enterprise. Without explanation, he had Austin grab his weapon, and they rushed off to the livestock yard.

Now Austin eyed the ramp and the long, sagging plank supported at each end by the corral encompassing the beastie pit. Shopkeepers, farmers and general citizenry, all carrying swords, formed a line at a similar incline on the other side. The first one tottered his way up to the edge.

"Magnificent," Po said, referring to his own idea. "A plait and five gills a go. Six opponents. Soon you'll have additional braids and we will be traveling like lords!"

A quiet horror crept over Austin. "Six. Six bouts while standing on a board."

"Only to three points." Po directed Austin's sight along the make-shift bridge spanning the sty. "See, it is your fencing strip, just as you described. You will have all the advantage."

Austin wrinkled his nose at an especially strong whiff from the mire. "It's supposed to be on the ground, not suspended in air. If you step out of bounds, you don't fall into—" Austin chocked. He didn't want to think about the composition of the earthy muck.

Po was giddy with pride. "That is the genius of my design. Fall and lose. They have not stripped before; you have. They will fall; you will not. No one will last to three points."

"What if *I* fall?" Austin asked.

Po sobered. "Then we must award the winner *ten* gills, double what they are paying for the privilege of being beaten by you. I hope that will not happen. There is a capital investment in renting the location and procuring referees. Two such catastrophes would devour our margin. A fourth would place us in serious trouble. There is no tolerance for unpaid debt here." Po brushed aside possible doom with the wave of a hand. "Do not dwell on that nor on the slop below you. Concentrate on preserving our earnings so we may continue to eat and perhaps purchase a pack animal."

Not having to carry his gear all the way to wherever it was they were going and having regular meals along the way sounded great. Austin would love to focus on that. But Po had told him not to think about falling into the foul mud and owing his opponents money, so naturally that filled his mind.

Po hurried to the other side to manage the opponents. Austin trudged up the ramp and cautiously inched onto the plank. Cabrill had disappeared. From the advantage of height, he scanned the stockyard but didn't see her. She was probably off somewhere retching up chowder from the nauseating smell.

Austin tested the footing and flicked his weapon. The wood groaned and shivered under him. He tried to imagine he stood inside a ribbon etched in the dirt in the arena back home. Flat land surrounded him, he told himself. Safe, flat land. He could almost see it, almost believe it. Except for the smell. And the quivering of the board. And the squealing of animals below his feet. Austin let the illusion go. He was stuck in this precarious reality and would have to deal with it.

The three referees stood outside the pit on barrels that elevated them to the level of the fencers. From habit Austin gave each one a salute, bringing his blade to his forehead then unfurling it downward. He did the same to his first opponent. Saluting was not part of the custom here. The round man grunted as he tentatively shuffled forward. The plank sagged, recovered, and sagged at each step. Awkwardly he returned Austin's gesture with his inelegant broadsword wrapped in a bark skin.

"Play," the main referee called.

The round man made a wide swing with his hefty weapon to test the range. The board wobbled with the redistribution of weight. Surprised, the man waved his arms, trying to readjust. He tilted to the left, sticking out his right leg to counterbalance. Grinning with relief, he successfully centered his bulk over his supporting leg. He tried to set his right foot on the narrow plank and missed. Crying out in disbelief and dread, he toppled into the muck with a wet splat.

Released from its burden, the board vibrated wildly. Austin bent his knees to absorb the flux, more like a surfer than a fencer. The spectators thought it was great sport, even though no contact had occurred. They roared with surprise, delight and disappointment. A referee pointed to Austin. "Winner!" he called.

Two of the waiting competitors demanded that Po return their five gills. Other spectators shoved coins at Po and rushed to the end of the line. Austin counted. Including the defeated man climbing over the rails of the corral, dripping in assorted shades of runny brown sludge, there were eight. The next one, a woman with many braids and just as many tufts of short hair, took two confident steps onto the board.

Austin took a deep breath of foul air and saluted her.

A referee called, "Play."

CHAPTER 26

"The cost of the animal and livery, a bit of grain to supplement the beast's grazing, a small fee to the livestock merchant for the use of the sty." Po ticked off the expenses as the travelers swayed from side to side with the stride of their new ploddel. "Our earnings were quickly depleted but well spent. At the next village we should gain enough for several meals."

The saddle had two seats on each side. They were little more than leather slings suspended from yokes across the animal's wide back. Austin sat on the opposite side from Cabrill and Po, unable to see them. He kept a hand against the rough hide to ease bumping against the ribs with each sway. "You want me to do that again?" He'd gotten through a total of twelve challengers without losing his footing. None of them had scored more than a single point. Only two had taken all three hits to defeat. Most had fallen into the pit because of their own mistakes.

"You did splendidly," Po said. "With no doubt, you will defeat all whom you face." He steered using reins that looped about the ploddel's head and thick neck. The beast needed little guidance on the well-worn road. "My family is grateful for the educational opportunity you and your sister provide. The English lexicon I'm compiling continues to flower with the buds that blossom from your lips. But, alas, knowledge of your language produces no income at the moment, and may never do so. Fortunately, we now have an immediate way to benefit from our partnership." Austin heard him slap the grooved hide. "And so we have this fine beast to speed us on our way."

Trees, grasses and farm fields crawled past. Austin wasn't seeing much speed exactly, but the animal ambled faster than Po could walk with his short legs. The ploddel tripped, slamming him against its solid side despite his efforts to cushion the impact. "I could teach Cabrill to fence on a strip. Then we could take turns sty fencing, or whatever you call it."

Silence was followed by the rustling of Po and Cabrill whispering intensely. They did that a lot, excluding Austin from discussions that often seemed more like arguments. He was sure Cabrill protested. Who would volunteer for such a bizarre, and smelly, sport? She hadn't been anywhere in sight while he'd faced a dozen grinning maniacs with heavy blades. It became quieter, silk against silk. Po, the negotiator, was making his case.

"That is an idea worthy of consideration," Po shouted from the other side of the animal. "Perhaps a lesson or two to determine if Cabrill has the aptitude for it."

Right. Austin knew he would be stuck doing all of it himself. At least he liked his braids and would be glad to get more.

"My friend," Po called, "you suggested we need a name for our new sport. You are most correct. Since it is on a strip of wood, I propose we call it stripping."

Cabrill closed her mind to the silly conversation. She was nauseous from the jostling and dizzy with images trapped in her head, pounding for release. She couldn't sketch because of the motion. She couldn't sleep. She couldn't think.

The beast's advantage was stamina. It could sway along all day with its giant, rolling gait and not tire. But even at a good pace, traveling from before dawn through twilight, it would take days to reach Wasbiln.

She had warned Po that his new sword sport made it more likely she would be noticed. They should be moving quietly, invisibly, not creating spectacles along their path. But they had to eat. The boy, not understanding the need for stealth, was right to suggest she help finance the trip by participating in Po's disgusting version of nicks and jabs. Even if she managed to gain enough skill to win, she couldn't take a turn at the game. People from Kriken's estate traded along this route, hauling goods as far from home as need be to find the right market. Every village brought the chance someone would notice her resemblance to His Lordship's forced guest.

Just as likely, Cabrill might be seen by another artist traveling from one commission to the next. Officially, according to the Guild, she was a resident of Seaba. Her presence elsewhere could be mentioned to someone who would tell someone else. Eventually it would be told to a master with the authority to send more mercenaries to imprisoned her in the Deld Mountains—or worse. Her location might reach the ear of whatever master or masters wanted her dead.

Her situation made it impossible for her to openly sell her

work, so she had no income. Her tiny savings had quickly evaporated. She'd sold the few possessions she could part with. She was down to living off money borrowed from friends and cousins—the few she trusted, the ones willing to let her in when she rapped on their doors after dark.

Food; clothes; camping supplies; this slow, smelly beast; a fee for Po, since she had hired him—she should be paying for everything. But she contributed nothing. Earning coin had to be left up to the boy, the skinny boy who played games and had no true experience with fighting and bravery. He was disappointing in real life, not the level-eyed champion from her art. This boy was no hero. Yet, he must become one. It was his reason for being here. He was supposed to save them and their world. Perhaps he would if it meant saving the sister he was determined to rescue, but Cabrill wasn't seeing the potential.

She hadn't lied to the boy. Lord Kriken had kidnapped Skylar but would not harm her or allow her to be harmed. He was not a bad man, just desperate. She was certain Skylar was safer at Wasbiln than traveling with her. For a long time she had been afraid that an assassin would not be able to tell them apart. Skylar could have been killed in her place, or a confused attacker might have decided it was easier to slaughter them both than to determine which one was the contracted target.

In her captivity Skylar was surrounded by guards and protected from the shadow in Cabrill's sketches. The Artists Guild would not harm her—no matter who they thought she was—while she was under the roof of an important landowner and client.

But those were small compared to the threat in Cabrill's art. She had sent her friend to the very center of what was going wrong. Kriken and his splendid guards and loyal allies could protect no one from it, not even themselves. If Cabrill did not deliver the boy in time to stop it, it would devour the planet, starting with Wasbiln. Skylar was at the most dangerous place on Saffrian.

CHAPTER 27

Using an augment lens to magnify the lines, Lian Sunang Shu inspected the rows of symbols Maoinge the younger had carefully reproduced on fine-textured paper meant to last a century or more. Expensive but necessary. Her great-great-great-great grandniece had inked a faithful duplicate of the motif on the ajrief cuff. The woman, barely past girlhood, sat silently at the small table that had been brought into the study for her to use. Hands in her lap, she didn't fidget, didn't finger the metal band resting beside the rack holding pens of different sizes, didn't quiz the matriarch about the reason for the task that had taken her many days to complete, didn't ask if her work was satisfactory.

Obligated by honor and pride to fulfill her agreement with the Yeawoche, Shu would have to relinquish the ancient prediction. That didn't mean she had to do so immediately upon leaving the Gregen Forest or that she had to lose the information. The adornment would not leave her presence until she was ready to let it go.

Ovals linked by twisting braids ran above and below the

main runes. She had noted the borders but given them little thought until she saw the almost identical motif on the seed bracelet. The design sent a Yeawoche song spinning through her mind.

> The past decays into soil,
> appearing to be gone;
> it feeds new growth today
> that ripens to tomorrow.

When she looked at the pattern, she did not see the past or new growth. She saw the ripening, the future that was almost here.

"Make another as precise as this one." Shu was moderately impressed with the performance and manner of Maoinge the younger. "Do not become sloppy because the materials you will use are of lesser quality. The second must match the first."

Maoinge the younger nodded. "It will be just as you say.

CHAPTER 28

At the next village Po searched for a suitable location for another competition. Not an easy task. The corral had to be in good repair and strong enough to support two people. That eliminated most of the possibilities. It seemed the livestock here was content to stay where it was put and didn't care to investigate broken or missing rails. He and Austin had argued over what to call the variation of nicks and jabs. Austin compared the balance needed to the agility of a cat. Skylar had described the animal to Po during one of their language lessons. He thought it might be similar to the furry inbiln, but inbiln jabs didn't seem right. He decided to call the new sport "cat jabs." The English word gave it an exotic edge, as if it were an ancient and noble contest discovered in a far-off land, instead of a quick invention to keep its creator from starving. The strange word would stir interest. Soon everyone would know of it and would want a turn on the plank.

He approached a man scattering grain in a pen full of strutting dybils. Clipped wings kept the birds earthbound. They seemed obligated to squawk their displeasure at the interruption to their meal. Even the plumpest could easily squeeze through the slates of the enclosure to freedom but chose not to. The structure was sturdy enough. Po engaged the man in casual conversation and was soon negotiating a price for the use of his property.

Po strolled away satisfied, but arranging the game was only a temporary distraction from troubling thoughts. Gram Shu continued to investigate the shadowy danger that hovered over them as if it were a matac, ready to snatch them up like carrion. But he had no messages from her. No new information, no speculation. He hoped for at least an acknowledgement of the reports he secretly sent her and a concern for his safety. Although, even that simple gesture would be a lot from the old woman, far more attention than she usually granted.

Grateful for the documents she had allowed him to study back in Astlia, he wished he'd had more than a single sleepless night to absorb the abundance of information. He would never admit it to her, but he already knew some of what was in the old scraps. He'd been a curious boy when he'd done his mandatory family service in the archives. There were rules, but he had often strayed beyond his assignments, poking through papers and artifacts at random. Mostly he had searched for forbidden tales of monsters. He'd found them, and more, not knowing the stories would become valuable to him later.

The misty beasts with glowing eyes had been created during the power struggle before the Separation. They had patrolled the areas around the stiavs, only allowing their masters to approach and travel among the connected worlds.

These new creatures he'd recently encountered roamed over a greater territory. He'd caught glimpses of them long before he'd reached the meadow. He'd stayed hidden until a downpour had dissolved some of them and had forced others to find shelter. Then he'd rushed almost blindly through the field. When the portal had revealed itself, he'd leapt through, hoping he had done so alone.

The master engineer who'd brought these nasty creatures, and others, to life had been punished with banishment. Stripped of his names so history could bestow neither blame nor fame on his family, he was referred to in the texts only as the First Exile.

Monsters that once existed and now existed again gave Po nightmares. But as he'd grown older, it was a diagram among the documents he'd secretly studied as a child that haunted his waking thoughts. A copy of a copy of a copy, the drawing that showed parts of a machine was generations removed from the original. Deterioration had set in before the initial duplication, leaving ragged empty spots and broken writing. Po had traced the lines of each piece and struggled with the phrases written in Ancient High Saffri that bordered them. Ajrief he knew of. Mniadd, which was frequently used, had baffled him at the time. The meaning of another word was still unclear to him. Conduct? Direct? Control? Po wasn't sure. A mark in the corner of the document looked like a guild sign. He'd never seen it before or since, which meant it was an original, abandoned after the Separation.

Po wished he could discuss what he knew with Cabrill. Before the Artists Guild had declared her mad, before the stiav had spit out Skylar, the young artist had hired him to identify the strange clothing and unknown locations in her art. The fee had been less than adequate, but he'd recognized the importance of her work. Besides, with his travels and knowledge of the many peoples on Saffrian, he had expected the project to be quickly done. Neither of them had understood it was an impossible task, since the drawings were not of this world.

When Skylar had arrived, there had been need for his translation skills—and his discretion. Po had been joyous to be in Cabrill's company again. They became comrades in the common cause of her art and in their affection for the sparkling girl from another planet.

But a Lian, especially a Ko Lian who continually had to prove his commitment to his Second Name family, never shared valuable information outside of blood. Never. The consequences and dishonor were too great.

Gram Shu had commanded he go alone to collect the boy. Po had thought it through, as Gram Shu had already done, and he'd had to agree. Suffering a gut-twisting pang at the disloyalty, he'd tricked Skylar into allowing him to take her necklace, saying it would help him obtain the meadow key by showing he had the ability to return home. Through careful phrasing, he had misled Cabrill and Skylar into thinking they would all travel through the stiav together.

Charging into that other world without Skylar as a guide had been the most frightening thing he'd ever done, but it had to be so. He did not doubt the depth of Skylar's affection for Cabrill and fondness for himself. He believed the sincerity of her commitment to protect her adopted land, but he knew the way of things. Skylar had spoken of her parents often. Encircled in their loving arms again, she would never have found the strength to leave, and they would never have let her go. And the brother, with his sister standing safely beside him on Callister, would never have been persuaded to rush toward an unknown danger to save a foreign planet.

Po regretted using Skylar as leverage. But as long as she remained on Saffrian, he could deal with Austin. In a way, Lord Kriken had helped them all.

Was his Lady of the Azure safe in her captivity? He was furious with Cabrill for allowing Skylar to take her place at

Wasbiln, even if it was shown in her drawings. Art warned of events; it did not declare they would come true. Skylar was smart and clever but she was too young. Her masquerading as Cabrill would not hold.

Po accepted he had his own blame to carry. He admired Austin's fierce dedication to his sister, and he had done well facing the unformed beasts. Still, he was only a boy, adept at swording but with no genuine combat experience. Po had done nothing to change that and didn't really know how. A silly game to give Austin practice and keep him diverted from the danger ahead was all Po could offer.

That afternoon Po presided over the first officially named cat jabs competition. Not feeling the excitement he tried to generate in the crowd, Po watched Austin face a string of challengers. While advancing to strike an agile boy barely older than himself, Austin stepped wrong and tumbled into the muck. The fat dybils pecked at him and seemed to laugh. Fortunately, that was his only loss. The earnings paid for baths and laundry services for all three of them. They usually camped out in the open at night to keep expenses low; but a cold drizzle set in, persuading Po to part with a large portion of the remaining profit for lodging. Listening to Austin snore, Po drifted into sleep, hoping the ploddel appreciated dozing in a warm and dry stable as much he did snuggling into a real bed.

***

Austin adjusted the yoke over the ploddel's back and attached the leather slings. Last night's rain dripped from the stable's thatched roof and sat in puddles. The chilly morning was slowly turning to sunshine. "Turnip. Not a very noble name."

"Indeed?" Po handed Austin his bundled possessions. "In what way?"

Austin lashed the pack to the yoke. "In English a turnip is a kind of vegetable." A dark-haired girl adjusted a bridle on the animal's snout. Austin stopped himself from blurting out to her, "Skye, what do they have here that's like a turnip?" He took a breath then said to Po, "Turnip. It's a tuber, a fat root you can eat."

Po produced writing materials from the many pockets in his cape. "'Too-burr,' a wonderful word."

Austin didn't want to think about the slip he'd almost made. He tried to remember the ingredients in Saffshier's famous chowder. "Like a smoocsh."

Po laughed. "A turnip is like a smoocsh? That would be a very un-noble name. In common Saffera, 'turnip' is the part of a mountain that extends from the base to where there is always snow." He pronounced it with almost no "u" sound and great emphasis on the "rn." "It is a word of size and strength, most fitting for our traveling companion." He scribbled some notes. The pencil and paper disappeared. "We'll save further discussion for our evening lessons."

Feeling shaky, Austin decided to walk. Without making eye contact, he took the reins from Cabrill.

Stupid, stupid, stupid, he thought. Was he forgetting his own sister? This somber, almost hostile, girl could never replace her.

Po and Cabrill hoisted themselves into slings. Austin gave the reins a tug. "Come on, Turnip, you old tuber. Let's see how fast you can go." The beast shuffled forward at its usual ambling gait.

CHAPTER 29

Master Forliani Morokr dismounted at the waterfall. "Splendid! I've heard so much about the beauty of the Angry Narrows."

Not so, Cheche thought. The artist's empty smile made him shiver. He grinned back and bobbed his head in a little bow as if he were humbly responsible for the splendor of the icy overflow.

"Beautiful," Forliani continued. "I have often heard it spoken of as a place one must see."

Not so, Cheche thought again. It was just a pinched spot where a stream spilled over a ledge. Melted snow from higher elevations had to go somewhere. Similar cascades spouted all over the Delds. Other falls were more powerful, more graceful, more satisfying to the spirit; but this was the one the Masters wanted to visit, so Cheche had led them here.

Today a thin veil of glistening liquid fell from the rocks above, churning to froth where it splashed into a rock basin at the side of the flattened path. Overflowing the pool, it plunged farther below to join the Angry Rill. The water gurgled and chimed, almost gentle compared to its fury when spring sun warmed the high, white peaks. At that change of season the roar blocked all birdsong and deafened the ear.

Cheche had been forced to ride, as if it were a privilege, when he much preferred the security of his own bare feet against the mountain trail. He dismounted then helped Grand Master Liaty Nobian ungracefully tumble from his saddle. Miles of up and down from Seaba, the Narrows was only slightly more elevated than the colony. The old man did not seem to be suffering from high sickness, but the long trip made his legs sleepy and weak. Leaning on Cheche, he took a few unsteady steps as if they were his first.

Master Forliani came to take the weight from the boy. "Let's explore, Liaty. The exercise will do you good and we can enjoy this lovely countryside and fresh mountain air."

Pretending to tend the goaddigs, Cheche watched them totter off toward the cascade. They didn't know about more of crazy Calbran's wild paintings just up the way. And he didn't tell them.

For explorers, they seemed to have a specific destination. The falling water obscured a cave but it was no secret. Everyone in this part of the Delds knew about the cavern. Too cold and damp to be good for anything, it was no more than a quick moment of fun. You could pretend it held treasure, but it didn't. You could imagine it sheltered a bandit camp, but it never had. You could convince a younger child it was the lair of a great beasty, filled with the bones of children snatched from villages all over the mountains; but it wasn't. You stood in it, watched the outside world through moving liquid for a little while and then went on your way.

Pelted by icy spray, the Masters traversed slick, moss-covered rock and disappeared behind the wavy curtain. To the left, concealed by shrubbery, a natural tunnel burrowed through the stone, providing dry entry to the cavity. Seems they didn't know about that part. Cheche could have called to them and pointed it out, perhaps guided them through. But he hadn't.

Seems they also didn't know the nature of caves. Like a huge mouth, the hollow projected sound. Even through splashes and gurgles, the boy heard everything.

"It's too dark," Liaty complained. "I can't see. We should have brought a torch."

"We walked through water." Forliani never used such a harsh tone toward the head of her guild when she thought anyone else could hear, even a scruffy servant boy. "It would have gone out."

"Then how do we find this thing?" the old man asked.

"You'll see it when you're near it. Hold up your arm and walk around."

Cheche listened and watched the falling veil, imagining the pair stumbling about in near darkness. Suddenly the shimmering water glowed as if it had captured a white flame. He forced himself to stare, afraid he'd lose it in a blink. And then it vanished. Had it been real or a trick of light? Possibly a reflection from the weeping wall on Bright Sorrow Pass just across the rill.

Had the Masters caused it from within the cave? If so, they made no comment. Truth be, they were silent.

CHAPTER 30

The road wound through hilly farmland. Austin soon tired of holding the ploddel's reins. He draped the straps over the saddle horn and kept walking. The animal dutifully followed as if still tethered to him, ignoring the tasty grass at the edge of the rutted path. It felt good to walk off his irritation and his loneliness. When he had traveled alone with Po, the Astlian kept the conversation lively with explanations of words and stories about cultures and customs until Austin begged for a little silence. Since Cabrill had joined them, it seemed she and Po dwelled in their own private bubble.

He'd been without someone to talk to for a long time. He missed the rambling conversations with Skylar about nothing in particular. They spent days teasing each other over some small thing and calling each other silly names. It drove their parents crazy. When they were feeling especially isolated at whatever research station happened to be home for a week or a month or a year, they'd do it on purpose. It was an easy way to get sent into town on errands. They would complete the tasks as quickly as possible then have the rest of the time to explore.

There was so much he wanted to ask Cabrill about his sister. But she was remote and serious, as if her mind continued to puzzle through the same problem, and there was no space for anything else. He was sure it concerned Skylar. He had to find out what she was thinking.

Austin swung up into his sling and tossed the mostly unnecessary reins over the ploddel's back to Po. As Turnip jostled the three of them to the next village, Austin worked out a strategy.

CHAPTER 31

Forliani Morokr, Guild Master of Bogoboln Colony, had seen many wondrous things, but nothing that thrilled her so completely as the circular room. Clothes dripping from passage through the waterfall, she turned slowly, devouring the grandeur. She felt encased inside a gigantic tree. No door. No window. No torch, yet subdued light formed a necklace about the ceiling, casting a gentle glow. Braids carved into the seamless wall twined around five oblong spaces scooped from the rich, reddish wood. The four vacant hollows looked like shadowed eyes, closed and dark. The fifth nest held a cloudy azure jewel.

Liaty shook himself like a wet chamapl, marring the sleek marble floor with droplets that quickly vanished. Moisture flattened sparse gray hair to his skull. "Where are we?"

"The manuscripts give no clues. We could be anywhere on Saffrian." Forliani shivered. She had expected the heaviness of a sealed tomb, but a strange stirring nipped dampness from her clothes and skin.

"What brilliant master crafted this?" Liaty stepped close to the polished scrollwork. Centuries had not decayed the sheen. He traced a metal filament that wove through the grain as if it had once flowed like sap along living wood.

Forliani ignored him. He would be humbled into distress if he learned that not one, but more than a dozen superb artists had used their skills to craft this space. He would know each of their names if he'd bothered to study the histories himself, as was his duty. At the time this room was constructed, the Artists Guild did more than create predictions. It also made things for beauty and utility, often commissioned by other guilds.

If only she wasn't burdened with her superior's presence, if only she had this moment to herself. But entering without him was impossible. By his office, he alone had the means to travel to this space and the right to be here. The stiav behind the waterfall was the only entrance. Its companion in the center of the room, which had vanished as soon as Liaty stepped away from it, was the only exit. The grand master did not carry an ajrief wafer for a key, as told of in the old documents, but an inked code infused with the rare metal etched into the skin on his left forearm.

Forliani suddenly regretted that sometimes she had behaved disrespectfully toward the grand master. Right now, Liaty could quietly step back through the guardian, leaving her in this sealed place to die, starving and alone. "It's best if you stay well back from the center until we are ready to depart," she said gently.

"Yes, of course." Liaty said as if not really hearing her, all of his attention on the artistry before him. "Extraordinary. I've carved since I was a child and never achieved this precision."

For her own safety, Forliani remarked on the importance of the statues Liaty had carved years ago known as the Famine Figures, which showed a major crop failure. The sweet, flattering words left a bitter tang in her mouth. The man was not a terrible leader; but, strangely for an artist of his skill, he was content with the present. His vision seemed limited to his next project with chisels and knives. It was Forliani who looked to the future of the Guild through a study of the past. She had easily convinced him to let her examine the histories meant only for a grand master's eyes.

"Any notes you make must be burned at my death," Liaty had told her sternly. "You must promise." And she had, not meaning to keep her word.

She'd expected a gigantic vault packed with ancient tomes. Instead Liaty had unlocked a small cabinet, revealing a few volumes and a slim packet of crumbling documents in High Saffri. The old script had seemed like tangled yarn. She'd had to spend many candle-lit hours researching words and phrases to unknot the meanings. Slowly, she'd discovered a tapestry of treasure.

It was she who'd told Liaty that the markings on his arm were more than a symbol of office. Had his predecessor known the true purpose of the tattoo? Had the grand masters before that? Or, like Liaty, had they ignored the documents in their care? She was furious that such important knowledge was so fragile, that it was granted to only a single person and could easily be lost forever. But she was grateful it had slept quietly, and that she had been the one to awaken it.

Forliani slid a hand into her sleeve, moving beyond the bronze cuff on her wrist. She eased her fingers into the hidden pocket and touched crinkled parchment. Delicate black strokes made by a brush with a single hair covered the scrap. The painting showed the curved wall before her adorned with intricate carvings, sad hollows, and the single smooth oval. Two unidentifiable figures stood in this most secret place. The moment Forliani had unrolled the canvas, she'd recognized the room from descriptions in the secret manuscripts, and she'd known in her heart that she would be one of those figures.

How fortunate Master Calbran Coriadler had brought his art to her, along with his concerns that movement had invaded his work and a madness had crept into his brain. She had sent him to Seaba—for his own wellbeing of course—and had kept the painting private, even from Liaty until she'd needed it to convince him they must seek out this chamber.

The mountain mural they'd visited proved she was right to have sent Calbran to the colony. She had pretended not to see the picture buried in the abstraction and hoped she had convinced Liaty it was no more than random colors. The huge scene was part of all this, although she didn't know exactly how. Not yet.

Through her efforts, other artists with Calbran's sensitivity had ended up at Seaba. It was a constant irritation that Cabrill was not locked away with them. When the girl had shyly admitted the strangeness in her art, Forliani had recognized it was more than the usual madness. As Cabrill's mentor, Forliani had convinced the girl to surrender her silk-point brushes, smoothly spun paints and finely milled chalks. Just for a short time, she'd assured Cabrill. Just until you return from a quiet retreat at the colony refreshed and clear of mind.

Forliani's mistake had been in allowing the girl to leave on her own. Cabrill had set out for Mount Wieldeld but never arrived. Something had happened on that journey. Forliani very much wanted to know what had caused the young, insecure girl to abandon her training, her teachers, her mentor, and the guild that provided her with home and family.

She rubbed her wrist cuff. Master Artist Mikol, not understanding the meaning of the pattern, had formed the room's lines and swirls into a band of bronze, not curved inward in concealment like the actual cavern, but outward in revelation. It seemed he too must soon join the other residents at the colony in the Deld Mountains.

Forliani thought herself fortunate not to be so afflicted by her talent. It was an arduous task monitoring the monthly shipments sent by that puffed up Master Jomaray Ganje, but worth the time.

She kept a watchful eye on Liaty as he strolled the perimeter, never taking a hand from the polished curves. Although her presence here had been predicted, she understood she was an intruder. That would change when she became grand master and the symbol of office was carved into her arm. That time would come. She was certain it would be soon.

"Whoever commissioned this is long dead," Liaty said. "But our masters crafted it. We are the rightful heirs."

Forliani agreed. She knew he meant the artistry, but she meant something else.

Once an oval had rested in each of the wooden cradles. Glowing like bright gems, they'd pulsed as if alive, surging with energy conducted through the stiavs. Together they'd linked the five worlds.

The Engineers Guild had designed the machine that was this room, and they had controlled the power it produced. But they'd hired the Artists Guild to build it.

When a world burned to ash because of the engineers' egos and stupidity, the Artists Guild, which had added secrets of their own to the chamber, had scattered four of the beautiful hearts, leaving only one.

Forliani gazed at the remaining blue egg. It had slept alone, dull and vacant for longer than she could calculate. But now she saw the sleek surface quiver as if a kindred spirit sang to it with a familiar song.

She'd been unable to determine the locations of the four

missing jewels, but she sensed that one was coming near. And she saw in the art of the mad Seaban colonists, that all of the ovals would be returned to their proper places, that this room would once again fuel devices and enhance minds.

Forliani knew she belonged here, that she was worthy to gaze upon the blue orb in its wooden cradle.

She imagined what this chamber had been and what it would be again.

She was the only one who knew the power that was to come, the only one prepared to make it her own.

CHAPTER 32

The public campsite on the edge of Dullwhittle huddled in a crater out of the wind. Austin outlined a fencing strip with sticks, glad that Cabrill had selected a stone-lined fire pit with enough space around it to practice. The area was already getting crowded, despite there being several hours before sunset. The day was fair, but the next village was far. Merchants, farmers and vagabonds no longer pushed on until sunlight faded then slept, fireless, on the side of the road wherever they happened to be. And they no longer set out in the gray mist before sunrise. Not anymore. Travelers sought the safety of villages, even though it slowed their journey. They gathered around bright fires with other peddlers and pilgrims, telling stories of monsters in the night and beasts in the daytime.

Po, usually one to socialize, so he could size up the neighbors and get the latest news, had trotted off to find food. And to set up a cat jabs competition. Austin pawed through his pack and pulled out his weapon. This was his chance to try out his strategy for getting Cabrill to talk to him, but he had to catch her before she took out her charcoal and the fine parchment Po had purchased for her with some of the winnings. She went into her own world when she worked, as if an image hovered in the corner of her eye like a shy animal and she needed to coax it into view.

"I promised I'd teach you the kind of fencing I do," Austin said. He hadn't exactly, but a promise felt like it carried more weight than just generally agreeing to do something. "How about now? I need the practice, so you'd be helping me out. I got dumped into the slime last time. I don't want that to happen again."

"The smell wasn't pleasant for those of us around you either." Cabrill pulled the protective skin from her knapsack and covered her sturdy sword.

Austin couldn't believe she'd agreed right away, especially since he was sure she thought cat jabs was silly compared to the more dignified nicks and jabs. Had her comment been an attempt at friendly banter? If so, she wasn't very good at the friendly part or the banter part. She should have picked up both from Skylar. The remark was water next to the acid his sister would have given him.

He showed Cabrill the outline. "This is a fencing strip. It's called a piste. That's a French word that became an English word too. There are lots of those. French, that's a language." He positioned her inside the long rectangle he'd marked out. "Pretend you're on a board and you don't want to fall off. Since you hold your sword in your right hand, your right foot is forward and pointed ahead. Keep your left foot behind it and turned outward." He showed her with his hands. "It's the *en garde* position. That's just French, not English."

"I don't find languages as interesting as Po does." Cabrill awkwardly tried the stance.

Austin got the message. No language lessons. He smiled

encouragingly. "That's a good start. Bend your knees. Move forward and backward in a straight line." He demonstrated with fluid ease.

Cabrill shuffled one way and then the other, as if unconvinced you could approach a real opponent from such a position. Austin had her repeat the moves—and repeat them and repeat them—until she seemed to feel the balance in each step. Then he showed her how to attack and how to deflect an attack without stepping outside of the rectangle. Although still sullen, she asked a few questions and nodded an understanding of his explanations. "Enough practice," she said. "We go for points."

Startled by his pupil's rebellion, Austin took his place on the strip and dropped into position. "Prepare to suffer, space monkey!"

In return Skylar would have yelled, "Beg for mercy, grit slug." Cabrill just leveled her blade at him.

Austin sprang forward in a simple attack. Despite the moves she'd just practiced, Cabrill immediately dodged sideways, crossing the stick boundary.

"Oops, you fell off the board," Austin announced. "I win and you need a bath."

Cabrill scowled. "We will try again."

Enjoying the role of coach, Austin almost forgot the real purpose of the exercise. Almost. "Cabrill, have you wondered how I knew you weren't Skylar?" He held his breath, afraid this attempt to talk about his sister would flop like the previous ones.

Cabrill took the stance he had taught her and held her sword ready. "You knew because she is your sister and I am not."

"At first I thought you were. Skye was a little girl when she disappeared. She's a teenager now. Maybe taller, like you. I don't know. It's hard for me to imagine her as more grown up. But there are things about her that wouldn't have changed, not ever. No matter what's happened to her here, no matter how old she gets. I knew you weren't my sister because you never asked." Austin watch the struggle crease Cabrill's face. He could tell she wanted to ignore him, as she usually did. She wanted to put down her sword and walk away, but she had challenged him and could not forfeit. And she was curious.

"Never asked what?"

Austin spoke softly. "You never asked about our mom and dad."

Cabrill planted her feet so she was square with him. She stuck the point of her sword into the ground, hands squeezing the hilt. Austin felt a challenge of a different kind coming.

"If it had been Skylar in the plaza," Cabrill said, "if she had asked the question, what would you have said?"

Austin swallowed. Would he have softened it, or would he have told the hard truth? "Skylar, Mom and Dad are crushed, destroyed by worry and grief. They miss you every moment of every day. They work and eat and sometimes they sleep, but they are barely alive."

"Children do not stay with parents forever."

"Sure, they become adults and go off on their own. This is different. She was there and then she wasn't. My parents and I and everyone searched everywhere for her."

"I have seen it. This is what some parents do. Their child is gone and they search."

Some parents? Not all parents? Austin had just wanted to hear Cabrill talk about his sister. He hadn't expected the conversation to get this raw, but he would use it to make things clear. "You and Skylar are really good friends—and that's great—but you understand, I have to take her back home to our parents as soon as possible."

Cabrill turned and walked away, tearing the casing from her sword. "There are things more important than parents."

Austin watched her set aside her weapon and take out charcoal and parchment. She would go into one of her drawing frenzies now and be unreachable. He wrapped his foil and tucked it away. His fencing strip no longer useful, he gathered up the sticks and piled them near the firepit for later. He was expecting a chilly night.

CHAPTER 33

"They're completely wrong." Skylar kicked the metal at her feet as if the incompetence of the people assigned to do her biding pushed her to violence. She had a clean room, soft bed, far too many pillows, laundered clothes, regular meals, and she didn't have to do a bit of work. She was so bored!

Of course the situation was more intense than that. She was still a captive and expected to produce an amazing, extraordinary work of art. And the people who followed her instructions were actually not obeying her but her guard and guardian Ishty. The hearth keeper sighed long and deep at Skylar's outburst. She pursed her lips so hard she made a fish face, and crossed her arms defensively. "Master Artist Cabrill, this is the thinnest metal the smithy can produce. I supervised the process myself."

The rigid shafts were less than two inches wide. Skylar recognized the crafting as exceptional for this culture's level of development, but praising the work would not get her what she wanted. "I need something that bends, but not too much, just the right amount, but only at one end. It has to move like this." Despite Po's excellent instruction, she didn't know the local word for "wobble." She held up her hand and jiggled it slightly.

"Perhaps if you describe the degree of bending, I can instruct Master Tlepel," Ishty said sharply.

Skylar was secretly delighted that she'd cracked the woman's shell. Hostility was much easier to manipulate than the calm that Ishty usually kept plastered over her constant irritation. Ishty's true feelings had started coming out after Skylar had insisted she needed a certain yellow flower that was often used by artists to make a dye. Anyone else would have sent an underling. Skye knew that Ishty, with her obsession to serve Lord Kriken perfectly, would go herself. It had really been a chance to be free of the woman for an hour or so. The bloom tended to grow among nettles, so Skylar had cautioned Ishty not to get stung. She'd meant *don't get stung by the prickly plants*. When Ishty was attacked by an insect, the woman had interpreted Skylar's warning as a foretelling that must have been revealed in one of the many drawings the artist had burned in the fireplace.

Cabrill had explained to Skylar that predictions didn't cause things to happen, although some people thought they did. Ishty had blamed Skylar for the swollen red knob on her nose. Now, even when Ishty's phrases were polite—which they sometimes weren't—her inflection make it clear she would rather scrub every charred pot in the kitchen to a shiny glow than look after His Lordship's prisoner.

"It isn't about the bending," Skylar said. "It's about the possibility of the bending. I must find something else that I can use, some other material to represent metal."

"How unfortunate you arrived at this realization now instead of a week ago," Ishty said.

Skylar gave her a sincere look. "Yes, that is unfortunate."

"What might this 'other material' be?" Ishty's tone said she didn't think Skylar cared about anything except tricking people, especially her, into running around on foolish errands.

"Hmm." Skylar pretended to considered substitutes for thin, lightweight metal. "There must be something on the estate I can use." She looked at Ishty thoughtfully. "You could search the buildings and grounds, and write down everything you find. Then we can review the list together, and you can describe the items to me. Or you can have them all sent here as you find them. That might save time."

Ishty put her bony fists on her almost nonexistent hips. "Or you could do it yourself."

Skylar wanted to laugh at Ishty's shivering anger over her own loss of self-control. An outburst toward her lord's guest was beneath her, no matter how annoying the guest or how much the guest's demands interfered with her regular duties. She shook her head, as if it were a serious suggestion. "I don't think His Lordship would permit it, even though it's essential to the sculpture."

"I will consult with Lord Kriken about how to proceed, for the good of the sculpture," Ishty said as if she wanted the thing done and this person gone. She directed servants to remove the offending metal bars.

Skylar wandered over to her weaving, as if she had too much on her mind to worry about anything Lord Kriken might decide. The long, bright banners taken from the great room dangled from a thick rod suspended across massive iron candlesticks. Skylar selected two of the strips and crossed one over the other, expanding the growing pattern. "I'll be getting more swords soon, won't I? I don't have near enough."

"You're certain that all of them are necessary?"

Skylar knotted a lizard to a serpent. "I could not use less than are required."

"Additional swords will arrive soon." Ishty turned to leave.

"Ishty," Skylar said sweetly, "I do so appreciate your help. Might there be fresh cwamets with lunch today?"

The woman kept her back to Skylar. She heaved a great sigh that raised then lowered her thin but sturdy shoulders. "I'll see to it."

"You are so good to me." Although Ishty didn't turn back to look at her, Skylar kept her expression pleasing until the door closed securely and she was once again alone. Then she danced around the room, keeping her laughter soft so the guard stationed outside wouldn't hear. Pickle-faced Ishty found the Master Artist Cabrill irritating, did she? Well, Skylar had a lot more fun and games planned.

A breeze squeezed into the room through the slim excuses for windows. Skylar had kept her promise to Cabrill. She'd let herself be kidnapped and she'd gone peacefully to Wasbiln Manor. But she hadn't exactly agreed to wait until her friend showed up and explained to Kriken that he had grabbed the wrong girl.

How much influence did Old Icky have with His Lordship? Skylar hoped it was enough to get permission for her to walk about the estate. She needed to see more than the slice of countryside she could view from her prison. If you don't know which direction to go, it's hard to escape.

CHAPTER 34

The stable master's second son gave Skylar a shy, almost flirty smile as he showed her a row of long-handled tools leaning against the stable wall. She pretended to consider them. Ishty sighed at her not rejecting them immediately so they could move on.

Skylar smiled back at the young man. "Tell me about this one." He stumbled through a nervous explanation. She nodded, as if interested, which she wasn't. Her monotonous days confined to the manor house were suddenly over. With Lord Kriken's permission she spent most daylight hours poking about the estate. Watched from a distance by guards and accompanied by a sullen Ishty, she searched every shed, smithy, and smelly barn, supposedly on a quest to find the perfect whatever for her sculpture.

At first the farmers, workers, and residents—old, young, and in between—timidly answered her questions in as few words as possible. That wouldn't do. She went on a campaign to put them at ease. She cooed over each baby, no matter how drooly, and she learned its name. She petted every single one of the dog-like creatures, no matter how dusty and disgusting, and she learned its name. She passed out compliments like candy, wished everyone good health, and she learned everyone's name. As brilliantly as she had sometimes lied to her teachers and her friends and her parents and her brother in order to get her own way, she told the villagers how much she valued their help.

Soon the entire complex was looking at the things around them anew, wondering if this or that might be what "that nice artist girl" needed. Among discussions about the flexibility of various reeds and berry canes, Skylar probed for the information she really wanted. Soon people were telling her more than she asked and everything she needed.

The stable master's second son was named Kensht. Most of the animals were out in corrals. Skylar glanced at the few tethered in their stalls. "Do you like working with animals?"

"Some," he said. "Some not."

As if on cue, a goaddig stomped and bellowed. Skylar jumped, as if alarmed.

Kensht flicked a thumb in the direction of the noise. "That one you want to walk up to slow. Needs a strong rein. Got its own ideas about where to go."

Ishty gave a "humph," as if she knew what that was like.

"Are they all dangerous?" Skylar asked.

Kensht swiped at his really cute, tightly curled hair. "Some. Some not. The large white out in the yard, that one looks like a terror but it's the gentlest of the bunch. It'll get you anywhere with no fuss."

Skylar smiled and nodded. So, the large white goaddig was reliable and best for an inexperienced rider. She tucked that away with the other useful bits she'd picked up. She knew the small path along the river led into the heaviest part of the Dobgronun Forest. The trail that crossed the river went to the main road. Once there, only the route that went through a sparser patch of the forest led to civilization. All others went to remote farmsteads or to the quarry.

She praised the row of tools as being of very fine quality but expressed her regret that none of them was right for her sculpture. As she left the stable and the disappointed boy, she made note of the big white animal standing serene and steady in the yard. Ishty pointed to a cottage that was their next destination. Skylar was grateful the woman conducted the exploration of the grounds systematically, even though it was so no one could accuse the hearth keeper of neglecting her duty rather than for the sculpture. Skylar didn't care about the motivation. The pattern of the estate was becoming clear to her. She could track its history from the oldest buildings close to the manor house to newer ones farther out. The progression showed a record of prosperity and growth.

From what she could tell, Kriken was not a bad lord. A Code of Fairness granted privileges to the residents and outlined their responsibilities. Some people seemed better fed than others, but no one went hungry or lacked a place to live as long as they did their share. His Lordship, who owned the land, gained from the arrangement through modest rent, made-to-order goods, and available workers. He maintained the buildings, trained and outfitted guards, and settle disputes.

Skylar was impressed with the rosy-checked people, the well cared for animals, and the strong structures. The master crafters, who made their living with metal, wood and stone, had formal shops. For other goods and services everyone knew that the chamapl herder had cheese for sale, and a certain family took in laundry if you couldn't get it done yourself, and the woman who sold dybil eggs often had freshly baked bread too.

This would have been a happy place except for dark clouds

that boiled out of the nearby forest. Skylar looked up and frowned. She couldn't see the gray slashes from her room, so she studied them during her expeditions outside. They rolled overhead like dying flowers. Each day the pattern looked more like the angry smears in Cabrill's chalk drawings. As menacing as the master artist had managed to make the scene, it was even more sinister and evil-looking in reality.

The breeze carried sooty particles that settled on Skylar's skin and hair, and attacked her nostrils with an acrid odor. Ishty brushed at a smudge on her sleeve with a gloved hand, which only increased the stain's size. "You'll fall in a hole if you keep your nose in the air." An uneasy tremor tinted her voice. "Best ignore what's above."

Ignoring something terrible doesn't make it go away, Skylar thought. *It just keeps you unprepared and helpless for when the beasty jumps out to devour you.*

Although Ishty tried to stop the villagers from gossiping in Skylar's presence, she still heard the rumors. Should she ignore those too? The really interesting stuff was always whispered and, despite being spoken softly, was eventually heard by everyone. The pollution was belched out by monsters (who must have eaten something nasty). Or was produced by an invading army (which suddenly appeared in the forest). Or seeped from a giant fissure deep in the earth (where apparently stinky stuff was burning). Or was tossed into the air by jugglers.

Jugglers. She might have gotten that part wrong. Still, she memorized each tale faithfully so she could relay it to Cabrill and Po later. Whether jugglers, fissure, army, monsters, or something else, at the core of the speculation was a truth: People and animals disappeared.

Kriken had sent guards into the forest to find the source of the billowing haze. Only one returned. Or rather, his goaddig brought him back, severely burned. He continued to waver between unconsciousness and delirium, unable to describe what had happened to him and to the still missing, probably dead, soldiers who had accompanied him.

Skylar saw the Bough of Vavder bent over the doorway as they approached the cottage. It seemed everyone in the small community displayed a sprig of the fragrant, spiky herb. A symbol of hope that a loved one would return safely, some wore woven bracelets of it. Some tucked it into braids. At the sight of it above the door of the small tidy home, Skylar wanted to drop to her knees and weep. She clenched her teeth and refused to think about families who waited for loved ones to return. Perhaps ignoring something terrible was a survival skill.

Skylar could almost forgive Lord Cranky for kidnapping her.

No, not really. Not even almost. Even though the guy just wanted a prediction showing how to defeat the whatever-it-was in the forest that killed his people and sent out false clouds. She'd learned from the villagers that Kriken had sent a formal entreaty to Bogoboln Colony for the services of an accomplished artist. No masters were available, he'd been told, certainly not the one requested, Cabrill Shistayia. The villagers expressed their thanks that the Artists Guild had changed its mind and sent her to them, as if she were their hero. That made her cringe with guilt.

Cabrill's being here wouldn't have worked anyway. To finalize her art, she needed to go to a special place that was strong with prediction. Skylar wasn't exactly sure what that meant. She hoped Cabrill's quest had already been successful, or soon would be, that Cabrill had drawn or constructed or something-ed a masterpiece showing the enemy. Before she, Cabrill and Po went to Callister to get her brother, Skylar wanted to see what they would be fighting when they returned. And she very much wished, with all her heart, that Cabrill's talent also revealed how to defeat the person or beasty or whatever causing the angry sky.

Skylar stopped and let Ishty approach the vavder-adorned door alone. The family would be waiting inside, wearing their best clothes in honor of their guest. She turned away. She was a lie. How could she bring false hope into their home? Ash-filled clouds churned overhead. The unfinished, bogus sculpture was just a pile of swords, and Kriken's stupid advisors were already arguing about its meaning.

My *unfinished, bogus sculpture*, Skylar thought.

Ishty was suddenly in front of her. "Perhaps you could sky-gaze another time."

Skylar glanced at her stone-faced escort. "I see the redness is almost gone from your insect sting."

Without thinking, Ishty put a hand to her face where the raised blotch used to be. She pulled it away quickly, obviously annoyed that Skylar had caused her to react. "It has healed completely and the discoloration went away over a day ago."

"I'm so glad." Skylar gave a pleasant smile. She walked toward the cottage, holding in a fit of laughter. The soot that had transferred from Ishty's sleeve to her glove was now a streak across the woman's long nose.

CHAPTER 35

The drizzle finally faded, as if it had grown weary and just given up. A patchwork of sun filtered through the clouds by the time Austin, Po and Cabrill reached the next community. Po said the place was more than a village but not big enough to be a town. The camping area for travelers held six communal fire pits. They claimed a space near one of the stone rings and started setting out clothes and gear to dry.

Cabrill's braids swung as she worked. Austin admired the number of plaits. His experiences with Po's new sport gave him an appreciation of their meaning. Po always set braid terms for the competitions along with financial ones, so Austin's collection had increased. He was relieved that he didn't actually have to keep the chunks of hair that defeated warriors presented to him, but he was embarrassed by the closely cropped sections where he'd had to give up some of his own.

Austin shook out a shirt. It needed a wash but was cleaner than the one he wore. "Skylar likes her hair in a single braid down her back. I suppose she can't do that here because she isn't old enough."

Cabrill checked her bundle of artwork to see if moisture had leaked into the cured animal bladder that held it. "Lack of sword bothered her more. While she is me, she can have both, braids and sword. And people won't act toward her as they do toward a child."

"She never tolerated being treated like a kid even when she was little," Austin said. Since the fencing lesson, Cabrill had started speaking to him a little bit more each time. They were getting close to having a real conversation.

Cabrill smiled, not at Austin but with her eyes lowered, as if at a memory. "At times it caused her difficulty."

They were using English. Po pulled out pencil and paper. "She is me or she is I?" he said to himself. At Austin's insistence, he'd agreed to making notes when he heard something that interested him then waiting until the daily language lesson after the evening meal to ask questions and get explanations.

"I'd like to see your drawings again, if that's okay." Austin didn't want to seem pushy, since he'd practically ignored them before. "Maybe you can tell me what they mean."

"An artist does not interpret her own work," Cabrill replied. "Trained advisors study a piece then explain the significance."

To Austin, it sounded more like a quote than something Cabrill actually believed. "I suppose that's straight from *The Artist's Handbook*."

Po scribbled.

Cabrill removed her drawings from the protective pouch and handed them to him. "It is what I was taught. But I no longer accept it as true."

Austin sorted through the creamy sheaves. He found several of himself standing in front of a Callister arch. "Did Skye describe this place to you? Or did Po?"

"Cabrill showed me those drawings before your sister arrived here," Po said. "They are how I knew the stiav had deposited me in the correct place. The portraits helped me recognize you."

Austin had difficulty thinking of the images as portraits. You gave your permission for portraits. You posed for them. They were an agreement between subject and artist. These were without his consent. They were stolen portrayals. But it wasn't drawings of himself he wanted to see. Cabrill seemed to know that. She slid a page from the curled jumble, placed it on top and carefully smoothed it. "Skylar tumbled out of empty air. I though her an imagining, but she was real. I had made a mistake of great size. Her arrival saved me from a larger one. She cared for me when the madness of creation came like a fever. She named herself my security blanket. I don't know how the words fit together, but I understand the meaning."

Po scribbled.

Austin gazed at the page. Skylar—single braid on her shoulder, loose strands swirling about her like black ribbons—stood determined and unafraid. The curved medallion hung at her throat against rough-spun cloth. She stared ahead despite the chaos enveloping her. Behind her, Austin saw himself, angular pendant like an emblem on his white jacket. The brother in the drawing focused only on the sister. The brother holding the parchment did the same.

He didn't want to cry in front of Cabrill and Po. Skylar had been his security blanket too. As their parents had dragged them from planet to planet, she had been his constant friend. He suffered through the uncertainty of moving more than she did. Skye seemed sure she would make new friends wherever they ended up. And she always did. It took Austin longer, and it was harder for him to let go when they inevitably had to leave.

It was the same way with their fencing. Skylar was

confident and spontaneous, while Austin was defensive and predictable. When he'd finally gotten tired of being beaten by his little sister, he'd forced himself to become more aggressive and versatile. That's when he'd started winning more often, against his sister and other competitors too.

"When I showed Skylar the drawings," Cabrill said, "of you on your world and also on this one, she told me she knew you would help us."

Austin handed the papers back to Cabrill. "I'd like to look at them again later, if that's okay." He didn't want to join a mission. He just wanted to get his sister home.

Home. They'd lived so many places the term had come to mean wherever he, Skye and their parents were together. It wasn't surprising that Callister hadn't felt like home since she'd disappeared.

As Cabrill rolled up the parchments, Austin caught a last glimpse of his sister's face, bold and steady against the turmoil around her, as if that's where she belonged. A strange doubt he had tried to suppress rippled through him.

Maybe Skylar didn't want to be rescued.

CHAPTER 36

A short rain before sunrise temporarily cleared the air of soot, making the sun seem a little brighter. Ishty led Skylar across the grounds on their daily exploration, despite her obvious distaste for the dirt and the people who lived in such conditions. Skylar sauntered along comfortably in the loose breeches, shirt, vest and soft boots that she'd had on when she'd been kidnapped. Ishty had immediately taken them away to be cleaned. Then she'd refused to return them, declaring them unsuitable for His Lordship's household.

This morning Skylar had decided she was done struggling with the ill-fitting gowns, awkward tunics and stiff shoes provided for her. When Ishty had arrived at her room, Skylar had sat like a monument, mouth frozen in a pout. She'd known Ishty was just fine with her unruly charge sitting like that forever, but duty required her to persuade Skylar to leave. Skylar, who desperately wanted to run out the open door, had refused to budge until she'd gotten her own clothes back.

Ishty seemed in a hurry today. She held up her long skirt as she stepped over a puddle. Mud bordered the hem like abstract embroidery. Although the hearth keeper would never give up her ankle-length dress, Skylar noticed she had traded her flimsy slippers for sturdier footwear.

In a grassy spot unoccupied by foraging dybils, off-duty guards practicing nicks and jabs. Skylar slowed, stifling a smile. All the metal weapons had been confiscated for her sculpture. Children played at the game using animal bones coiled in rope or wrapped in rags, but that would humiliate trained fighters. These soldiers wielded crude wooden swords they had probably made themselves.

Oh, how Skylar wanted to join in! She could teach them something about technique. They were experienced fencers, yet they stabbed with clumsy, hesitant motions. A pair at a time flailed at each other, laughing at their own awkwardness. Used to heavy weapons, perhaps their balance was affected by the lighter weight of the wood.

Ishty urged Skylar to continue on. "Do not let a fad and the fools who follow it disrupt our schedule." Skye shushed the woman, knowing she would pay for the rudeness later. Ishty would add it to her stubbornness about the clothes.

Confused, Skylar watched the gawky interplay, not sure what she was seeing. She had gotten used to sweeping strokes and circling steps. Those typical actions were gone. Duelers who slipped into them from habit were disqualified, and roared at by the others. The fencers struggled to keep their movements in front of them. They lumbered forward and backward in a tight shuffle, thrusting their swords straight out from their chests. Forward and backward. Advance, retreat.

Ishty folded her arms at the latest irritation with her young burden. "When he returns, we will go to see Master Hobben, the wood smith."

Skylar realized that Ishty misinterpreted her interest in the swording, thinking her focus was on the false weapons. "He's not here?" That made sense. A clever wood worker would have fashioned a far more refined sword substitute for His Lordship's guards.

"He has gone to Lady Wist's estate," Ishty said.

"To get wood."

Ishty pulled in a startled breath, as she always did when Skylar made a guess that seemed like a prophecy. She sent a furtive glance upward at the sooty trail thinned by the recent rain and wind. "A certain kind of wood."

Safe wood, Skye thought, not from a forest belching unnatural clouds where seasoned fighters disappeared.

The guards seemed to enjoy swinging their crude swords. The next pair launched into a bout. Shuffling feet, elbows tucked in tight, they flailed about, as uncoordinated as those before them. The woman took a bold step and thrust her weapon forward in an attack. Her opponent performed a parry and riposte. She seemed uncertain how to counter and tried to move away from him. For a moment she balanced on one leg, as if about to fall off a tightrope, free foot waving to the side.

If Skylar had been the woman's adversary, she would have easily scored a point by now, but the man held his cramped position, as if waiting for the woman to topple over. And if Skylar had been the woman, she would have taken advantage of his hesitation and scored a point on him.

There's plenty of grass available, Skye thought. *Just put your foot down and attack.*

The woman wouldn't give up. She bent her knee, leveled her shoulders, and pulled her loose leg under her. Both feet on the ground, she joined her companions in laughter, letting her sword arm drop and her pretend blade hit the wet dirt. Except it didn't make a dull thunk. It clunked, like wood on wood. There was something in the grass. A board? A long, narrow plank? Like a strip? Skylar grinned. Somehow nicks and jabs had turned into straight-line fencing.

Skylar Swiftbrooke wasn't sword age here, but Master Artist Cabrill was. She felt like a fraud, wearing the older girl's numerous braids. She'd won plenty of bouts that would have earned plaits and crossovers of her own, but victories before you turned sixteen didn't count here—wherever here was.

Curiosity and her new bit of freedom overpowered her. Since she was a captive, she wasn't allowed to have the borrowed sword Cabrill had gotten for her. But no one, not even the hearth keeper, could object to her having a little practice with a wooden weapon. The guards would not be much competition. She'd have to give them some training first to make it a fair fight.

Skylar left a frustrated Ishty stamping her foot in the mud and rushed to join the fencers.

CHAPTER 37

At the cat jabs competition in the next village, a long line of opponents waited for the opportunity to defeat the boy from somewhere far away who wielded a strange sword. Po was glad to take their money, but the popularity of his creation worried him. The new sport was spreading faster down the road than a ploddel could carry them. He heard that similar tourneys were springing up like weeds in places they hadn't been.

At the moment he was less interested in Austin's current game against a nimble but frightened boy and more concerned with the spectators. The usual friends and relatives of the brave participants milled around the sty. Farmers and crafters stopped by to gawk. But there were also onlookers of a different sort. Vendors hawked food, drink, and trinkets. Master sporters made bets and chatted about technique.

Po kept an eye on three uniformed soldiers. From a distance they watched Austin dump a few opponents into the muck, then they visited a nearby smithy. Their business finished, they strode purposefully toward the crowd. Two men and a woman, dressed in black and red. Calf-length pants over high boots. Loose shirts cinched by leather vests marked with crimson and gold emblems.

Po looked for Cabrill to warn her. She had already melted into the crowd.

Austin carefully stepped down onto a barrel, then to a box, and then a low stool. The makeshift stairway got him to the ground so he could take a break. He'd just won a match against a guy who backed up every time Austin attacked. He finally fell backwards off the far end of the plank, defeating himself.

Po puffed up to Austin, out of breath. "We're getting close to the honorable Lord Kriken's land," he said in a low voice. He tilted his head toward three figures in impressive black, red and gold uniforms. "That lot belongs to His Lordship's guard. We would be wise to avoid their scrutiny."

Are they the ones who kidnapped Skylar? Austin wondered. *Do they patrol outside her prison cell?* He wanted to smack them into the muck.

"Finish these up and we'll be on our way." Po scurried back to the other side of the corral before Austin could complain.

Finish these up! Po made it sound easy. Austin's muscles ached. Covered in slime, he stunk so bad he could barely stand it. Some of the sworders had obviously been practicing, eroding his advantage. Five of the bouts had gone to the full three points. Twice a blow had dumped him into the pit.

Stool, box, barrel. He climbed back up onto the plank. To give his sword arm a rest, he experimented with different moves. If he shuffled his feet and leaned to one side, pretending to step in that direction even though it was impossible on the narrow board, his opponent took a counter side step out of habit from years of circling in nicks and jabs. It worked on the next opponent.

Splush!

And the next.

Splush!

He ripped through a string of challengers with a combination of honestly scored points and his new trick. Maybe he *could* finish this up fast and make Po happy.

A figure in black, red, and gold stepped onto the sagging board. One of Lord Kriken's guards. Austin's muscles clenched. So much for avoiding scrutiny. The woman's pale braids—with no stubby gaps, as if she hadn't lost in years—were pinned high up on her head. A polished hilt rested lightly in her hand. Austin could sense the balance in it from the way she rolled her wrist in a practice stroke. The rest of the serious weapon was cloaked in a smooth fitting skin that must have been custom stitched for this specific sword. Austin had gotten used to heavy blades, designed more for hacking firewood than swording. They were like bulky plow horses compared to the guard's Thoroughbred.

The woman bent her knees and dropped into a starting position, just like the one Austin had tried to teach Cabrill. She attacked quickly, as graceful as her weapon. Her elegant motions surprised Austin. Twice. It had been a long time since he'd faced a skilled opponent. In the past he would have been excited by the challenge. Now he was embarrassed by his inability to defend himself. His training had been comfortable and routine for far too long. He could blame it on not having Skylar to practice with, but the truth was he had gotten lazy.

One point away from being defeated three to zero, Austin felt desperate. Ashamed at using a trick on someone of her skill, he made a feint to his right. Disciplined, the woman held her line like a seasoned fencer. She lunged. Austin felt the delicate strike as if it were a punch. Point number three. The referees declared the woman the winner.

Another uniform faced him, with the same sword and the same style. Determined to redeem himself, he scored against the man but still lost the bout. He fought the third black-red-and-gold combatant to a two-point tie but couldn't get past the man's defenses and lost again.

Austin ruffled the short spots in his hair where braids had been, and watched the three guards saunter away laughing. Not just skilled, not just well practiced, they were trained. In fencing. On a strip. He was too exhausted to think about it, and Po probably wasn't pleased with the tally. Austin's vision of soaking away his aches in a steamy bathhouse while his clothes were being properly laundered was fading. When he finished here, he'd be bathing in the cold river and washing his own reeking clothes.

The last sworder inched onto the board. The wood groaned, protesting the red-haired man's considerable weight. "You've gained quite a crop since I saw you last," he called across the vibby sty, his voice like tumbling boulders. "But there's also been a harvest."

Austin flushed at Ryster Brimbren's reference to his missing braids. "I suppose you want your plait back." Thanks to Po's lessons, he was gaining confidence speaking Lynawic.

"There's a bit of that," Ryster said. Inching closer to the middle, he held his massive sword ready to attack. The board trembled with each shuffle. Suddenly, he flipped his weapon and snatched it in the fist of his other hand. Then he planted the tip into the wood. He held on to it for stability and gave a tentative bounce. The vibration forced Austin to fling out his arms like a tightrope walker. "More of it being, I only have to pitch you into the fragrant soup to put five new gills in my pouch." He gave another bounce.

Austin flailed but kept centered. "Not a very sporting approach."

Ryster grinned. "You're the one who invented this chancy game, or so's I hear. Can't blame a guy for trying a different way of it. Noticed you have your own special clevers."

Already embarrassed, Austin lunged, his foil aimed at Ryster's ample chest. Sword stuck in the board and useless for defense, the man jumped back, harder than intended. Released from the considerable weight, the plank sprang up, lifting off the corral rails supporting it at each end. Ryster's descending bulk slammed into it midair. It bowed toward the mire then snapped back, sending both occupants flying. Austin managed to land on it with his feet under him. Ryster swiped at his sword to steady himself, but instead jerked it from the wood.

The plank bent deeper, almost touching the slop. Austin stumbled forward into the downward curve. The board rebounded, launching the two fencers even higher. Almost nose to nose, they dropped their weapons and clutched each other's shoulders. "Ahh!" they yelled. Together they smacked against the center of the strip. A thunderous crack tore the air as the wood shattered. Austin felt his stomach jolt into his throat.

Splush!

Shock silenced the crowd. Stretched out in the foul slop, Austin was too drained to move but strongly motivated by the stench and the fat vibbys poking at him to see if he might be food. Coated with putrid mud, he struggled to his feet. Ryster sat up, looking dazed. Assured that both competitors were unharmed, the crowd erupted in deafening laughter, scaring away the snorting vibbys.

Austin found his foil and staggered to the rails. He tried to wipe gross filth from his face with dripping hands. His muscles refused to work properly. He could barely grasp the post. The big man grabbed him from behind and tossed him out of the pen as if he were a rag. Ryster climbed out and shook himself like a wet animal. Soaring clods pelted the crowd, causing a rain of shrieks and curses. He gave Austin a slap on the back. "I'll be trying a different way of it next time."

Austin hoped there would never be a next time.

CHAPTER 38

Skylar knotted a swatch of cloth embroidered with a wildcat's claw to one adorned with a fish, as if the feline were about to scoop the scaled creature from its orange habitat. The rest of the furry form snarled over and under other ribbons. It intertwined with beasts and beasties of lesser landholders sworn to support Kriken during difficult times.

Where are they now? Skylar wondered. *Are the fish and the wildcat at Old Kriky's side? Or are they huddled in their homes with the doors barred?*

The huge iron candlesticks could not hold the supporting pole high enough to put the right tension on the colorful strips, but she made do. When she was a child, she'd taught herself the knotted and woven craft of yatyaka, not so she could make things, just to understand the technique. Once she'd figured it out, she went on to something else, not knowing she would someday need the skill. The transformed banners were turning into a sloppy, but interesting, wall hanging, although that was not her goal. Kneeling, she stretched the growing construction across the floor of her prison room to gauge the next weave. After another day touring the grounds she was happily exhausted but stomach-growling hungry. *What will supper be tonight that I can only nibble at?* she thought.

When the food arrived, it was not in the quaking hands of a nervous servant, as usual. Ishty plopped a cloth-covered basket on the table. "The baker sent this for you." Skylar remembered meeting the man that morning. Round of face and body, sweaty from the ovens, he had enthusiastically invited her into his fragrant shop. Breads, pastries, two kinds of soup, and roasted fowl were available for sale that day. You could purchase a single bun or an entire meal to take home and eat. She noticed Icky Ishty never referred to the man as a master, although his guild sign was clearly carved into the door.

Of course there had been nothing of use for her sculpture at the bakery. If there had been, Skylar would have ignored it. As they were leaving, the baker tried to give them each a pastry. Ishty rigidly declined for both of them, saying they did not wish to decrease his profit for the day. The man winked at Skylar behind the hearth keeper's back. Now she understood the secret sign. A goodie could be refused at his shop, but a present sent to the manor house could not be turned away.

Skylar sat and slipped the cloth off the reed basket. Her stomach rumbled in response to the rich odors. For a moment she wondered if this was a test. Ishty had become suspicious of her eating habits. The woman might have prepared it herself to observe Skylar's reaction, but that soon seemed unlikely.

Ishty wrinkled her nose with disgust. "I would have tossed it out, but you should at least see it so you can appropriately acknowledge it with a thank you. You're under no obligation to eat any of it. His Lordship's master cook has made a proper meal of roasted dybil with ground hialn nuts and crushed jrookr leaves. I'll have a plate sent to you when it's ready."

"Mmmm." Skylar unwrapped a pouch of warm biscuits. She pulled out a potpie large enough for the hearty supper of someone twice her size. A wooden spoon left over from breakfast still sat on the table. She wiped it on her sleeve and plunged it through the crust. She scooped out a dripping brown mass, and shoved it into her mouth. That should assure her custodian she hadn't gone on a secret hunger strike.

Ishty looked away. "You've no idea what might be in that."

The spicy filling was like a thick stew. "Wonderful," Skylar mumbled. She offered a mound of mystery meat and vegetables to Ishty. "Taste?"

The woman put a protective hand over her mouth. "I'm sure it's delightful, but I prefer the fare prepared in His Lordship's kitchen."

Skylar dunked a biscuit into the center of the pie and swirled it around, sopping up fatty juices. She shoved the whole thing into her already full mouth. Austin would have appreciated the effort. They'd had contests to see who could cram in the most food and still chew and swallow without chocking. Skylar had gotten pretty good at it, but she usually only won if she made exaggerated chomping faces, forcing Austin to laugh so hard he started gagging. Oh, how she missed having a brother around to be gross with! Cabrill was wonderful, but she didn't understand silly.

Skylar gave Ishty a puffy smile. The golden bun that deliciously rolled across her tongue threatened her escape plan, but she couldn't pass up getting a reaction. The woman placed a hand on her stomach, as if she might be ill. "There's a small cake. The frosting is a local specialty made from beetle larva. It doesn't appeal to me, but I'm sure you'll find it delightful."

"Beetle larva, my favorite!" Skylar managed to say. "I'll save it for last." The sweet would be tempting, but she would have to resist. The biscuit had already been enough of a setback to her scheme.

Ishty gave a hard swallow. "We'll start again tomorrow at sunrise." Rigidly she stalked from the room, forgetting to close the door after her. Apparently afraid the prisoner might attempt a dash at freedom, the startled guard quickly swung the broad chunk of wood into position with a screech.

Still horribly hungry, Skylar put down her spoon. Her sword sculpture, although incomplete—in fact, deliberately incomplete—was keeping Kriken and his advisors busy, squabbling over its meaning. Their stupidity was beyond laughable. The serious-faced old men and women in their stodgy robes wanted an unfinished pile of stuff to tell them what to do. Instead of analyzing a piece of art, they should be examining the real situation that was right in front of them and figuring out a plan. People in this village needed protection. Kriky and his gang were wasting time arguing while a dark cloud scattered soot on everyone and something snatched away armed soldiers.

Sure, knowing what might happen could come in handy, but Skylar had a lot more confidence in her brain and her gut than in a sculpture or a painting or the pattern on an old vase. She'd given it a lot of thought during her captivity. Art was information, not destiny. And it most certainly was not a solution. She'd allowed herself to be kidnapped, not because it was foretold in Cabrill's drawing, but because she'd freely chosen to help her friend. She, Skylar Swiftbrooke, had decided. And then she'd acted. Because it made sense.

Obviously on Saffrian art couldn't be ignored. The sketches

of Austin had confused her at first. How could Cabrill draw a guy she'd never met standing in a place she'd never seen? Back then, they'd been at the point-at-yourself-and-grunt-your-name stage of understanding one another so the artist couldn't explain. Skylar had looked at page after page filled with her brother's face. There were pictures of her too, even though they'd been drawn before she'd tripped into the meadow.

She accepted Cabrill's talent as normal for Saffrian, but she didn't think of it as telling the future, even after Po had explained it to her. Predictions didn't turn themselves into reality. People did things and then more things happened—or not. Cabrill's art was simply a record of the doings and the happenings. Okay, so the drawings and paintings and whatever were created before the doings and the happenings. That didn't mean they caused any of it.

Kriken's missing soldiers hadn't disappeared because certain art existed. The dark smear across the sky wasn't there because Cabrill had drawn it. There must be a real, live monster in the forest producing the foul clouds. Maybe it was an ogre who liked huge bonfires. Or a fire-breathing dragon with a fondness for belching out smoky cartoon figures. She had to admit neither of those was native here, as far as she could tell. But something could have fallen in.

Just like she had.

Skylar was hoping for a dragon. The planet Ursuwa had them. Well, dragon-ish creatures. Sort of. She sighed. A girl could dream.

It didn't matter to her who defeated the thing, as long as it was stopped. She would do whatever she could to help her friends save Saffrian. She knew Austin would too, once she told him how important it was.

Leaning back in the carved chair of her posh prison cell, she put a hand to her breastbone and felt the absence of her pendant. She wondered where Po was now. He was her friend and she loved him dearly, but she suspected he kept things from her, especially about his search for the key that would get them to Callister.

What would she say to her parents when she finally saw them again after such a long time. Hey, I went through this amazing doorway that instantly took me to another planet! Austin would be star-smacked for ages when he found out. And how would she convince her mom and dad that she and Austin were critical to the survival of that world? She wanted to see her parents more than anything, but this would be so much easier if Austin would just pop out of a portal on his own as she had.

Well, she would figure out how to handle that later. First, she had to deal with her present predicament.

The usual trembling servant arrived with supper from the kitchen. Skylar kept the water and the butter-like toont. She refused the food, showing the boy the full meal from the baker already on the table. When he was gone, she tossed the potpie out the narrow window. The remains would quickly be devoured by the dog-like creatures that were supposed to keep predators from entering the village at night. She put the empty tin where it would be seen, as evidence that she'd eaten. The biscuits she hid in a chest. Tomorrow she would crumble and scatter them during the daily outing while her nursemaid wasn't watching. Wandering dybils would quickly snatch up the morsels. She wished she could save the fluffy breads, but they would go moldy before she would need them.

The basket was almost empty. Almost. Skylar took out the cake, nestled in its own little cloth. Pale blue frosting swirled over golden perfection. She stared at it in agony. Her breeches were definitely roomier today, although not loose enough. Not yet. But one teeny little bite wouldn't hurt, would it?

Ishty burst in without giving the traditional greeting before entering a private room. Even as a prisoner, Skylar had been granted the courtesy. Considering the abrupt way the hearth keeper had exited only a short time ago, it seemed Ishty was having difficulty with her etiquette tonight.

Skylar acted as if she were delighted to see the woman again. "How sweet of you to collect the dirty dishes yourself instead of sending the kitchen boy."

Ishty ignored being compared to a child servant. "A message arrived from the Artists Guild. It seems there is concern regarding your presence here."

A message. Skylar could deal with that. But did Ishty seem more than a bit smug? "Under your kind supervision, I am perfectly well cared for and content. Tell Lord Kriken that I will gladly write a response saying so. He has been a splendid host. I would not want him to be chastised."

"I'm sure His Lordship would be most appreciative of the gesture. However, the interest is not in your welfare. The artwork you're producing is to be assessed by the Guild. It seems there is a question of quality due to your—hmm, I believe the word used in the text was instability. Before you came to us—"

You mean before I was kidnapped and dragged here by armed soldiers, Skylar thought. And this seems like more information than a lord would tell a hearth keeper. *Did you snoop in your boss's private papers, Icky?*

"—there were events that forced the Guild to ban you from making art. Yet, here you are, still presenting yourself as a master artist."

The room felt stuffy and small. Skylar kept a rigid smile plastered on her face while her insides churned. Cabrill had warned her, but it had seemed unlikely the Guild would be a danger. Kriken certainly wouldn't advertise that he held an artist captive, but somehow the Guild had found out. She was suddenly glad there were guards outside her door, but a more immediate threat stood before her.

Think, think, think, Skylar told herself. *When you're at the end of the strip, lunge!* "How wise of Lord Kriken to share a private letter with you. Your counsel must be as valuable to him as his advisors'." Ishty blushed, proving that Skylar was right about her secretly reading the message. "I look forward to having my work examined by other artists. And I will enjoy conversing again with masters who have a more worldly perspective than my recent company."

"I'm sure you're most excited to hear the names of the delegation." Ishty waited for a reaction.

Skylar gazed at her as if mildly interested. She would not feed the woman's enjoyment by asking. Her thoughts ran a marathon. If she was exposed as a fraud, there would be no need to hold her captive. She could eat her cake and walk out the front door. She very much wanted to do both. Would Kriky let her go without some kind of revenge?

Ishty smirked, as if sure she had won this bout. "We are to be honored by the presence of Grand Master Liaty Nobian and Guild Master Forliani Morokr. I believe Master Forliani Morokr was your teacher and mentor."

Skylar knew the name. Forliani was the one person in the whole world, or all the worlds, who should have given Cabrill encouragement and support. Instead, she had ordered the young artist to report to an asylum, to be locked up as if she were a dangerous criminal. Skylar couldn't hope to fool the former mentor and wouldn't expect her to go along with the charade.

She isn't here yet, Skylar thought. *Keep the deception going. Don't defeat yourself.* "I look forward to seeing Master Forliani again."

Ishty gave an insincere frown. "This is such a terrible confusion about you and your art. You can understand that His Lordship is inclined to believe the tale, since you arrived without the usual brushes and paints."

"My escorts appeared suddenly and were in a hurry to bring me here. In the excitement they neglected to take that bag."

Ishty smiled sweetly. "So you have said. Of course that is all the explanation needed. I'm sure everything will be clear when the masters arrive."

A little too clear, Skylar thought. "When are they expected?"

"Three days. No more than four."

Skylar relaxed. That was a long time.

A sly curve twisted the corners of Ishty's lips. "But you won't have to wait until then to catch up on Guild news. The young man who brought the letter is no village bloke but an artist himself. Perhaps you know him, from before the events that caused you to—well, to practically be disowned by your colleagues. He says he has met you. It must be true since he appears unimpressed by your character. His Lordship has invited him to stay at the manor. In fact, this is not the first time he has been our guest. He is Master Mikol Wilsheem."

Skylar wanted to puke up the meat pie and biscuit. Cabrill had spoken sparingly about the mysterious Mikol; but her feelings for him were obvious to Skylar, even if Cabrill denied them to herself. Maybe he had feelings for her too. He would see the deception in a flash. Skylar's three to four days had evaporated. "Master Mikol also received his training at Bogoboln, as I did."

Ishty seemed pleased by the formal way Skylar referred to the new guest. Perhaps she was even delighted that the charming young man couldn't possibly be friends with a disgraced ex-artist. "I'm sure you'll have an opportunity to visit with him tomorrow." She ignored the dirty dishes, leaving them for a lesser servant to collect. "No doubt you would have predicted this through a drawing or some trinket had you not been occupied with that horrendous sculpture." This time Ishty closed the door triumphantly as she left.

CHAPTER 39

Austin sat huddled by the fire pit wrapped in a blanket, still shivering from his dunking at the local bathhouse. Po had taken pity on him, parting with enough coin for a proper soaking, but Austin's opponents had beaten him to the establishment. The place could not draw water and heat it fast enough to keep up. His sore muscles had grown stiffer in a bath barely warmer than the river that supplied it. At least the soap had been strong, and the owner had laundered his clothing for free as compensation for the temperature and in appreciation for Austin's having sent so many customers his way.

Cabrill gazed at the fire from the depths of her hood as if she peered from a personal cave. Po held his daily language notes but seemed uninterested in them. The day had not been a triumph, but Austin felt good about his spontaneous comments to Ryster Brimbren. "That was the first time I said something in Lynawic—other than to you two—that I hadn't rehearsed."

"Yes, very good," Po said. "Did you notice the speech of the woman guard, the first of them to beat you? Lynawic is new to her. Her accent tells me she's from the northern city of Tueu."

"Kriken is recruiting from far away," Cabrill said.

"Perhaps His Lordship has expanded his army," Po said. "Or the locals are reluctant to serve. Or there are few jobs in Tueu and its people must travel to find suitable work."

Austin lifted his head, listening to a creaking that had been distant but now seemed close. *Too close*, he thought. It was after dark. Travelers had claimed campsites and settled in hours ago. Cabrill gave Po a look then slipped away into the cloaking evening. Austin grabbed his pack and dug for his sword.

"Friend asks a chat," bellowed a gravelly voice. "Not likely a sneaking robber with the noise I'm hauling." Ryster Brimbren tugged a groaning cart into the firelight. A bulky goat-like animal with two thick horns twisting out of its head was tied to the back. It gave a fierce bleat, then docilely sniffed the ground, looking for something within easy reach to munch on.

"Chamapl's gone lame," Ryster said. "Can't find a new one strong enough to draw this lot. I'm a metal smith. Master, truth be, with the Smiths Guild. My wares have heft. Stable Keep says you got a ploddel. And I wonder, might you be going my direction."

Po and the big man discussed terms using a speech pattern Austin wasn't used to. He had to think hard to follow the rhythm. Ryster would pay a fair fee, and Austin no longer worried that they would end up starving because of the cost of his bath.

Ryster plopped a cut tree stump next to Austin as if it weighed no more than a fluffy cushion and sat on it. "Can I see that whip of yours again?"

Austin took out the foil, checked that the cover over the controls was locked, and handed it to him. The smith mumbled at the slim, four-sided blade; indented grip; and curved hand guard. "Don't see the making of it. Would like to meet the master."

"He lives beyond the known countries." Austin didn't have the words to explain his weapon to someone who worked metal with hammer and tong at a forge.

Ryster handed it back. "Learning would be worth a far trip." He patted his own weapon in the scabbard hooked to his belt, the one he had used against Austin. "Mine's not a sword to do work for you. Makes you think before you swing. Hilt to point, not what you'd expect a crafter to carry. Heavy and plain, as I made it." He squeezed his hand into a fist and held out his ample arm. "Keeps me strong. As it be, no thief wants it. Might get striped of my fine wares, but I'll always be left with a weapon." He leaned close to Austin and gave him a serious scowl. "Here be a lesson: Some swords be more dangerous than others. Can't tell them apart by the look."

Austin wasn't impressed by the great wisdom, but he didn't want to offend his new friend—his very large, new friend. "I'll remember that."

Ryster went to his cart and returned with a bundle. He put it on the ground and folded back the cloth. "This be my best." He slid a shining shaft from a familiar-looking casing.

In awe, Austin grasped the hilt. He twisting his wrist so firelight dance along the blade. The elegant weapon was designed for serious duels where people actually bled and died from the wounds it inflicted. The perfect balance made it light in his hand.

"There's responsibility with any weapon," Ryster said. "More so with this like. Take care or there'll be slices out of things you'd rather have whole."

"I know this sword." Austin had seen the hilt but not the blade until now.

"Aye, nine times," Ryster said. "I be talking guild business with the local smithy when Lord Kriken's crew came looking for a finery. Paid me well for the use of it."

Reluctantly Austin relinquished the blade, but it wouldn't leave his thoughts. Later, bedded down under a clear sky, he watched constellations slowly parade overhead. The three guards who'd defeated him had all used the same sword. A rented sword. Not one of their own. They'd moved as if trained in the formal fencing he knew, but that didn't exist here.

Weird, Austin thought, as sleep snuffed out the stars and faded Ryster's snoring.

CHAPTER 40

From what Ishty said, Skylar thought she had the evening to herself, uninterrupted by a confrontation with the new visitor. But Lord Kriken apparently felt an urgent need to confront his prized artist with the letter discrediting her. And with the person who'd delivered the letter. She trudged down the stairs, feeling very small sandwiched between two towering escorts. They took her to a room on the second floor just below her cushioned cell. During the short walk she devised a plan for how to handle the meeting. Simple. She would bluff her way through. The guards motioned her inside. They stayed in the hall and closed the door. Feeling very much alone and on her own, she resisted leaning against the solid wood for support.

An abundance of candles lined the walls and cluttered the central table. Were the plentiful tapers meant to flaunt wealth or to offer false security with fake sunlight? They sucked oxygen from the room and smeared a sallow yellow across the musty advisors who somehow still found breath to argue with one another. The two grayed men and two grayed women stood, as if height gave their competing arguments more substance. They pointed and poked at the single item stretched across the polished wood. Skylar knew it well. She had stitched together chunks of parchment to get the length she needed for her sketch of the prophetic sculpture. Crude lines showed swords, planted hilt down and point up, lashed to a wooden scaffold. Tiers of decreasing sizes formed a tower. A single weapon, impossibly thin, aiming skyward, rose from the top. More swords circled the base. Behind the structure, knotted banners hung from a stout pole.

A burly man, Lord Oliak Kriken sagged at the head of the table in his high-back chair. Light brown hair infested with white, he seemed more creased and sadder than the last time Skylar had seen him not that many days ago. Beside him sat The Visitor. Master Artist Mikol Wilsheem. She knew him immediately, although she'd never seen him before. Not clearly, anyway. She suspected he was the dark statue almost hidden in the background of many of Cabrill's sketches. Cabrill wouldn't admit the possibility and seemed embarrassed when she'd suggested it. He had the blue-black hair and bronze-brown skin of the Floriklian people. Scattered braids were gathered at the nape of his elegant neck. He seemed to listen to the arguments of the dusty advisors with polite interest.

Skylar set her jaw and approached the table. She was Master Artist Cabrill Shistayia. Her friend would denounce her as a fraud and she would say he was mistaken. Or he was lying because—

Okay, so the strategy was a bit thin, but it would complicate the situation. For tonight, that was all she needed.

Mikol's gaze swung away from the counselors and locked on her. His slate eyes showed no surprise. Deep as any ocean, they captured her in a private gaze. He tilted his head toward the robed bunch and gave an almost imperceptible twitch as if to say "Fools." The subtle message was seen only by her, meant only for her. It was their secret, just as her identity was now a confidence they shared.

Skylar inwardly seethed. How dare he slip into her conspiracy, pretending he belonged there! No, it was the other way around. He was not joining her. With a half-wink and the hint of a smile he meant to pull her into *his* sphere and make this his game.

A kaleidoscope of Cabrill's stories suddenly clicked through Skylar's mind. There were nameless friends who had performed brazen feats. There were anonymous acquaintances who had said bold, clever things. Cabrill had made it sound as if they were all different people. Now Skylar fit the pieces together and saw the complete pattern. Cabrill had talked about Mikol. Frequently. Often. All the time.

He came toward her, arms stretch to pull her into an embrace. Skylar stiffened and glared at him. Without a stumble he turned the hug into a single hand on her shoulder. He leaned in and whispered, "Everyone knows Cabrill and I are very close. They'll think it strange if you don't show me some affection."

Skylar knew it for a lie. Cabrill might have a nova-sized crush on him, but there had been no romance or even close friendship. For the past years it had been her, Cabrill, and Po. This guy was not a part of their lives. She whispered back, "We had a fight and I'm mad at you."

Mikol grinned to cover his shock. She could tell he had expected her to throw herself into his arms with squeals of delight. His hand slipped from her sleeve. "I haven't named you yet. You'll be in less trouble as Cabrill than as a child playing grownup with borrowed braids."

Ocean-eyes glowing with candlelight, he was magnificently tall and handsome—and arrogant and insulting, calling her a child and thinking she had no swording skills. "Give me a weapon and we'll see who deserves to wear braids," she whispered.

Mikol's grin drooped to a mocking pout. "Yes, we had a terrible spat, but I think you'll get over our little disagreement very soon, especially since I have a present for you."

Oooh, a present. Did he expect her to go all zonk-brained over the promise of something shiny? "The fight was your fault, and I'll never forgive you."

Mikol stepped back, bowed, and said loudly, "How wonderful to be in your delightful company again, Master Cabrill."

Skylar gave a reserved smile. His scheme was as short-term and unformed as hers. In a few days Cabrill's old mentor would arrive. How did Mikol expect to convince Forliani that he'd been deceived by a girl too young, too short, and too absolutely unartistic to be Cabrill?

Skylar would like to see him try. But not enough to stick around.

CHAPTER 41

Wasbiln Manor should have been quiet with the gentle inhale, exhale of sleep. Weary servants had gone to their beds long ago, but candles still blazed in Lord Kriken's study. A slice of amber reached through the window into the darkness, as if to escape the agitated voices rattling the room.

Wedged sideways in the window one floor above, the glow was all Skylar could see. Wider on the inside and tapered through the two-foot deep wall toward the exterior, the slit was designed to give an archer a good view for shooting while providing protection from the enemy. The common-sense design was not unique to this planet. She'd noticed it in historical records of fortresses on other worlds. Some narrowed to the width of a hand on the outside of the building. Fortunately for her, the space here was enough to accommodate a small caldron, allowing the boiling liquid of your choice to be pour onto invaders below. Unfortunately, the narrow gap was still effective at keeping a prisoner from escaping.

She stretched her right arm toward the open air and wiggled her shoulder, gaining an inch at most. The voices below vibrated through the stones. Her head throbbed with the droning. She could hear a few of the words and could guess the rest. Arguing over the meaning of the sword sculpture, the moldy advisors kept rolling the same barrel back and forth.

—What she has made means nothing because she is no longer sanctioned by the Artists Guild.

—A dispute with her guild does not make her talent vanish.

—Does it take away the prediction in her art?

—The girl was born with the ability, even if her style is unusual.

—More than unusual, it's rough and crude.

—Perhaps that is by design, to convey a certain mood.

—Or it shows she has the madness that sometimes comes over artists.

—The madness is a myth.

—If she had the illness, she would be confined to Seaba Colony instead of roaming around as she pleased.

It had all been said right in front of Skylar a few hours ago. She and Mikol had deflected the dusty old goats' questions by insisting Guild Master Liaty Nobian's presence was necessary for a complete explanation. Since the two master artists would not cooperate, the advisors had ventured into their own speculations, ignoring the only two people in the room who had any worthwhile knowledge. It had been a relief when she'd finally been sent back to her room and Mikol had been kept to smile and nod at their ridiculous babbling.

Squeezed into her new prison in the window opening she squirmed another inch toward freedom. She regretted eating the gravy-soaked biscuit just to spite Ishty. Using her toes through the soft boots, she scooted her right foot forward, careful not to become tangled in the streamers shoved against one side. The tight space reeked of rancid toont. Eating her bread plain day after day, she had saved up the oily spread. Tonight she had slathered the paste onto the casement to make it slippery. Although most of it had become foul with age, the odor still made her mouth water. She pressed her hip toward the amber light from the room below but felt no progress.

She decided to pull out of the window and start over. If she coaxed the last film from the toont container, she could grease her clothes—although the thought was positively gross—or smear more on the stones where her hips needed to slide through.

Supported by a wobbly table shoved against the wall, her left foot was slightly below the windowsill. She shifted her weight onto it and pushed with her right to pop herself back into the room. Her hips wouldn't budge, not even a little. She was stuck, unable to move outward toward liberty or inward to her cell.

She had planned her escape for four days from now, when an early moon would cut the darkness. And she would be skinnier. And the yatyaka would be finished, instead of dangling with loose ends.

Four days. The Guild bigwigs would be here before then, bringing the end to her masquerade. And while she waited for doom to descend upon her, she would have to endure the company of the too handsome, too clever, too arrogant Mikol.

She tried again to pry herself from the opening.

Stuck!

Skylar swallowed panic. A terrible, horrible thought paralyzed her: Ishty would discover her here in the morning, pinched between rocks like a bug. The woman would smirk and probably laugh outright. Her joyful shrieks would echo through the manor house.

Blood burned Skylar's cheeks. She couldn't be found in this

uncomfortable and embarrassing position, especially not by Ishty. Again she tried to shove her right hip toward the sooty evening air. She had to get out of here and it had to be tonight. There was no waiting until she lost another pound. She had already tossed out her pack. The yatyaka pole, supported by the candle holders, was braced horizontally across the opening. Its knotted embroidery hung into darkness. It was a good plan, a perfect plan—if she could just get out of the window.

Concentrate! No, that was wrong. It made her tense up.

Relax, she told herself. *Think about finding Cabrill. And whipping her butt for getting me into this.*

The window was slightly taller than Skylar. She stretched an arm into the cool night and felt around the exterior. Her fingers found the keystone. Her stubby nails crumbled away a bit of grit, giving her a crevice to dig into. She sucked in her stomach, exhaled and pulled, using the triangular rock for leverage. Her hips scrunched forward a few inches. She braced her left hand and elbow against the casement behind her. Chest pressed tight, she panted shallow, crushing breaths. Suck in, exhale, pull with the right, push with the left. Suck in, exhale, pull, push. When she got out of this vise, she promised herself she would devour every scrap of food in her pack.

Her right foot felt the outer edge and the emptiness beyond it. Almost in a fencer's pose, she shoved hard against the wobbly table with her left. It clattered from under her, but the force scraped her hips free into vacant air. She teetered on one foot, fingertips gripping the keystone. Dizzy, she slapped her inside hand against the top casement to halt the pitch forward. Her cheek stung with scratches from the rough wall. Half hanging out of the window, she slammed her left boot onto solid stone and took long, deep breaths. Had someone heard the table fall?

Voices from below continued. Cautiously, she probed the dangling woven banners with her right foot until she found a gap to support it. The bar tightened against the window casement with her weight. The weaving stretched under her and held.

The yatyaka didn't hang all the way to the ground as she'd hoped. Much of the length had been gobbled up by the knotted pattern. In the dark she couldn't tell by how much the artwork failed to reach its goal.

Slowly she climbed down the embroidered ladder that swayed as she repositioned each foot. Below her, gold threads in the rainbow macramé flashed as they caught the sliver of light from Kriken's study.

"Are they the banners of lords—"

Skylar froze. During the long, boring session earlier that evening, she had given each advisor a nickname. She recognized the whinny voice of Yeti Beard. At least being caught scaling the manor wall was better than being found wedged in a window.

"—who still stand with Your Lordship or are they the banners of those who have abandoned you in this time of crisis?"

Relieved, Skylar continued her descent. They'd simply moved the discussion from the sword tower to the cloths she'd chosen from the great room, not discovered her out the window clinging to them.

"My Lord, you must confirm the alliances with those provinces," Toxic Breath bellowed.

"This is all speculation," Stork Neck shouted. "The sculpture's meaning will not be clear until it is complete."

Yeah, Skylar silently agreed, *let an artist finish putting it together before you go dissecting it.* She was almost even with the light. She hoped the old moldies were too occupied with outshouting one another to noticed a girl half climbing, half hanging on their precious banners. If this went badly, would they hear the thud of her fallen body? Possibly preceded by a scream of terror and maybe accompanied by the crunch of breaking bones.

"The meaning is clear from what has already been constructed and from the plans," Yeti Beard said.

"A design for the sculpture is not the genuine art," Stork Neck said. "You cannot determine a prediction from schematics."

Lumpy Grumpy interrupted, "It means nothing because the girl is no longer an artist."

A breeze chilled Skylar through the sweaty fabric of her shirt. As she passed, she peeked into the candlelit room, hoping no one was peering back. Stork Neck faced toward her, ebony eyes glaring at his colleagues. She stifled a gasp. If he should shift his gaze—

Skylar's foot probed for another rung in her incomplete ladder and found only loose streamers. She wrapped her legs around the cloth strips and shinnied down them like a rope.

Yeti Beard was roaring now. "A single sword above the rest, a weapon never seen in this world. That is why she cannot find the right one to place at the pinnacle."

"Our champion will come from another world?" Lumpy Grumpy almost chocked on her disbelief. "Ridiculous!"

"That was not my meaning," Yeti Beard shouted.

Skylar crossed from the slice of candlelight into full night. She grasped the last bit of a lizard's tail, her body twisting. She let go. Suspended in black, touching nothing but air, for a moment she was nowhere. No one watched for her. No one missed her. No one expected anything of her.

The ground slammed against her. Shaking, she patted around her with sore, clenched fingers, searching for her pack.

She grabbed the rough animal hide and propelled herself unsteadily to her feet.

Each day during her tour of the estate, she had propped a bright bolster in her window. As she'd walked the grounds, she'd used the yellow pillow in the row of third-floor slits as a waypoint, orienting the stable and the road to its position. Her plan had been to dash into nearby bushes then crouch behind carts and stumps while working her way across the yard in moonlight. But that was meant to be four days from now. The moon rose weaker tonight, and Skylar was suddenly impatient with independence. She shouldered her pack and rushed straight toward the stables.

Something tangled her feet. She plopped into the grass, landing on one of the wooden swords she and the guards had played with. She'd beaten them all at the new game with a strange name they couldn't remember, and she'd shown them a few moves to practice. Little more than a stick with a carved grip, the toy blade was hardly a weapon. She took it anyway.

A champion from another world. She was surprised the stuffy advisors had enough imagination to even think such a crazy notion long enough to reject it. Good thing the idea hadn't surfaced earlier when she'd been in the room. She would have been tempted to encourage them just for fun. They were sure to be shocked when Austin finally got here, proving it true. If he got here.

Po's negotiations might fail. Despite Cabrill's predictions, Austin might never arrive. Skylar might never find a way back home. She'd thought it through many times. Fluent in Lynawic, she also knew enough of two other languages to barter in the markets. She could apprentice to Po and become a master, earning her living translating for merchants. She'd make the best of her situation, just as she always had. She could have a good life here, doing good work. Except this time, it would be one place forever.

Quietly, she approached the stable and called the name of the dog-like beast that kept watch. Instead of banging a gong as it had been trained to do when a stranger entered at night, it greeted her with an affectionate nuzzle and twitching tails, following her to the stalls. The drowsy white goaddig objected to being led from its cozy bed. She didn't know its name, so she dubbed it Buttercup. She soothed and coaxed until the gentle creature gave in.

She climbed into the saddle and urged the goaddig toward the road. The dog-like creature ambled back to its duties. Although Skylar couldn't see it in the dark, the menacing cloud churned in the sky above her. She could smell it, acrid and foul. Not so far off something burned in the forest. With or without Austin, she would do what she could. But she was no champion.

CHAPTER 42

Standing in the hallway, Mikol announced himself through the closed door. The guards outside the captive's room had been doubled to two. They cared little that he had Guild issues to discuss with the girl, but they softened when he hinted at a personal relationship that needed repair. Gossip of the cool meeting earlier was sure to have spread through the manor house. There must be plenty of speculation that a romance between the two artists was stormy at the moment.

His greeting answered with silence, Mikol pretended to hear an emotional reply. "Don't let it upset you so, my darling," he said. "It was a small mistake. I want to forgive you, if you'll just explain it to me." He listened again to the silence. "Yes, of course, I promise." The door was watched but not locked. Without glancing at the guards to see their knowing grins, he let himself into the room.

Inside, the overturned table and the weaving hanging out the window told him she was gone. The escape was completely unnecessary. His plan all along had been to support the charade then get her away from here before the masters arrived. It was the least he could do, since he was responsible for her being here. He shoved a pile of bright pillows out of the way and sat on the end of the bed. The intense colors made his temples throb, or maybe he was just irritated by how poorly the evening had gone.

The imposter was no stranger to him. He'd observed the girl traveling with Cabrill. Even from afar he could see how alike they were. A few times he had approached Cabrill, but only when he was certain of her identity and that the girl was off at the market or getting water. When he'd found the artist by herself at Moon Valley, he knew who must be at Wasbiln in her place. He'd expected the girl to appreciate his playing along with the deception and was surprised by her hostility. What had Cabrill told her about him that angered her so?

Months ago the Artists Guild had refused Kriken's petition for a resident artist, causing him to offer Mikol the position in a shadow deal.

Although not opposed to generously paid, illegal work, Mikol had another idea. Humbly, he'd explaining he was not the right artist for the job. Master Artist Cabrill Shistayia, and only she, could give His Lordship the quality of prediction he needed.

Mikol viewed the scheme as perfect. The Guild kept it quiet that Cabrill had been declared crazy and ordered to Seaba, so Lord Kriken thought she was in good standing. He would keep her presence at Wasbiln a secret. No one must know that his lordship had hired an artist under an illegal arrangement.

Cabrill would be protected from the Guild and would earn some coin, which she desperately needed. The deception wouldn't hold forever, but Cabrill would be safe for a time.

Or so Mikol hoped. Seeing her at Tarafalla was a shock. Blinded by the pattern of ovals that filled his art, he hadn't anticipated her rejecting the shadow contract. Or foreseen the botched kidnapping and that Kriken's estate would grow dangerous.

He'd ached to chase after her as she'd walked away from Moon Valley alone that day, but he still had his own challenge to wrestle with.

A short time later he heard from a certain friend, who always had news not commonly known, that the Guild had learned Cabrill was at Wasbiln. A scorching letter of complaint from Grand Master Liaty Nobian was on its way to Kriken. Mikol hustled to the Tumble Tavern, only a town away from Wasbiln, arriving just before the courier. Over a pint, he offered to deliver the document himself since he was going to the granite quarry farther up the road past the estate anyway. The nervous young artist, still a student, had heard of the tragedies on Kriken's land and was quick to shove the pouch at him.

Now in the ornate bedroom Mikol punched a vivid blue pillow. If only the girl trusted him. There was no reason why she should, but people usually did. Although Cabrill didn't.

He imagined the girl fleeing through the dark in this dangerous place, lost and alone. Cabrill would slice him open like a fatted vibby if anything happened to her. Truly, Cabrill would put his heart on a spit and roast it to ash.

Lian Sunang Shu might kill him too for not delivering her package to the imposter before she disappeared. He'd already been paid for the task and spent too much of the coin. He hadn't asked how the Lian clankin found him at the Tumble, or why he had to make the delivery instead of the man who pressed the bundle into his hands. The deal, the Astlian said, came directly from Shu. Mikol couldn't pretending he'd fulfilled the contract and saunter away, temping as that was. Shu would find out it was a lie. Given enough time, Shu found out everything.

He massaged his temples, trying to ward off the fit descending on him. His joy in his art was balanced by the curse of it. The closer he'd gotten to Wasbiln, the more severe the seizures had become. Paint and paper rested on a table only a short reach away. It would be ease to grasp them and let his madness do what it would. He willed himself to rise and step toward the door. He had to get back to his own room, to his own chalks. He rushed past the guards, his vision going dark with the pain. Let them think what they would. That the lovers still quarreled.

He could feel the piece would be another like the bronze and the seeds only bigger, greater. The power in the design was not done with him. Perhaps it never would be. Would the scroll work move and twist as it had before? Would the ovals again pulse in unison like colored flames?

Mikol could do nothing else until he defeated this demon. He could never take a position at Lady Tren Ne Seine's estate or any other. Flooded fields, illnesses, the fate of ships, births and deaths—this was the information lordships and ladyships needed to run their estates. These were the predictions they paid for. Such revelations escaped him no matter how faithfully he performed the meditation exercises.

The artist's affliction was strong in him, connecting him to Cabrill as intensely as the lines in his art twined the ovals together. Or was that just a wish? Someday Mikol would tell her. Someday.

He stumbled into his room, latched the door, and let the madness take him.

CHAPTER 43

Stars sparkled across the satin dome. A lazy moon rose, slim and ashen, casting weak shadows across the road. No insects sang. No wings fluttered. No claws scampered across tree bark. The rutted path stretched empty and silent, except for the escaped girl riding a stolen beast, and carrying a crude wooden sword.

Skylar sensed she was being followed. More like stalked. The certainty of it prickled her skin. Lord Kriken's soldiers would have already swooped in and grabbed her. This was something else. More than one something else that fanned out behind her, making the goaddig rattle its bridle. The terrible tales whispered about the manor house and the village swirled through her mind. She clutched her only weapon in one hand and grasped the reins in the other.

Strobed by trees and bushes crowding the edge of the path, sparks flashed to the left and right. In pairs. Like eyes. She urged Buttercup to a quicker pace. How fast could it run in the dark on the uncertain track? And for how long?

Four bulky shadows suddenly blocked the way ahead. Eyes

set in smoke burned at her. Beasts appeared behind her and to the sides. Surrounded! She pressed her mount into a gallop and charged. The goaddig screamed as it hurdled the strange barrier. Searing heat raked Skylar's legs.

Buttercup raced down the dark road. Leaning flat into its neck, Skylar felt the animal's pounding heart and labored breath. Still it ran as angry howls chased them.

Exhausted and burned, the steed stumbled. Skylar soared over its head and rolled on hard dirt. She sprang up, surprised she still clutched the wooden sword. Shadows nipped at her limping mount, sending it shrieking into the woods. Swirling hulks trotted after it, as if disappointed by the lack of challenge in running down the injured animal.

Bulky shapes encircled Skylar. Canine in head and body, they swirled like dark ghosts set with unblinking lava eyes. She flicked the mock weapon at them. Burning flesh and charred cloth tainted the air. "Stay back, you stupid swamp gas!" The shapes growled. Skylar sensed it was laughter. "A whole pack against one little person. You're all cowards." She'd been speaking in Lynawic. She repeated the word in English. "Cowards. Cowards."

Low growls rippled around the ring. Slowly, they stepped back. Except for one. Keeping her in its gaze, it dipped its head, as if agreeing to honorable combat between the two of them.

Skylar lunged, shoving the wooden sword straight into its eye. The tip flamed. The shocked ghost screeched and reared on its haunches, huge and furious. It shook its great head and crouched to leap. She held the flaming weapon steady. She'd made the challenge and she would not run from it.

Streams of water blasted Skylar and the beast. Her fiery sword sizzled as it went out. She threw an arm over her eyes against the torrent. A clear, stormless sky covered the night, yet wave after wave drenched her. She gasped for air and instead gulped liquid. Coughing and unable to see, she wildly swung the sword in front of her.

The pelting suddenly stopped. Skylar swiped moisture away from her eyes and looked around for her attackers. The smoky canines had vanished. She stood in a puddle, shivering and panting, clothes soaked to her skin. Droplets slid down the stray strands of hair plastered to her face and dripped from her chin.

A stubby tree trunk, heavy with bark, stepped from the forest into a streak of pale light cast by the curved moon and spoke. "Your presence brings the joy of soft rain."

CHAPTER 44

In the morning Po invited Ryster to ride on the same side of the ploddel as himself. "To balance the load," he said. But it was really to find out what the stranger knew about their destination. The lame chamapl stayed at the stable while the group traveled on. Harnessed to the rear saddle braces, the cart carrying the master smith's wares clattered and creaked, causing Turnip to twitch her ears. She twisted her neck, attempting to see the source of the racket that followed her, and stepped a little faster, as if trying to stay ahead of it.

"You're traveling far to sell your swords," Po said.

"And I wonder what your business be at Wasbiln," Ryster countered. "You don't seem the army type."

"Is the noble Lord Kriken increasing his troops?" Po kept his voice low so Cabrill and Austin couldn't hear on the other side of the rocking animal. He hoped Ryster would do the same. "Surely his land is as safe as a baby's cradle."

Ryster seemed unconcerned that he bounced against rough hide with the animal's every stride. "Rumor be, a fire-belching monster took a fancy to his forest and calls it home. Don't take that for much. But there's the steep coin His Lordship's putting out for swords."

Po pretended to find that unimportant. "A man of Lord Kriken's wealth and stature is likely to want a new sword now and again."

Ryster nodded. "Steady customer to be appreciated. But this time he sends gills up front. Take my whole stock, every weapon in the smithy. No matter practice, competition, battle, chore. Wants them all and quick. Lad who brought the deal can't take them. Says he's not turning about just yet. And I wonder if he's to visit other smiths in other villages and make other deals. Says he, 'Not your concern.' Which tells me I be right."

"There could be any number of explanations for why he needs numerous swords." Arming more guards did seem the most logical reason to Po, one worthy of a note to Gram Shu in the Lian family language.

"Truth be," the big man agreed. "None of them good. Won't know till we be there."

"I'm surprised you're making such a long trip yourself instead of sending an apprentice."

Ryster frown and shook his head. "The roads be danger these days I hear. Couldn't pack up pups with valuable weapons and shove them off on their own. So's I be touring the countryside while addle-brained children the Smiths Guild sends me to mentor have most like turned my shop into a tavern." He laughed, deep and loud, startling Turnip into a little skip.

Austin wondered what was so funny on the other side of the ploddel. He strained to hear Po and Ryster's voices through Turnip's snorting and the creaking of the cart. He could only snatch fragments out of the noise.

Monster. Battle. Danger. *Nothing to laugh at,* he thought.

He imagined his sister being led into the forest by Lord Kriken, who was probably a sharp-faced villain with beady black eyes, to serve as a sacrifice. He leaned toward Cabrill. "Is my sister okay? Really?"

The artist had been silent, perhaps also trying to eavesdrop. Austin thought it strange she accepted Ryster's presence as if she'd expected it. Most of the time she seemed tangled in her own thoughts. Her evenings were spent by the fire filling sheaf after sheaf with drawings that made her increasingly upset. "The images I've made show her to be well."

For Austin, that was no better than a guess sprinkled with hope. Worry stayed with him like a toothache.

Cabrill slipped out of her sling to walk, probably so she wouldn't have to talk to him. She seemed to be studying the sky. Facing forward, Austin's view on one side was blocked by Turnip, but he could still see plenty of clear blue. Then he noticed the gray streak. As they traveled closer, the charcoal ribbon carried by the wind became a stormy river. Fed by churning clots rising above the trees, it flowed from a spot anchored in the distance. It was right where they were headed, right where his sister was.

When dusk set in, they tucked themselves back into the trees out of sight of the road and camped beside a pond. Cabrill unrolled a drawing showing the four of them—Austin, Po, Cabrill, and Ryster—stared up at an angry swirl. Austin remembered the gray smears in the background of other scenes. Master Ryster seemed undisturbed by seeing himself in a prediction. He was far more interested in the dark plumes roiling from their destination. He studied them in the parchment and the sky. "Not so bad as the stories going 'round."

Singing a discordant tune, Po built a fire. Ryster volunteered to provide supper. Austin wondered what that might be as he watched the burly man pick his way across the small lake's pebbly shallows, searching for just the right something.

Eager for a chance to shed the day's dust, Austin stripped to his breeches and waded into the cool liquid. Po had assured him no Droombians lived beneath its placid surface. Other fishlike creatures might be annoyed by the intrusion, but they would stay out of his way. It felt renewing to stretch and glide through the water in long, smooth strokes at twilight. His cramped muscles eased in the buoyant release from gravity.

In a sleeveless shirt and short pants, Cabrill paddled into deep water, sending out golden ripples that caught the last of the light. She sunk out of sight then burst upward, throwing her arms in great arcs as she propelled into the air. Ruby and amber droplets rained down. She laughed and did it again and again.

Floating on his back, eyes closed, Austin pretended a different body of water supported him. Before Callister, the Swiftbrooke family had lived near a lake on Gabrietta. His parents would set out a picnic meal while he and Skye ruffled the water. His sister would cup her hands together and give a squeeze, squirting him with skilled accuracy. He'd return the fire. The war often escalated into a submerged wresting match that ended in near drowning and happy exhaustion.

There hadn't been a family picnic, or a family anything, in forever. Austin so wished his parents were with him now, helping him rescue Skylar. Instead, they were alone. Two children and both of them gone. He had watched his mother and father fade, going through the motions of living while less than alive. The weight of their grief and his own dragged him deep until he thought he might sink to the muddy bottom and never resurface.

A shocking spray hit his face. He pulled himself upright, treading water. A faint rosy gold tinted the sunless horizon. A figure silhouetted against the glow giggled. She clasped her hands together. With a swoosh she sent a jet splashing into him.

Too late, Austin put up a hand to block it. "Cabrill, stop it." She looked so much like Skylar; now she was acting like her too. He didn't want a substitute. He wanted the real thing. Angrily, he swam toward shore.

"Austin!"

He halted, staring at the land. A trick of the mind. He'd been thinking of Skye so he heard her voice exactly as he remembered it. The bulky shape of Ryster and the compact form of Po stood backlit by the fire. A female figure clambered up the bank of the pond to join them.

The hallucination behind him yelled, "Turn around, you slimy sea slug."

Austin pivoted. A shrieking banshee pounced on him. He barely gulped air before they sank. Instinctively he made a familiar counter move, slipping out of his attacker's grasp.

He resurfaced with barely enough breath to shout "Skye!"

CHAPTER 45

"You want me to go back." Skylar shook her head emphatically at Cabrill and broke from Lynawic into English. "No way. Zero chance. Zilch-trino. Nill-tronium."

Reflected stars glittered the pond like tiny fireworks. Within the comforting sphere of the campfire, Austin picked at roasted root of water reed and fresh fish, both provided by the resourceful Ryster. A fin circled the gilled creature like a tutu. The narrow snout and plump body made it appear as if it had tried to squeeze through the ruffle and gotten caught. The curved shape wobbled on the shallow wooden plate. One vacant eye stared as it rocked.

Although hungry, Austin had yet to take a bite. Finally, it was really Skylar sitting next to him. After a splashing reunion, she'd asked, as he knew she would, "Mom and Dad?"

"Bad. Worse now that I'm gone too, I suppose." He was older; he wasn't supposed to cry. Joyous at finding her and suddenly deeply homesick, he hadn't cared that tears rolled down his already wet cheeks. "We'll be back with them soon." It was a promise.

Now he watched Skylar attack her food as if it were candy. She had grown a little taller but not much. The baby roundness had melted from her face, leaving pronounced cheekbones. She was thinner but a good weight, a healthy weight, not scrawny like some bird-boned adolescents. Unfortunately, she was developing breasts and hips. Austin lamented her maturing figure. More adult now than child, she still seemed so young. Her intensity had not dimmed during those absent years. He was embarrassed that he'd mistaken the quiet artist for his boisterous sister.

"I am not going back there. I am traumatized," Skylar said. "I will need intense therapy and lemon-chocolate gelato for the rest of my life."

"You won't be a prisoner this time," Cabrill said.

"*You* will be. With old Kriky's guards for muscle, your guild is going to grab you and hold on. I haven't told you about all that stuff yet."

Stabbing the fish with a knife to hold it in place, Austin stripped back the scaly skin with his fingers, tore off a fat flake and popped it into his mouth. The taste was like oily peanut butter. Too bad the reed root didn't taste like jelly. The chewy onion-shaped tuber reminded him of bland, unseasoned crackers.

"This is *so* good," Skylar said. "Po, I have missed your cooking."

"I'm glad you find it tasty," Po said. "Master Ryster provided the ingredients."

Skylar shoved a chunk of pale flesh into her mouth. "You wouldn't believe what they fed me. Everything was over cooked, and drowning in sauces and creams." She shuddered. "Disgusting." She took a swig of cider. "I had one good meal, but I couldn't eat much of the pie and only one biscuit because I was getting ready to escape."

Austin poked at his unadorned fish. Sauces and creams sounded wonderful. He didn't see the connection between eating and escaping, but he was used to not immediately understanding his sister's chatter. Eventually she'd add the right details and it would make sense.

To him, the discussion of what might happen if they continued on to Wasbiln Manor was pointless. At sunrise he and Skylar would leave for the portal in the meadow. His sister should remember its location, since that's how she'd arrived here. There was still the whole "save the world" thing, but her refusal just now told him she was ready to return to Callister. With a little persuading, he knew he could get her to agree to a quick getaway.

He wasn't as sure Po would give up the key to the stiav. The master translator had been evasive every time Austin had asked about it. Tonight after everyone was asleep, he would search Po's belongings and take it. He'd feel bad about it, but he'd do it anyway.

Po scribbled ecstatically. "'No way.' Perhaps a shortened phrase for 'not going that way.' Meaning you refuse to take the path in the expected direction? The other words will need more explanation. My Lady of the Firmament! It is delightful to once again be enriched by your company."

Skylar freely talked with her mouth full. "Cabrill, I know I was supposed to wait until you came to get me, but that Mikol guy showed up and your mentor was going to arrive any minute so there was no point in my hanging around pretending to be you anymore."

"Mikol!" Cabrill blanched then blushed.

Skylar explained Mikol had delivered a letter from the Artists Guild announcing the arrival of the masters.

"Fortunately, I'd been working on a plan. Uh, just in case something like that happened."

"Oh, sure, just in case," Austin said in English. "I don't know why I thought I had to rescue you. You were going to escape by yourself all along."

"I don't need you to swoop in and save me," Skylar replied in English. "I take care of myself."

Ryster didn't understand a word of it. Cabrill's English wasn't good enough to catch the quick exchange.

Po grasped it all. He spoke in Lynawic. "Whatever the circumstances of your release, Azure Lady, we are grateful you are with us."

Skylar switched back to the local tongue. "I'm just sorry I had to take the goaddig."

"You walked into camp." Ryster was on his third roasted root. "No goaddig."

"I named it Buttercup." Skylar used the word *toont* for butter combined with the Lynawic word for cup. "It got burned but it's okay now."

Austin wanted to ask how the animal had gotten burned, but he needed to pout for a minute. He *had* expected to swoop in and save Skylar. He was disappointed she'd taken that away from him and that she didn't want it in the first place.

Ryster picked his teeth with a fishbone. "Why put butter in a cup? Does His Lordship melt it and drink it?"

"Buttercup isn't a cup for drinking butter." Skylar stuffed more fish into her mouth. "It's a flower. I don't think there are any here. They grow in other places."

"In these places do they truly keep their butter in cups?" Po asked.

Skylar thought a moment. "Some do. Or in a dish. Tub. Boat. On the Xent colonies butter is kept in a turn. Except, it isn't exactly butter."

"Butter belongs in a pot," Ryster said firmly.

Po chuckled and scribbled.

Skylar chomped into a tuber as if she'd never tasted anything better. "Buttercup the goaddig is on its way back to Wasbiln. I certainly wasn't stealing it. I just borrowed it for a while. I was worried about how to get it back."

"I'm sure it'll find its way home by itself," Cabrill said. She'd been quiet since the mention of her friend Mikol.

Skylar nudged the crumbs on her plate. "Not on its own. It's being delivered. I met these really nice people. They said they'd sneak Buttercup back into Kriken's stable."

Ryster groaned. "More like thieves be having themselves a new goaddig from a gullible little girl."

"I am not *gullible*," Skye said. "And if they *were* thieves, it should worry you that they know exactly where you are, Master Smith. Or did you think I found you by accident, way off the road like this?"

A burning log crackled and split in a burst of sparks. Ryster jumped and looked about, as if bandits crouched just beyond the firelight.

Po had been scribbling about "butter" and "cup." He set aside his notes and put his full attention on Skylar. "What language did they speak?"

"Lynawic, to me. I didn't recognize the tongue they used with one another. I'm sure you know it, Po. I hope you do. It sounds like music, like birdsong. I learned a little bit and I want to know more, right away. It's so beautiful."

Po, Cabrill and Ryster stared at Skylar in silence. Worried by their reactions, Austin wondered if his sister *had* been with thieves.

"Usually this one guy talked to me," Skylar said. "I think he was the leader because he had the most marks on his skin. From a distance they look like tree bark. Up close they're really symbols. He knew Kriken thought I was Cabrill but he knew I wasn't. He said to call him Lawheleo. That must be a Lynawic translation of his name because it isn't what the others called him and it doesn't sound much like birdsong. Cabrill, Lawheleo said you know what's happening in the forest and you should 'accept the way your gift grows.' Po, you'd like him; he talked like that a lot. Every word felt important."

"You had this conversation with Lawheleo," Po said.

Ryster saw it differently. "And I wonder why Lawheleo talked to a small blade of grass like *you*."

Po stood and gave Skylar a deep, formal bow. "You strolled directly into a Yeawoche encampment and boldly conversed with their esteemed chieftain! Lady of the Brilliant Zenith, you are the most amazing of creatures."

"It wasn't exactly like that." Skylar relayed her encounter with the shadowy beasts. "I stabbed the leader of the wolfie things in the eye."

"In the eye?" Austin said.

"That's the only part that seemed solid enough to stab."

Austin wished he'd thought of that.

"So I stabbed it in the eye and that just made it more mad," Skylar said. "Then these people popped out of nowhere and sprayed the big scaries with water from sort of squirt guns attached to big pouches. Like portable plant-watering thingies." She pulled up the patched leg of her long pants and showed off an angry red burn on her skin. "I'm supposed to keep using the salve for a few more days." She poked at her now healed cheek. "It worked on the scratches too. Lawheleo kept apologizing as if my getting hurt was his fault. He said something about being late and having trouble finding me because I wasn't wearing cheese. I'm pretty sure I'm wrong about that last part. Sometimes his pronunciation was hard to understand.

"They brought me here through the forest. Safer than the road, I guess. And the best part—well, other than saving my life—they gave me a present. Austin, I wanted to show you right away, but it was too dark for you to see when we were swimming."

Skylar rolled back her right sleeve and stretched her forearm toward firelight. Blue-gray runes framed by curling scrollwork snaked across her skin. "It's a poem. Lawheleo sang it for me in his language, but I don't know what it means. He said it couldn't really be translated."

Austin stared at Skylar's glowing face as she excitedly showed off the design. He had feared he would find his sister broken by her exile on this foreign world. Maybe he had even hoped for it, so he could heroically whisk her away. Instead, he discovered she had allowed herself to be kidnapped, had escaped on her own, had survived being attacked by burning-eyed beasts, had gone off into the forest with strangers, and had gotten a *tattoo*.

Why, for even a second, had he thought she needed her big brother's protection? She would never go home with him until this—whatever it was—was over. She was having too much fun.

CHAPTER 46

Cabrill shoved a stout log into the flames, afraid to let the fire collapse to embers. *Accept the way your gift grows.* Hadn't she done that? Hadn't she embraced the strange, twisted branches of her talent? Sand drawings that flowed and changed. A sculpture that flew across a valley of moonlight. The Yeawoche were oldest of all the peoples and Lawheleo was an elder among them. It seemed he could have sent a more straightforward message.

She watched her friend's peaceful breathing. The moment Skylar closed her eyes, she was completely asleep. The girl had been safe in the manor house and should have stayed there as instructed. She was lucky to reach them with only a fright and a few burns.

The boy sprawled under his blanket. For a long time he'd pretended to sleep, until he could no longer fight it off. Perhaps he worried his sister would vanish into his dreams. Ryster snored with gusto. If only his grating roars generated light and could show Cabrill a larger perimeter around the camp.

A restless Po sad down next to her and handed her a

drawing. She studied the borders of ovals and curling ribbons, then the center runes. Inked with precision, parts of it appeared traced. The low-quality paper would not last through the next rain. "I won't ask how you suddenly have this." Cabrill never saw a messenger, yet Po would surprise her with information he hadn't had just an hour before.

"You understand the way of my family."

She nodded.

"I ask your counsel as a master artist, and the secrecy of a friend," Po said.

"You have both." Cabrill said. "I've seen the border motif done in a metal cuff." She didn't add it had also been in an unfinished seed bracelet, so he wouldn't quiz her about it. What would upset him more? That she had been to Tarafalla or that she had shared a meal with Mikol, who had then shown up at Wasbiln as an emissary for the Guild? "The rows of many ovals serve as a frame, which says they support the meaning of the work but are not the focus. On the other that I saw, there are only five ovals. And they are the center design, which gives them importance." She ran her finger along the paper. "This, of the many, is old. The other, of the five, is new."

Po studied the page. "It is freshly drawn. How do you know the design is old?"

Three runes sat between the strips of ovals. Cabrill no longer felt bound by loyalty to those who had betrayed her. She pointed to a figure of circles and slashes set in a rectangle. "That's the original mark of the Artists Guild. From before."

Po wagged a finger at her. "Oh, you're in trouble now for breaching your vows by telling me that."

Cabrill chuckled. "For punishment, they'll try to send me to Seaba." Their laughter interrupted the night-bird song but did not disturb the exhausted sleepers. It felt good to sit by the fire with a friend when worry clung to her like cobwebs.

Lawheleo was right. Even though she didn't have all the details, she knew what was going on in Dobgronun Forest. The terror of it filled her dreams with ancient stories, making her over-tend the fire and dread sleep. "I don't know the other two symbols."

"I know them," Po said. "The middle one is the Engineers Guild, from before. Forgive me that I dare not share the identity of the other. They were not on the metal you saw?"

"No. Only the ovals and the lines connecting them. That doesn't mean that the new cancels the old." Cabrill ran her finger along the repeated design. "The guild marks are gone, but these are in both. They were significant once and now they are again. I think they're part of what is in my own art, but I don't understand how."

"Yes. I believe you are correct." Po sighed, as if making a difficult decision. "I will tell you a story, which is just a story and no more."

Cabrill tensed. "A campfire on a starry night is a good place to tell stories."

Po took a deep breath. "There was once a machine unlike any in the land. It was not a single device but a number of engines, let us say five, that together produced an energy that we might call mniadd. There was a guild that knew how to manage its flow like candle light through a pinhole and how to sell it like the treasure it was. The clever guild had a way to withdraw it from those who would not, or could not, pay for it, and from those who abused the abilities it granted. For a while it was glorious. Masters constructed buildings that sang. They painted the sky with symphonies. They formed seawater into creatures they would ride.

"Then something happened, as it always does in stories. The pinhole ripped open, allowing the flame to blaze in all directions. The guild could no longer govern it or control how it was used. Anyone, everyone, with a certain natural ability was suddenly immersed in the energy. Those with the ability enslaved others, moving them about like marionettes and forcing them to serve. They lived out their whims, destroying what generations had built."

Cabrill closed her eyes to her own nightmare. Is that the monster she would become if the energy feeding her madness continued to grow?

"Power is always dangerous," Po said. "Those of strong will and honest hearts dismantled the machine. Its engines were distanced from one another. One might choose the word separated."

Cabrill looked at the dark lines of the connected ovals, knowing she'd been told protected, Lian family knowledge. If Po's indiscretion was discovered, he would be punished far more harshly than she ever would for identifying a banned guild mark. "People," Cabrill said. Like Po she had to pick her words carefully. "Not the great leaders who divided the machines, but regular people like us who suddenly found they could do things—some of them must have resisted the temptation to be selfish and cruel. I hope they moved heavy carts for neighbors who didn't have the power to do so themselves. I hope they built barns, mended broken bones, saved villages from mudslides, coaxed fish into nets to feed the starving."

"Perhaps they did. But if you want something gone and never explored again, it is wise to repeat the horrors so they become common lore." Po shrugged. "And to relay the narrative correctly, the story does not say who accomplished the—the division of the engines. It may not have been great leaders but ordinary people. People like us."

"What if the engines were found?" Cabrill asked. "What if the machine was assembled again?"

Po crumpled the paper. "One could imagine that would be a terrible thing."

"Yes, one could imagine that." Cabrill rubbed her temple and sighed. "There is another story, which, of course, is just a story and no more."

"Meant only for a starry night and a campfire," Po said in agreement.

"There were once five tapestries. Braids of silver chained them together. In the arrogance of the time the magnificent needleworks were ignored. Each showed an entire planet wrapped in a death. Fire. Flood. Quakes. Cold. Plague. Five worlds no longer able to hold life. All stitched by those infected with power."

For a moment they sat in silence. Po seemed to be waiting for more, but that was all she knew.

"A tragic tale." Po tossed the drawing into the flames. "Not my favorite kind." He stood and went to his bedroll, leaving Cabrill with her thoughts.

Lulled by the dancing flames, she watched the tissue curl and blacken. Mniadd. She now knew what caused the madness that sickened her. She took out her charcoal and parchment. Again and again, she tried to draw the figure who was rebuilding the machine. Each time, the face became Austin's.

The boy tossed in his sleep. Although about her age, he seemed like a child. Would he, or any of this strange company, be of use in the battle they would face? In frustration, Cabrill threw the images of him into the fire. If they failed, if mniadd enveloped the world, she dreaded what she would become.

P o curled into his blanket. The page he'd shown Cabrill had been part of a message from Gram Shu. A cousin had surprised him while he'd been relieving himself behind a shrub. The man had pressed the paper into his hand, recited the speech that went with it, then bowed and disappeared into the greenery.

Loyalty was a difficult thing when blood conflicted with friendship. Po had broken family protocol by showing the page to someone who was not a Lian. By speaking of the machine. By naming mniadd.

He'd tipped a jar of sand. Only a few grains had spilled out, but they were gone just the same, and could never to be recovered.

CHAPTER 47

As they approached Wasbiln Manor, Austin steered the ploddel hard to the left to make room for a cart coming toward them on the narrow road. The billowing cloud was larger and darker here, as if a storm threatened to break loose from it. Ashen particles in the air dulled the sunlight. A stooped man guiding the weary chamapl that pulled the squeaking contraption thanked him with a warning. "Best turn 'bout. Only sorrows at our backs." A child slept in a basket of clothes wedged between cooking utensils and farming tools. A woman, eyes red from crying, walked behind, nudging the cart along the ruts without disturbing a baby cradled in a sling across her chest.

Turn back. The well-meant alarm stayed with Austin like a rock weighing him down.

Swaying together against the ploddel's side, Cabrill and Skylar huddled in serious whispers. Their shared secrecy chaffed Austin like sandpaper. Ryster pretended he could tell the two girls apart, but Austin knew he relied on height and

Cabrill's braids for identification. Even more annoying, Po knew one from the other without effort, no matter the situation. Braids or no braids. From the back. In the dark. Probably even blindfolded. Skye's connection with Cabrill and Po felt permanent. She'd matured into a space of her own, while he'd stayed paralyzed, like a bug in amber.

His plan to stay awake last night and steal the key from Po had disintegrated into sleep. It didn't matter anyway. This morning Skylar had forgotten her refusal to return to the site of her captivity and declared that of course she was going back. She wouldn't even argue with him about it. Her new friends and their cause were more important than family.

Stone and wood, Lord Kriken's home defiantly monopolized a prominent rise, making it impossible for visitors, or invaders, to sneak up on the place. A mix of practical shelter and defendable fortress, it was far from the grand display of wealth Austin had expected. From the size and style, he guessed His Lordship held a modest fortune and a no-nonsense approach to ruling.

Cabrill and Po strode straight for the large entrance. Behind them, Austin stayed close to Skylar, uncertain how she was managing under the veil Cabrill had devised. Ryster hung back, taking charge of the ploddel and his cart. Scowling guards scurried to form a barricade in front of them. Austin recognized the red accented uniforms from his embarrassing loses at cat jabs. The three he'd faced probably stood as living posts in the intimidating fence. He tried to take it as a good sign that the group had been allowed all the way up the slope to the building before being challenged.

The somber row of soldiers split open. Out rolled an irritated boulder of a man, his light brown braids streaked with white. He glowered at the arrivals. Three robed dignitaries flanked him. Several others appeared content to remain behind armed defenders. The guards, the dignitaries and the man who must be Lord Kriken looked like formidable chess pieces. Austin wondered if they had a version of the game here.

Kriken confronted Cabrill. "Your sculpture is about to be dismantled, since your guild tells me you are a fraud." Austin was relieved the man accepted the dark-haired girl before him as the same one he'd held captive. His Lordship didn't look like the kind of guy who laughed off being fooled.

Cabrill seemed unshaken. She acknowledged the two people on Kriken's right. "Grand Master Liaty, Guild Master Forliani, I am honored to be in your presence again. Lord Kriken, I apologize for the unannounced departure. There was something I needed to seek out."

"I would have provided you with anything if you had only asked," Kriken said.

"It is not yours to provide." Cabrill looked from him to the artists at his side. "Just as I am no one's property to lock up." She continued in a softer tone. "Your Lordship, I want the same thing you do. The danger in the forest threatens us all."

The robed man on Kriken's left smirked. He seemed to be in a snit over the prisoner's return. Bushy hair cascaded about his face and blended with a long snowy beard so they seemed to be one growth. "Is that what your sculpture tells you? You presume to interpret your own work?"

Skylar leaned close to her brother and whispered from behind her veil, "That's Yeti Beard, one of Kriken's advisors."

"More like Mossy Face," Austin murmured. He stifled a smile. His sister hadn't whispered to Cabrill or to Po but to him. The moment had been theirs, so comfortable and familiar that it was hard to pull his concentration back to the tense meeting.

"I have been to Tarafalla," Cabrill announced.

Everyone except Austin and Skye suddenly needed a sharp breath. Austin didn't have a clue where or what the place was and why it was so shocking that Cabrill had gone there. He guested his sister wasn't surprised because she already knew.

Grand Master Liaty flushed crimson. "Forbidden!"

Cabrill calmly addressed the guild master. "And still artists go there when craft demands it."

Yeti Beard sputtered. Finally, he squeaked out triumphantly, "And how did you journey to that foul valley and return in so little time? You have only been gone a few days."

"It was done," Cabrill said. "That's all you need know."

Yeti Beard nervously twisted a strand attached to his chin. "Your foolish decent into that putrid place was pointless, since your sculpture is here."

"That's not what I needed enlightenment about." Cabrill pulled coiled bark and parchments from her bag. "I sought clarity on these." A breeze rustled the pages, lifting them from her fingers. "And these." She pulled out curled scrolls and set them aflutter. "And these." She grasped more and set them free.

The crinkled creatures flew together as a flock, white wings in a sooty sky. They whirled high overhead then danced low. Yeti Beard gave a whinny cry of distress as they darted past him. Master Liaty put his hands over his balding head in fear. Forliani crouched from the attack, scowling in anger but not surprise.

Austin heard his sister laugh behind the curtain draped over her. Awed by the wondrous sight, he watched them rise again. Many of the bark-and-paper birds were etched with black, but the leaders shimmered with blues, reds, yellows and veins of silver. They pulled the others along in their wake, as if connected by invisible thread.

His own face swirled past. And his sister's. Or was it

Cabrill's? Austin, Skylar and Cabrill. The brother, the sister, and the artist. A sword led the flight, a silvery blade amid fiery colors. Sword after sword appeared through the pages, like shafts of shinning water. The impossible birds spiraled before Cabrill. They floated to the ground at her feet and were still.

"It is only a trick of the wind," Forliani said. "Nothing more."

Lord Kriken clenched his jaw, as if wanting to believe the easy explanation despite what he'd seen. "Yes. Of course. Wasbiln is known for sudden gales."

The pale-haired guard Austin had fenced snatched up a slip of bark and handed it to His Lordship. Her eyes flicked to Austin in recognition.

Kriken examined the drawing. "Master Artist Cabrill what did you learn in Moon Valley?"

"More than I ever expected. But you only want to know the part that affects your estate and those under your protection." Cabrill raised her voice so everyone could hear. "I need your help to fight an old enemy. The safeguards our ancestors set in place no longer hold. A dangerous power invades our world through a fissure in your forest."

Kriken looked grim. "Does your art predict how to prevent the disaster it will bring?"

Yeti Beard burst out, "My Lord, that is not a question to ask a mere artist." He gestured to the white scraps that littered the ground, as if that were their proper place. "The other advisors and I will study these and determine if they are worthy of consideration."

Cabrill waved a dismissive hand. "Do as you please with them. I'm beyond what they reveal." She strode past Kriken, past the masters, through the row of soldiers as if she were beyond them as well.

She paused at the towering doors of the manor house. "I

hope you haven't damaged my sculpture." Taking the hint, Skylar scurried to Cabrill's side to herd the artist, ever so discretely, toward the artwork she had never seen. Austin followed, eager to discover what had leapt from his non-artistic sister's imagination.

CHAPTER 48

ikol looked down on the spectacle from his room on the third floor. This time it was really Cabrill, the caped translator Ko Lian Po at her side. Hidden by a veil, the girl who was not Cabrill stood behind them. And there was the boy, protectively near her. A broad man trailed after, as if torn between human company and the cart-hauling ploddel being led away by a stable hand.

The manor house had burst into chaos when the hearth keeper had discovered the pretend Cabrill was missing. The sour woman had acted as if the disappearance were a personal insult. Searchers were sent out. Vibbys were used to track the scent of the goaddig she'd taken. At first energetic, the snout-nosed creatures had abruptly stopped where the path from Wasbiln joined the public road, as if the mount and its rider had vanished from that spot.

Mikol wondered if she'd manage that herself or if she'd had help. And who might have been the source of that assistance? He couldn't come up with a feasible guess. At least she'd returned, although for a moment he couldn't think why that was important to him. Oh, the package from Lian Sunang Shu. He rolled the gritty blue chalk in his hand. How could he have forgotten his contract with the revered and feared matriarch?

Cabrill's drawings spiraled up past his window, so strong and beautiful. The movement didn't shock him. He'd seen her soaring kite pursued by the matac. And he recognized the charcoal and vivid paint. On the mountain ledge while Cabrill had slept off the effects of Tarafalla vapors, he'd examined the drawings in her pack. He too had journeyed to the valley seeking a new revelation. Despite being surrounded by the mists and mysteries of the valley, old patterns had continued to fill him. He'd climbed out of the rift feeling unsatisfied.

Then a different kind of enlightenment had tumbled into his hands from Cabrill's worn pouch. In the moonlight he'd smoothed the drawings over his knees. Strokes curved elegantly across the mix of creamy paper and crude bark. The boy in strange dress against a barren landscape. The girl laughing before a stone structure.

He saw no connection between Cabrill's art and his own, yet he felt it, like a thread stretching from the horizon. Was it bringing the distance toward him? Or pulling him into the vanishing point?

Mikol watched the sheaves settle at Cabrill's feet. He turned his back on the window. He'd had a difficult time preventing the overly attentive hearth keeper from entering his room. The woman would fly into an angry fit when she saw he had pulled the furniture to the center and torn down the tapestries, tossing them into a heap on the floor.

He rolled the stub of blue chalk across his palms and surveyed the walls. A ring of elliptic gems dominated the canvas, each in its own color like the seed bracelet. Each linked to the others by elaborate whorls. The surfaces should be bowed together, instead of flat and joined by corners. He didn't have the power to bend the wood, so he'd done it with illusion. He lacked Cabrill's level of madness, but his own was strong enough. When the hearth keeper finally entered, she would think herself transported into a circle.

Mikol's breath came and went with the rhythm of the room. He put a hand to his chest. With the other he swept a final stroke around the curve of a vibrant oval. It pulsed with life, as if it were a beating heart.

CHAPTER 49

Pretending to be an attentive apprentice, Skylar slyly guided Cabrill into the great hall. Austin, trying to figure out how Cabrill had pulled off the flying papers trick, followed the others. The cavernous room echoed strangely with their footsteps.

"Well, I'll be a swift nonan," Ryster muttered.

Austin stared at his sister's creation, trying to take it all in. He didn't know what a nonan was, but he felt Ryster's amazement. On the floor a ring of weapons, like spokes on a wheel, pointed to a central structure. Wooden braces and globs of clay supported an upright circle of swords. Balanced on the grips, their sharp tips rested against an elevated platform. That stage held a slightly smaller circle, mimicking the first. Up and up, tiers of blades formed a tower rising toward the high ceiling.

The weapons were of varied sizes and shapes. Their hilts, polished by the many hands that had wielded them, seemed to shout stories through their carvings of horned beasts, winged creatures, runes, and family symbols. Or they were silent in their plain and unadorned strength. The blades whispered tales in metal dark as wet bark, ashen as mist, russet as rich earth. They were smooth and keen, nicked and haggard, according to the lives of their owners.

Light from a slit window fell across the topmost object. Austin squinted. What stood on the highest platform of this magnificent sculpture? What rose above all these noble blades? It must be splendid, something of great symbolism and significance. He shifted until he could see it clearly.

A bucket. A dull, overturned wooden bucket that looked as if it leaked. A sheaf of torn parchment tacked to it showed straight, heavy black lines. A childish stick drawing of a sword. Was that all his sister could think of to complete this wonderful formation? What about a rainbow, or a lightning bolt, or a lightning bolt splitting a rainbow?

Cabrill and Skylar stepped nimbly over the swords fanned across the floor. They stopped at the bottom platform where a crude ladder allowed access to the level above. A series of similar, and equally unsafe-looking slats led to the top. The boards seemed hastily pulled from elsewhere and forced into this service.

"Austin." Cabrill motioned for him to join them. He stumbled through the metal sunburst, wondering how the artist and his sister had found places to put their feet. The guards chuckled at his clanking missteps. The girls didn't seem to notice he was red-faced with embarrassment.

"It's even better than you described," Cabrill said softly to her friend. Skylar whispered back. "I don't have your gift. It isn't art, just something I made up."

Cabrill gazed at it and smiled. "The form guides the eye to a pinnacle, just as my work leads to a single time and place. Your tower is a part of the prediction as if I had created it myself. There is much of the artist in you."

Austin knew Skylar beamed at the praise from behind the curtain concealing her face. He wondered if he would ever get her home.

"It's time to finish the sculpture," Cabrill announced to Lord Kriken and the others crowding the room.

Skylar nudged Austin. "Turn around."

"What?" Confused, he let her twist him so his back was to her. He felt her digging into his sling pack. "Hey!"

"Hey, yourself. I need this."

He turned to face her. "No." He grabbed for her wrist, but she had already handed his foil to Cabrill who climbed the splintering scaffolding.

"It has to be," Skylar said. She pulled him away through the wheel of swords where they could get a better view. No one snickered at the clattering. All attention was on the artist ascending to the highest tier. Austin barely noticed a figure moving in close to them.

High above the great hall Cabrill examined the parchment for only a moment. She ripped it free and tossed it in the air as if it were one of the drawings she had released in the yard. She picked up the bucket and pitched it to a startled servant. The man caught it in self-defense so it wouldn't hit him in the head.

Austin watched, mesmerized. Master Artist Cabrill Shistayia reshaped the mound of clay that had held the bucket in place. No longer the sullen traveling companion or the girl who hid from crowds while he fenced for food, she moved with skill and confidence. She held the foil over her head for all to see. With a swift stroke, she plunged the hilt into the clay, crowning the sculpture with a single sword, a weapon like no other in this land. The metal sparkled, absorbing the slash of sunlight streaming through the high window. It burst into a brilliant star. The glow shimmered down the tower, blade to blade, until every sword shone with its own light.

Cries of wonder echoed around Austin. He gasped in a long breath, as if to pull the energy into himself. He accepted it all now: Cabrill's images of what she'd never seen, drawings fluttering about as if alive, the rightness of his being here. The radiance flashed and faded but he continued to stare up at the single sword and Cabrill beside it.

"Aha!" A shout of triumph broke the spell. A granite-faced woman snatched off Skylar's veil and gleefully shook it in his sister's face.

CHAPTER 50

The Masters were shut up in Lord Kriken's council room discussing the big to-do in the great hall, giving Cheche time to roam past the ovens and fire pits behind the manor house. Tending to two artists in the lowlands was easier than dealing with one Master Jomaray at Seaba Colony. There was a great fuss about clothes and grooming, but everywhere on their journey other servants changed bed linens and scrubbed floors.

Forliani and Liaty did not need a boy to fetch and carry for them. Seems their asking, which was really telling, Jomaray to allow Cheche into their service was only to remind Jomaray they had power in the guild and he didn't. Cheche figured he was like the chamapl that would never be returned. Except he wasn't bound by any rope. He'd go back to the mountains when he felt the going was right.

For now, he truly enjoyed this adventure in the lowlands, although it wasn't always to his liking. The variety of birds, animals, vegetation, people, customs, and especially foods made having to wear shoes most of the time more tolerable.

He'd never seen so much sword play. Bouts popped up in the street on a whim. Some sworders took their braids too seriously, twining them with colored cords and dangling ornaments, as if to give the game more fat than it deserved. In the Delds, there were herds to feed and crops to coax out of rock during the short summers, leaving little time for sport.

The monotony of flat land stretching to the horizon and the lack of a proper pitch, plagued him with dizziness. He often closed his eyes, envisioning the drop from the top of Ten Mile Plunge to regain his balance. Lowlands were impractical. You couldn't look down on a grazing herd, judging where they had eaten grasses to the nubs and what patch you should move them to next. You couldn't watch the society of an entire village from an up-wise path before entering it. You couldn't gaze upon a valley and see the twist of a river, the image better than a map for deciding where to farm and where to build.

He knew the local folk didn't think of their land as flush. They complained about hills and mounds, as if it were a hardship to climb minor ripples in the soft, forgiving earth. Worse, they seemed unaware of the potential their land held. Large swaths were planted and prosperous, like plush carpets in a giant's house, but patches that could grow enough vegetables for an entire mountain village or graze a large herd were left to thorny scrubs and bitter grasses. You could feed the whole world off this much level land with ease! Yet people toiled and struggled and were lean, just as in the mountains. He hated to see it so, since he'd balanced on the edge of starvation a time or two, during years when the snow came early and the thaw came late.

As it is, he thought. He certainly wasn't starving now. He'd tasted fish, fowl and fruit unavailable back home. He'd devoured pastries and sweets beyond his imagining. Today the outdoor roasting pits of Wasbiln Manor crackled and hissed with juicy drippings from beasts he couldn't name. He searched for Cook among the spits and found her drizzling citrus sauce over bird carcasses, golden and crisp from the licking flames. A fine day was becoming a fine evening, and there was a large party to feed.

Every available servant was here or at the ovens. The hearth keeper was in a rare good mood, making her a bit lax in her supervision. That caused Cook to feel especially jolly and willing to give a taste to a boy from far away who appreciated her skill. She sliced off a chunk of fowl, rolled it in a thick reddish liquid, and offered it to him. Cheche took it with many thanks and compliments. The fragrance alone was enough to make him weep. He bit into the soft flesh, sauce sliding across his tongue, tart and sweet.

The commotion in the great hall had given him this moment of joy, although it had gone badly for others. He'd missed the excitement outside the main entry with the flying paper. He'd been examining the sword tower when a crowd had filled the room. The bitter-faced hearth keeper had suddenly become merry when she pulled off the girl's veil, as if she'd been given a gift she'd wanted all her life. She'd almost danced around the room waving the limp fabric while she'd shouted, "You can hide your face, but I know those ugly boots and beggar's clothes. My Lord Kriken, you have been tricked. This is the one who came to you as the artist, the one who built this monstrous jumble."

His Lordship had puffed up with anger, directing most of it at Master Cabrill Shistayia. Cheche had learned much about the artist from overheard conversations during the trek here with the Masters. With the unmasking of the other dark-haired girl, who looked to be of the same family as the artist, he understood Kriken's ire. The graying lord was as hard willed as he was hard muscled. The sole arbiter of law on his land, he seemed unlikely to forgive being deceived.

Now the visitors were caged in the stables. Kriken, his advisors, and the Masters argued loudly in the council room. They would resolve nothing. Silly Liaty Nobian and cold Forliani Morokr knew much of what was going wrong here, but they would never tell Kriken and his fossils. Cheche had overheard them, speaking almost in code. Having served Master Jomaray, he was used to how adults dressed the truth in ornate clothes so it appeared to be something else. He'd learned to strip away the extra drapery as easily as the hearth keeper had snatched the veil from the startled girl. Regaining control of Master Cabrill and her art meant a great deal to the Masters. More to Forliani than Liaty.

Mad Calbran worried them too. They'd traveled all the way from their plush houses to the spare mountains to look at his art. Then Forliani had pretended the huge painting on Hopro Leap was nonsense. Liaty couldn't see the shape of it for himself to know she was lying. Forliani had immediately ordered Jomaray to capture Calbran.

As if every colony worker hadn't already spent days trying to do so.

As if saying it sternly would make it happen.

Cheche chuckled. The crazy artist was probably still roaming the Delds as the demons in his head told him to.

Master Jomaray might think himself finally noticed, finally favored by the head of the herd, but he was just someone to blame if the milk soured. He'd not been asked to take them to the Angry Narrows. He'd not been invited behind the waterfall with them.

That day when the Masters had turned suddenly silent, Cheche had slipped through the dry tunnel and poked his head into the cavern. Damp footprints had halted in the middle of the hollow. For a moment the emptiness had made him think dangerous bandits had snatched away the two, or savage beasts had swallowed them whole. But those were just tales for dark winter nights.

The Masters were gone by their own doing. That was the only way of it, although he couldn't say how. No reason to rush about the space pushing at the walls, searching for secret doors. He'd done all that before many times when a bit of a lad.

He'd waited in the tunnel until the Masters reappeared, stepping from sparkling light. Then he'd snuck back to the goaddigs before Forliani and Liaty emerged through the chilling falls.

He could have guided them back to the colony by way of Sallor's Octave, but he didn't. They had their secrets and he had his. Painted with urine and vision, a battle washed across the cliffs and fallen boulders from the Narrows to the Octave. Rock after rock held figures attacked by smoke and flames and rushing lava.

Cheche remembered the colors as he strolled among the firepits, savoring the best roasted bird he'd ever tasted. He didn't know if the story Calbran scattered across the mountains was destined to happen. Maybe. Maybe not. It wasn't about him. He wasn't in any of the images brushed across the stones. The real, living beings of it were locked in Kriken's stable.

From early, Cheche knew he had few choices of his own compared to others. He'd rolled around each possibility like the egg of an unknown creature, speculating on what was inside. He could tend one relative or another's herd, and that would be an honest life. Instead, when he thought himself old enough, he'd gone to Seaba and convinced the Keep to give him a job. His parents, aunts, uncles and cousins had objected, but not stopped him. If they had locked him up, he never would have found out for himself the good and bad of it. And it had been mostly good, because he'd made it go that way. He'd taught himself to read. He'd observed and learned. And now he traveled.

So who could say what dwelled in Calbran's art or what the prisoners in the stable would do if that future truly was theirs.

Cheche licked a final drop of sauce from his fingers. Citrus and sugar, tart and sweet. He surveyed what he could see of the estate. Stable, manor, smithies, houses. He checked the position of one building to another, wishing he stood high above on a cliff to get a proper view.

While the manor house vibrated with arguments, Cheche glided through the servant's route to the deserted great room. He did what needed doing then picked his way unseen to the stable. Guards strolled around the outside, enjoying more pleasant air than the dung-pungent interior. Cheche easily slipped past them. The warm, familiar odors were comforting but made him long for crisp mountain air. Already used to his visits, the animals made low, welcoming noises. He gave the new ploddel a friendly pat then hurried to the makeshift jail.

This was a soft land. Unlike at Seaba, he'd seen few doors with proper locks. One small bolt kept the saddle room secure. Slowly, quietly, he eased the shaft from the catch. He gave the rough door a wisp of a tug so it might drift open on its own. The prisoners could choose for themselves what to do about it.

The thin, silvery blade he'd plucked from the top of the scaffolding felt good in his hand. Perhaps someday he would be a sworder. He placed it on the floor so it pointed toward the cart holding the prisoners' possessions.

Light-footed, Cheche returned to the roasting pits. He teased Cook and got in the way of the other servants. Later, when questions were asked, his presence at the fires would be remembered.

CHAPTER 51

Finally within the shelter of the trees, Skylar slowed Buttercup's pace. It seemed she was making a habit of fleeing Wasbiln. Just now she heard shouts of alarm from the village and saw specks of torches bobbing about.

This time the escape was more mysterious. The saddle room's suddenly unlatched door had creaked open to reveal Austin's foil in the straw. It felt like a trap with the sword as bait. They'd cautiously crept from the small room that smelled of leather and animal sweat. When no one had jumped out from behind lazy Turnip, who hadn't seemed to have missed them at all, and shouted "surprise," Skylar had been, well, surprised. They'd quickly saddled goaddigs and retrieved their personal gear from Ryster's cart. Unfortunately, his bundle of wonderful swords was gone. Then Po had lured the two guards into the stable. The mighty smith had knocked them out with quick blows and trussed them up like straying chamapls.

From her outings with Ishty, Skylar knew the estate well. In deepening twilight she'd guided Cabrill, Po, Ryster, and her brother away from the stable and the manor house into Dobgronun Forest.

Now that they were within its shelter, she couldn't say exactly where they were going. To the source of the ugly clouds, she supposed, except she couldn't see them. Until the sun rose, it was dark woods, dark sky. There was no trail here. Easy to get turned around. Easy to get lost forever in the thick foliage. She followed the sound of a gurgling stream to its bank. "We'll stop here a moment."

"I'll watch behind us," Cabrill said. She turned back and melted into the darkness.

Skylar dismounted. She'd been pleased to point out to Ryster that Buttercup had been returned to Lord Kriken's stable as promised and its burns were completely healed. Of course, now she'd stolen the animal again. Austin steered his coppery mount next to her. "We have to keep going. They'll figure out we came this way. They'll be right behind us."

Ryster leapt from his mount to the ground. "Not so. Won't put a toe toward here just for us. Consider us dead and be done. They know we're making a long run toward our own graves." He helped Po climb off a saddle made for the taller peoples, rather than Astlians.

Po was more optimistic. "Perhaps His Lordship allowed us to escape so we would do exactly what we're doing. Taking care of the problem for him."

Ryster shook his head. "And I wonder how he thinks three youngsters, a word smith, and a metal smith can slay a beast where his trained soldiers failed. It be a hard swig to swallow myself."

"You should have stayed at the stable," Skylar said. "Kriken knows you were only bringing swords to sell, nothing more. There's only one image of you in Cabrill's works. The drawing of us all gazing at the angry cloud."

"Doesn't mean I'm not in the tangle of it," Ryster said. "I know personal there be tragedy in ignoring a potent foretelling. I ride with children and a wee bit of an Astlian. No offence given in that. You all be smart as you'll find and good folk, but a fragile crew. You need me. That be the right of it. Life's heated me red, pounded me keen, and tossed me in cold water plenty. I'll not turn from what stalks this forest."

"We are truly honored to have you in our company, Master of Metals," Po said with a bow. Ryster gave an embarrassed "humph" and fussed with Po's saddle, as if he could somehow make it fit the smaller rider.

Austin did a sliding, falling dismount. He led his goaddig to the stream for a drink, but the animal backed away. He wrinkled his nose. "The water smells funny."

Skylar crouched and dipped a small branch in the current, feeling its movement. Rivers twisted and turned but the water only flowed one way. This one tumbled down to the village. She'd heard it talked about. Its source was upstream toward the cloud and their destination. She sniffed. "It's more than just an odor of decay, like in the creek that one time back home when there was a chemical leak. There's something nasty here."

"Do you even remember Callister?" Austin asked. "You don't act like you miss it."

She understood what her brother didn't say. *You don't act like you miss Mom and Dad and me.* Skylar put a hand to her medallion, glad to have it back from Po. The familiar odd shape was a reminder of her past home yet it was of her new home too. In a way, it dwelled in both worlds, which was how she felt. "You're disappointed I haven't been terrified and teary eyed the whole time I've been here?" She'd shed tears, buckets of them, until she thought she'd shrivel up from dehydration and die. She didn't want Austin to know that. The less pain he thought she had gone through, the less guilty he might feel about not having been here to watch over her. He was her big brother. Protection and guilt were hardwired into his brain.

"No. No, I'm glad you've been okay here. It's just, what are we doing? Who or what am I supposed to fight? Cabrill doesn't know, even though this is all her fault."

Skylar stalked to Austin and poked the branch at him. "That's not fair. It's blaming the geologist for warning you there's going to be an earthquake."

Austin countered, "It's blaming the geologist for warning you there's going to be an earthquake and insisting you have to straddle the fault line in order to stop it."

Laughter bubbled out of Skylar. She doubled over and sank to the ground. "I have missed my favorite brother."

"Only brother." Austin sat beside her. "I don't know what we're charging into. I only know the 'nots.' It will not be tournament fencing. It will not be cat jabs, or nicks and jabs. And, according to local standards, my foil is not a real sword anyway."

"You forgot there will not be any rules. Or referees to make sure everyone plays fair." Skylar cast aside the stick and tossed a pebble toward the splashing and churning of the stream. "Okay, let's puzzle it through like we always do. Your foil is not a regular sword according to local standards, but it is a weapon. Focus on what it can do, not what it can't."

The sound of rushing water seemed unaffected by the pebble. Yet, the stone was there, subtly changing the flow. Austin stood abruptly. Maybe that's what he could do in all of this, just change some little thing that would make a difference "Time for an equipment check, radiation eel."

Skylar bounced up, grinning. "Yeah, an equipment check. That's what I was thinking too, astro sludge.

Austin grabbed his glove and foil. He'd locked his blade

into the most rigid setting when he'd faced the smoke wolf and kept it there for the cat jab competitions. Only the last few inches still flexed like a whip. He switched on the electrical charge. The digital controls beeped. Skylar watched them flash as her brother stepped through the menu. Since they were kids, they'd experimented to see how far they could push the settings. Their parents would have fainted if they'd known some of the things the siblings had tried with one another as test subjects.

The system complained and made Austin confirm and confirm and confirm. Yes, he really did want to set up a loop, which was usually only used for diagnostics. And yes, he really did want to raise the voltage to the highest level. And yes, he really did want to disable all safety protocols, turning it into an old-fashioned stun gun. He gripped the weapon in his gloved hand and aimed it at his sister.

Skylar was tempted to snatch up her own clumsy sword and engage her brother in mock battle, making him work for it. But she stood still. Without padding to protect her, the touch would cause an unpleasant jolt. Would it be strong enough to convince an attacker to back off? There was only one way to find out. She scrunched up her face in anticipation. "Okay, hit me."

Austin pressed the tip of his super-charged foil to his sister's rough-spun shirt. Skylar heard a clink. Wide-eyed, she jerked. Her body spasmed out of her control. She twitched and crumbled to the ground.

"Don't play around, Skye," Austin said. "That's not funny."

Skylar propped herself up on an elbow and put a hand to the spot. It took a moment of ragged breathing for her to recover. "Ouch. Really, seriously, truly ouch! You hit my necklace. I think it sucked in the charge. I declare the equipment check an ultra-nova success."

Austin dropped beside her. "I could have shocked you into a heart attack! How would I explain that to Mom and Dad?"

"I think you could bring me back to life with it too, Dr. Frankenstein," Skylar said. "Let's hope the evil thing you have to fight is carrying a stiav key."

Austin helped her stand up. "I'm going to change into my uniform."

Skylar nodded. "You need to be wearing your whites, just like in Cabrill's artwork."

"Actually, I have to get out of these clothes," Austin said. "I think I sat on dead fish."

CHAPTER 52

Hooves on moss. Rustling in the waist-high ferns.

Cabrill grasped the hilt of her sword and eased it from the scabbard. Two years evading her former guild had sensitized her to the sounds of stealth. She'd tethered her mount then retraced the route on foot to ambush the single rider that followed them.

Rattle of thorny branches.

"Ah!"

A cry of pain. Not so stealthy after all.

"Mikol," Cabrill said.

A tall, lanky figure on a goaddig, hand to his injured cheek, emerged from the crosshatch of leaves and branches. "I'd forgotten how dangerous it was to stray from the path."

Cabrill kept a firm grip on her sword. "Seems you do it frequently enough that you'd remember."

He swung from the saddle. "I went to rescue you, but you'd already vanished."

A lie, Cabrill thought. If Mikol went to the stable, it was for another reason. She'd hoped he was the one who'd released them, but it was not his nature to do so anonymously. If he had unlatched the door, he would have taken a bow so he could revel in their thanks. "And now you've come to join us?"

"I don't believe I was in any of the drawings that flew about His Lordship's lawn like snow." He stepped nearer. She kept her weapon between them. "I have a package for your charming duplicate. Perhaps you would deliver it for me."

"Her name is Skylar and she is no one's copy," Cabrill said. "In all things she is very much herself." He'd met her, he must know that. "If you have a present for her, then give it to her, not me."

"I thought I'd found her," Mikol said. "I expected you to be leading the troops. Forgive me, I never would have made that mistake in even the thinnest light. I didn't know it was you until you said my name. That lovely voice could belong to no one else."

Cabrill couldn't see his expression, but she knew his persuasive smile well enough. "You trailed fugitives into a dangerous forest. This present must be important."

He shrugged. "It's a small thing."

Which meant it was much more. In his brief encounter with Skylar had he been so entranced that he felt compelled to risk his life to give her a gift? Cabrill would not run his errand for him. She would not. She wouldn't even ask what the token was. She wouldn't.

"I'm glad I found you instead," Mikol said, his voice soft and sincere. "I *should* have been in your art. I have a role in this too, although you don't see it yet." He came close. She let him take the sword from her and toss it to the ground. Gently he held her hand—and clamped metal around her wrist.

A shackle? She shoved him, cursing herself for being so foolish as to let her guard down. She dropped, grabbed her sword, and rolled away from him. She came to her feet with the blade pointed at his chest.

Startled, Mikol backed away.

With her free hand, Cabrill pulled her sleeve back. In the darkness she couldn't see the metal but she could feel it. Warm. No clasp. No lock. Not a shackle but a band. "Your bronze cuff?" she tried to choke out, but Mikol was gone.

Cabrill stood alone, sword drooping. She did not yell an apology after him. She did not shout she was sorry for misunderstanding his actions and treating him like an enemy. She was not sorry at all. He had slapped an ornament on her wrist, expecting her to present it to another girl in his name.

She should have run her blade through his heart when she had the chance.

CHAPTER 53

In the shaded night, not needing light or mirror to perform the familiar task, Skylar divided her hair and folded strand over stand. She tied a cord around the end and draped the ebony braid across her shoulder.

Since she was going into battle—against what, she didn't know—she would go in like a warrior.

She wished she had her uniform to change into. She'd hauled the pieces around for over a year, not able to wear much of it. The unusual clothing would attract unwanted attention, yet she couldn't just leave the items by the roadside. They seemed too important, and they were all she had of home.

She'd worn the socks until they'd become more holes than comfy, soft tubes. The pants she'd abandoned when she'd grown too tall for them. The insulated jacket had been useful on cold days, hidden under a heavy shirt and cloak. She'd hacked off the sleeves and shortened the torso as her arms and hips changed. When she could no longer fasten it shut over breasts that surprised her with their fullness, she'd given the modified silvery garment to a little girl shivering in an early snowfall.

Tight shoes and a single glove—that's what she had left, so that's what she put on. She flexed her covered right hand, wishing for the millionth time that she'd been holding her weapon when she'd fallen through the stiav.

Buttercup nudged her for attention. Ryster and Po were no more than blotches against an array of other blotches that must be trees and shrubs. Austin, in his whites, moved like a faint ghost. Beyond him, the embers of twin campfires glowed.

Skylar absently patted the goaddig's neck. Who was out here building fires? How could she see so far through the dense vegetation? The distance must be an illusion. The fires must be closer. They reminded her of sparks she'd seen before.

In a cold flash she realized what they were.

"Get into the stream! Now!" Skylar swung into Buttercup's saddle. The fires moved, betraying their true nature. Beastie eyes. The burning coals flamed around her. She urged the goaddig into the water, reassured by sounds that the others followed. The stream was shallow but wide enough to keep the monsters from Buttercup's hooves. They snarled and snapped along the bank.

"Cabrill!" Ryster, Po and Austin were near, but Skylar could not sense her friend.

"I'm here." Cabrill splashed toward them from downstream. On foot, she stumbled over exposed stones. Embers on both sides of the flow matched her pace. "Those things took down my goaddig. I barely made it to the water."

"Here, my friend," Po shouted, offering a hand. Cabrill swooped up onto the mount behind him.

Skylar counted the eyes. Fifteen, maybe twenty pairs. She urged Buttercup against the current, deeper into the forest.

From the dry banks, their angry escorts glared and growled.

CHAPTER 54

Forliani was furious with Lord Kriken, but it was not wise to let it show. She spoke to him in her concerned voice. "You must bring Cabrill and the others back for their own safety." *And stop them from interfering,* she thought.

The great hall was eerily empty. Swords had been reclaimed from the sculpture, leaving gaps in the pattern. Guards had been sent to the forest. To capture the runaways or to assist them? She wasn't clear what the orders had been. The seasoned fighters now limped home, burned and babbling about monsters that could not be fought with blade or mace or fist.

"I have recalled my soldiers," Lord Kriken said. "Good men and women all, I will ask no more of them for the sake of a deranged artist and her reckless group."

"The Guild thanks you for your efforts." Forliani's gentle words masked the sarcasm under them. There was no help here and no other resource available. She could only hope that Cabrill failed.

CHAPTER 55

Austin jolted awake, shocked he had dozed in the saddle while bright eyes watched from the river bank. Dawn slowly leaked into the forest. His goaddig kept a slow, steady pace through the stream. Skye rode in front of him. He twisted around to make sure Po, Cabrill, and Ryster followed.

The misty beast that knocked him into this world had hunted him in his dreams. He put a hand to his chest where its burning paws had pressed against him, and he felt the heat of its breath on his face. A spasm shook his lungs. He remembered the chocking brine that had poured into them, almost drowning him but causing the vaporous wolf to disappear.

Water had saved Skylar as well when she'd been attacked. She'd described a spraying device the Yeawoche had used to douse the creatures, as if they were fires. Had it killed them? Or had they dissolved then re-formed? Was the same beast who'd charged him on Callister the one his sister had challenged? Did it prowl beside him now?

He wondered if the stream took them in the right direction.

The air stank of soot and decaying fish, so it certainly seemed they were heading toward the destruction of the world. What would happen if they reached the first trickles where the creek began and still hadn't found the—the whatever?

The rushing path they waded through suddenly spread into a vast lake veiled in muted sunlight. Austin immediately knew they were in the right place.

<hr>

Ember-eyed smoke wolves angrily prowled through withered vegetation along the lake shore. Trees sagged, their heavy trunks pulling weakened roots from the earth. Skylar eased Buttercup from the stream into the broad expanse of water. She put a sleeve across her nose to filter the foul smell. Dead fish and amphibians floated on the surface of the once beautiful lake, blotching it with dingy greens.

She stared at a ragged wound twenty feet up, suspended in the humid air. Sooty clouds billowed from it like grimy pus. A slow blue-gray tide bled from the threshold. Creatures made of burning, reddish rods pushed the sluggish liquid with long-handled tools, forcing it to the end of a ramp that sloped across the sky. There the substance cooled, adding length to the structure. Excess sloshing over the lip and sides, dripping into a lattice of stalactites like hanging blades.

Ryster stared, awestruck. "A metal road spilling out of the sky. Never seen the like."

"It's coming from a stiav," Po said.

"A guardian? For truth?" Ryster said. "Thought they be just stories. Strange place to put it. Not very handy."

"There might have been an island under it," Po said, "or a

finger of land with a well-elevated hill. This part of the lakebed seems shallow enough for such a scenario."

"Whatever it sat on is gone now," Skylar said, "so they had to build a bridge. Since those things are all flame-y, they're probably not good swimmers."

Austin pointed out the short distance from the end to the shore. Ten more feet and the eerie structure would hover over the land. "Hope they're not good jumpers."

"Cabrill, was this in your art?" Po asked.

Riding behind him on the mount they shared, Cabrill shook her head. "It may be in another's work. It's not in mine."

"Took years, this," Ryster said. "But it be an unskilled crafter beyond that hole. Can't tend a decent fire that burns clean. And I wonder how one came to find all that ajrief. Didn't know so much existed. Enough for thousands of blades."

Skylar put a hand to her necklace. "That's what stiav keys are made of."

"The ones that are known," Po said. "The metal is rare beyond rare here. It must be abundant in the world on the other side."

They rode closer to inspect blue-gray drops crawling down already cooled spindles like candle wax. Ryster pulled a sleeve over his fingers and tapped at the substance. "You'll burn yourself!" Skylar cried.

Ryster's pokes left indentations. "Lived in a forge since a bit of a lad. Used to hotter. Never worked with ajrief but heard tell of it. Only a few pools I know of. All in spots that addle your brain 'till you forget why you're there."

"Tarafalla," Cabrill said.

Ryster nodded. "That be one. Takes skill to treat it gentle, work it slow. A smith's nightmare and a smith's dream. Not much heat to keep it soft. Stays pliable till near to tepid. Once set, never melts again. Never bends. Get the edge keen, stays sharp forever. No pits or scars or breaks unless it be struck by itself." He shook his head at the towering road. "This be a wasteful use of it." He gave it a critical eye. "I be thinking hard about the construction. Must be anchored well up top in that other place. Then these drippings rooted it to rock that could be your sliced off island, Master Po. Not much support for a span this size. Seems the balance be wrong. And I wonder if it needs mooring to shore to be anchored in a proper way."

At the top near the belching gap, a ledge jutted out. Rigging attached to it supported an empty platform that swayed over the water. A fiery rod-being reached out a long crook to snag an off-center post on the wooden square and pull it closer. Smoky wolves slunk out of the bridge's cloudy opening. Their swirling forms turned thicker, almost solid. One by one, they reluctantly hopped onto the suspended raft and cowered in the center.

"It's a raft," Skylar said. "That's how the wolfies are getting to shore—until the bridge is finished anyway."

The last creature stayed crouched on the ledge. The beasts already on land and on the platform snarled, as if taunting it. The misty ball leapt. It missed the mark and fell into the water, releasing a wispy puff. The other beasts growled.

"Definitely not good jumpers," Austin said.

A rodder carrying a pole seemed to stare with its single black-hole eye in its elongated, flaming face at the rodder with the crook. The crook guy gave in and tugged the raft flush with the ledge. The pole rodder jumped on with the wolfies. Crook guy released the post.

The wolfies whined as the deck under them swung on cords fasted to each corner and twined to a central rope slung over a pulley. Burning creatures on the bridge worked the stout main cable, slowly lowering the deck. Off balance, the pole rodder grabbed one of the corner lines with its flaming hand.

The cord flared in the tight grasp and gave way. The raft dipped, tumbling the occupants into the lake with a great splash and steamy plumes.

The beasts pacing the shore howled for their lost comrades. The bridge workers seemed unconcerned that one of their own was gone. They ignored the extinguished skeleton growing stiff amid the remains from earlier spills and stared expressionless at the platform tilting from the three cords that still held. In unison they dropped the long, thick strand that controlled it, letting the end dangle free. The pulleys squealed at the release. No longer anchored, the raft plunged downward and smacked into the lake, sending out great waves. Turning their backs on the botched job, the rodders disappeared into the soot-belching opening.

"Definitely can't swim," Skylar said. "But once the bridge reaches land, those things won't need a raft. There could be a million of them on the other side, waiting to rush down and swarm over Saffrian." She thought of the baker and the woman who sold eggs and the other villagers who had been kind to her. "We have to stop this and slam that door shut."

Cabrill shivered. "Po, this is a dangerous place."

"It is indeed," Po said to them all. "And you who are here to confront it must know the scope of the peril." He sighed. "I cannot tell you what you need to know while bound to silence. With all of you as witnesses, I renounce my sacred oath to the Lian family."

Seated behind him on the goaddig, Cabrill wrapped her arms around him, as if she could force him to keep silent. "Po, no. No, don't."

Po leaned back against Cabrill, as if needing her support. "I dissolve alliance to my second name. From this moment I make no claim on its properties or fortunes. I expect none of the protections and privileges it provides. Further, I ask for no rights from my first name family. I declare that I am no longer Lian, no longer Ko. I am of a single name. Po, and nothing more."

"That be a harsh thing," Ryster said softly.

"But necessary," Po said. "For some time I have gathered knowledge. What I've learned is a heavy weight that I now place upon all of you. Our task is much more than preventing beasts from terrorizing the land. If we are to save this planet, you must know the full nature of the danger we confront. A great mechanical gem dwells on Saffrian. Alone it is dormant, but another engine reaches out to it through this stiav. What Cabrill senses is mniadd, the energy that grows between them. It creates power that leads to destruction. Ajrief provides the conduit. Should it connect the two machines, the Separation that has protected us will be undone. As my wise Lady of the Zenith said most concisely, the progress of the structure must be halted before it grips the earth, and the guardian must be sealed."

Cabrill sobbed into Po's shoulder. Skylar wanted to weep too, but not for what Po had given up. Astlian blood loyalty was legendary, but he had chosen his friends over his family. He'd chosen Cabrill. He'd chosen her. And that filled her heart.

"I didn't follow all that," Austin said, "but I got enough to know you should have told us this before now."

"My information was incomplete," Po said. "It is only as I view this surprising sight that threads collected over time weave themselves into whole cloth."

"I know the Astlian clans," Ryster said. "Don't know if you be brave or a fool, but it be done." He studied the silvery bridge. "They've a length to go and it be a slow job. Gives a chunk of time to sort it out. Slug work to take down the beasts. That be the first toil."

Like Ryster, Skylar knew that the enormity of Po's action

had to be set aside for now. She put a hand close to the hanging wall then jerked it back. It might not burn the calloused master smith, but it was too hot for her. She dismounted into the contaminated lake, feeling muck and silt layered over stone. Melted snow pack and icy mountain rain sent rivers to feed this pond. They carried fresh fish and aquatic life that did not survive long in the sweltering hollow as the frigid water warmed from the heat of the bridge. But the liquid that covered her knees was still a lower temperature than the dripping metal. She put her hands in the water and quickly squeezed them together, sending a spray against the lacy wall. "Maybe we can cool it down enough to climb it." Ryster dismounted and mimicked her but with less accuracy.

CHAPTER 56

Austin glanced at Skylar and Ryster spraying the bridge with water. That approach was too slow. He had to find another way to reach the opening. Hoping the plow-pushers were unaware of anything except their work, he rode close to the lowest part of the structure. He eased to a standing position on his saddle. Balanced precariously on the fidgeting goaddig, he stretched up with his gloved hand but was far short of the uneven edge. "I can't reach high enough," he shouted to the others.

A flaming head suddenly appeared over him, staring at him with its dark eye. It ducked away. Scalding ajrief rolled over the edge. Austin scrambled into the saddle and urged his mount away from the scorching wave.

He splashed to where Po and Cabrill examined the damaged platform, floating in the graveyard of fallen rod-beings. The bridge was at its highest point here. Straight up, the stiav belched out soot. He dismounted and examined the long rope dangling from the rigging. The twined strands were spotted with singe marks, making it difficult to judge strength, or lack of it.

"Hey, I've got an idea." He explained it to Po and Cabrill. The three of them piled rodder skeletons onto the heavy wood deck. Austin got his foil and gave it to Po, then he grabbed the rope and hoisted himself upward, using the loaded raft as a counterweight. As he rose higher, he could see fiery rods busy at the low end of the ramp. A soaring fish slammed into one. It teetered on a bird foot then toppled into the lake with a splash and a hiss. Ryster gave a victory yell. The confused rodders jostled together and fumbled with plows, too busy to notice Austin at the top getting his footing on the ledge.

Po fastened the foil to the dangling rope. Austin hauled it up, not sure how to use his blade against the strange enemy. More flying fish pelted the creatures, knocking the thin bodies into the water. He was sure Skylar tossed some of them.

A burning rodder stalked out of the stiav, so close Austin could feel its heat. He sucked in his breath and froze on the skinny landing. The end of a long chute rested on the worker's shoulder, blocking its view of Austin. It marched down the ramp. The other end of the gutter appeared, cradled in the spindly arms of a rodder who plodded along with bent legs as if it held the heavier part. Three more followed single-file. The first carried nothing. The second held one of the long-handled plows. A bucket hung from each stiff arm of the third. Any of them could have swiveled a dark eye to the side discovering Austin, but they trudged down the curved track with their focus straight ahead.

There was no room on the narrow ribbon for the chute parade to get past the rodders Skylar and Ryster hadn't yet smacked with fish. The leader elbowed them over the edge, clearing the path. It sloshed through flowing ajrief to where the bridge stopped in midair, set down its burden, and steadied it. Its counterpart at the other end dropped the chute with a splash and stepped into the flat-bottomed canal, adding an anchoring weight. The next in line shoved the gutter forward, knocking the unconcerned leader off the edge.

Sliding on liquid metal, the chute cantilevered over the withered land. With the additional length, the bridge could now reach its goal.

A fishy blitz knocked off the anchoring rodder. The pusher stepped into the chute to take its place. The worker with the plow stepped in, adding more stability. The bucket carrier dumped lava along the fresh joint where the channel overlapped the bridge. It stood immobile while the plower smoothed the goo.

Austin could see Cabrill below, wading near the shore. Sword in hand, she hacked thick branches from a tree that dipped into the water. Smoke wolves, their forms so thick they were almost solid beasts, paced the bank, snarling and snapping. One ventured onto the leaning trunk, getting dangerously close to her.

Imitating Ryster with the fish, Cabrill threw chunks of wood at the chute. They smacked it with dull clunks, nudging it out of alignment. After each hit the anchoring rodders wiggled the channel back into place and the plower again smoothed the goo.

As if in frustration, the bucket carrier nudged aside the plower and dumped the second container. A white substance hit the ajrief, sending up a steamy plume.

Snow. In horror Austin remembered what Ryster had said. Once cooled, the metal was set.

The hours they thought they had suddenly evaporated. Nothing could dislodge the chute now.

A steady stream of ajrief flowed past Austin. When it reached the end of the chute, it would cascade onto the land, connecting the two worlds, linking the two engines Po had described. He had to stop it.

A small space on the other side of the portal looked solid, like the ledge. Austin jumped over the blue-gray stream, not wanting to step in the stuff unless he had to. He examined the stiav. It appeared to be a rough cave entrance, only there was no mountain around it, just sky. His lungs protested against the foul air with barking coughs. His eyes stung. He hoped no wolf beasts hid in the onrush of smoke. Holding his weapon ready, he probed the frame with his free hand, just as Po had done to the arches on Callister. The surface seemed no more than ordinary stone. Blackened moss flaked off at his touch. His fingers slid into a depression with an irregular shape similar to his medallion. He dug at the lock, finding nothing but dead lichen. No key. Whatever kept the guardian active was on the other side. He groaned, but he wasn't surprised, since that's where the ajrief and the creatures were coming from. He'd have to slip into that other world without being noticed, do a quick grab, and rush back.

Okay. He could do that. He took a breath, put his face close to the rift and squinted into the obscuring cloud.

Flames exploded before him. He staggered back. Before the thought could reach his brain, he shoved the tip of his blade into the lock. The air sizzled. Through his glove, he felt a shock from the super charge he'd programmed into the foil. The cave mouth spit out inky puffs then vanished before the thing could grab him.

The air cleared. Was that it? Austin teetered at the top of the ramp with nothing but sky around him. Cautiously, he peered down at the lake far below. He had actually climbed all the way up here? Wobbly with vertigo he stepped back from the edge. Slowly he turned to look down the path to a lower altitude.

Skylar trudged toward him, her indestructible fencing shoes splattering goop. The silly wooden sword that rested on her shoulder smoldered along an edge. "Ryster and I took care of the fire guys. That man can hurl fish! Their skeletons make a great ladder—the fire guys, not the fish. Ryster tossed up stuff and I damned up that flume thing. I jumped on it to see if I could get it to break loose, but its in solid. That should be okay though, since the doorway is closed now. When you did that, the wolfies on shore sort of dissolved." She looked him up and down. "You been mining coal?"

Austin's whites were dulled with soot. He swiped at his sweaty forehead, smearing grime onto his hand. Then he wiped his hand on his already blacked sleeve. "I did it." He didn't have to admit it had been out of panic and sort of by accident. They couldn't get whatever had been keeping the guardian open on the other side, but now they didn't have to. "I zapped the circuit. I broke it." His foil had saved the world, just as Cabrill's art predicted. Everything was okay now. They could go home.

"Oooh, my perfect brother broke something," Skylar said. "I am so proud!" She twirled. "Great view. Too bad we're the only ones with heat tolerant footwear. We should check with Po on the zapped circuit thing. Do you want to get off this by rope or demon ladder? I'll warn you, demon ladder requires thought before you move so you don't get everlasting goo on you. Ryster says that would be grim."

Austin felt limp. He ached, as if his muscles had been on alert for a long time and were suddenly allowed to relaxed. He didn't glance at the rope that dropped down and down to the water. "Demon ladder."

They walked single file down the narrow slope. Austin tried to think about the future—the mountain range of homework that must be waiting for him, the ruined caterpillar experiment (had his parents fed the crawlies?). An itch wormed through his brain. It seemed that for a world-saving event, this had been much too easy.

Skylar's braid swung with each step. "Ryster told me—"

A blast of air slammed into Austin's back, pushing him against his sister. She staggered. Quick reflexes kept her on her feet and blocked him from falling.

Austin turned. The re-opened portal flamed with burning rodders who trudged toward him. "Jump," he urged Skylar. She didn't budge.

The first rodder swung a plow. Austin crouched, feeling the wind ruffle his braids. A blue-gray line trickled between his feet. Ajrief flowed again!

Hefting her rigid sword with both hands, Skylar swung over Austin's head, slamming the creature off the edge. "Mine's better at this than yours," Skylar shouted. There wasn't enough room to trade places so they swapped weapons. Austin blocked the next attack with a clunk. Double-handed, he used the dull wood like a club. Smashing down at an angle, he swiped the skinny enemy off its feet. He jumped over the fallen creature and slashed at the next. Skylar transferred the foil into her left hand. She grabbed the bird leg of the downed body with her insulated glove and tossed it over the side.

Crude sword scorched and smoking, Austin worked his way up the blue-gray ribbon. Behind him, Skylar disposed of carcasses that did not tumble off on their own. The two made progress toward the gap, but fresh fires emerged. No longer clogged with charcoal clouds, it shimmered behind the advancing flames. Austin needed to get close enough to zap the key slot again. He thought he could slam creatures with the wooden sword in his right hand and jolt the guardian with the foil in his left. He yelled this back to Skylar. It felt good to have a plan, but they were still too far away.

Abruptly, the flame creatures stopped coming. Austin sent the last one spinning into the lake. "Switch," he called. Now grasping his own foil, he slogged toward the guardian. A blinding sight stopped him. He squinted at the unexpected brightness that was not walking fire. A glittering white-clad figure strode onto the bridge. Golden braids like rays of sunlight framed an angular face set with intense blue eyes. Just Austin's age, just Austin's height, the fencer carried a thin metal blade.

Austin stared at himself.

CHAPTER 57

Standing on the narrow bridge facing a doorway into an unknown world, Austin would have been less surprised by a fire-belching dragon or a giant, bull-headed minotaur than what actually appeared. He was stunned. The light-haired, blue-eyed boy his height and age, clad in fencing clothes, could be his twin.

But not exactly.

The white pants were too long. Past mid-calf, they tucked into sparkly boots that must provide a barrier against the hot surface of the bridge but were definitely not regulation. Both hands were gloved. Silvery filaments glittered in the jacket, mimicking the sheen of the sensor-embedded target area of Austin's uniform, but a stiff gray emblem dominated the chest. *Easy to aim at*, Austin thought. It seemed as if the boy wore a costume constructed from a description. Or from drawings not as detailed as Cabrill's.

But the sword. The sword was remarkable. Slate-gray, like the emblem, the stiletto thin blade lacked the quadrangular shape of Austin's foil and instead was flattened into sharp edges. The tip, not blunted to give an electrical charge, was tapered to a lethal point.

The young man stood balanced and confident in his false uniform. His pale eyes quickly surveyed the now stagnant progress of the unfinished lava road and the frozen carcasses of workers sticking out of the water below. Frowning, he scanned the charred shore, empty of the smoky beasts that had patrolled it. Then he broke into a charming smile and spoke to Skylar and Austin.

Austin didn't know the language. "We speak Lynawic."

The stranger seemed pleased and responded in kind. "The traditional language of the engineers. Then you are educated."

Austin took a slow breath. You had to fight a monster, but you might be able to reason with a person. He wished Po, the experienced negotiator, stood beside him. "I am Austin Swiftbrooke and this is my sister Skylar. Our friends below are Master Artist Cabrill Shistayia, Master Metal Smith Ryster Brimbren and Master Translator Ko Lian Po." Po's name was inaccurate now, but this guy didn't have to know that.

The young man stood erect, sword relaxed. "I am Orliando Breckt of the Engineers Guild. You may call me Master Orliando, as is the way of the First Engineer. I am pleased that such fine people are here to welcome me."

Ryster shouted up at them, "Master? And I wonder if you're no more than a young apprentice."

"I assure you I have earned the title," Orliando shouted down to him.

"And I wonder," Ryster called. "if your mentors think the same."

"My guild has cautious leaders who are wary of exceptional ability," Orliando said. "Their vision is limited. They have forgotten the greatness of our founder. Their council is no longer useful to me."

Creaking and squealing came from the strained platform rigging. Po called loudly but calmly from that direction. "Talent is not always appreciated by those closest to it." He and Cabrill rose into view on the raft, repaired but less than level. Ryster must be providing the muscle to raise it.

"You wear an emblem I recognize," Po said.

Orliando put a reverent hand to the gray plate on his jacket. "The symbol designed by the First Engineer. I am a humble student of his life and accomplishments."

Po clutched a cord supporting one of the raft corners with both hands but spoke as casually as if he stood on even ground. "I can tell he has inspired you to greatness. For what purpose have you journeyed to our humble land?"

The young man held his sword in front of him, blade pointed upward as if in salute. "I come to make this world more magnificent than it has ever imagined. I bring you a gift, a taste of the power from my world. I suspect you already feel it has enriched you. Soon you will flourish beyond your dreams. With my guidance, your world will become like my own, a paradise full of joyous people who want for nothing."

Skylar murmured in English behind Austin's back. "Blah, blah, blah. 'I brought you a present delivered by snarling, wolfie monsters.' Come on, Orly, get to the real stuff."

Austin recognized the young man's stance from several of Cabrill's charcoals. Now he wondered who the fair-haired fencer in the portraits really was, himself or this new guy? Who were the predictions really about? Skylar must be having similar thoughts. She spoke in Lynawic. "Looks like you practiced that pose in front of a mirror. I bet you stole it from a drawing of someone else."

Orliando's smooth confidence slipped. He scowled and leveled the tip of his sword at the pair. He had obviously prepared a speech and Skylar had ruined it. "So you have predictions here, despite your planet's weak energy. You'll be sorry you mocked me, girl."

"Just as so," Skylar said sarcastically, using an expression she'd heard one of the guards mumble.

Orliando sneered at Austin's soot-streaked uniform, face and hair. "Your manner of dress will not bring you victory. You are far from the likeness. I am the true image. I have carefully analyzed the prediction. It is shown in a hundred drawings and paintings. It is glazed on urns and woven into tapestries. *I will take this world as my own.*"

"Now that's the real stuff," Skylar said in English.

Po said, "So you do not mean to be our benefactor, as you presented yourself, but our oppressor, using mniadd and this conduit. We banished that energy, along with the First Exile, who, I believe, is the one you call the First Engineer. We respectfully reject your gift."

Orliando smiled, his poise back in place. "You are of a small people."

Po bowed, as best he could while standing on a tilted base. "I am Astlian."

Orliando ignored Po and brushed his gaze across Cabrill, Skylar and Austin. "You know of mniadd but you don't understand it. Its power has been hidden from you by those who want to use it for themselves."

That didn't make sense to Austin. The people here had done that Separation thing. They'd purposely flipped the mniadd switch to off.

"A secret group has a plan to shatter all you hold dear," Orliando said.

Austin felt dizzy. Not surprising. He'd breathed in sooty air and probably toxic fumes from the hot metal. He didn't know who was in the secret group, but he was suddenly, deeply afraid of them.

"They will destroy your families," Orliando said. "They will enslave you and steal your future."

Austin could think of nothing he had seen or heard that supported the blond boy's statements. Oh, that showed just how crafty and dangerous those people were. They kept it all hidden, hundreds of them, thousands of them, in their private meetings, with their private codes. Orliando said it was true, so it was true, because he said it. Austin didn't need any more evidence than that. He *believed* there were enemies and so the enemies were real. And they plotted in the shadows to take over *his* world.

"One of these thugs stands with you pretending to be your friend," Orliando said. "But he lies to you and keeps secrets from you. That is what Astlians do. They want to crush you and walk on your bones."

Austin accepted it almost before Orliando voiced it. Po *had* lied to him. Astlians could not be trusted. They were arrogantly *small* and haughtily *smart*, and they were not *us*. Po and the Astlians must be stopped. But how? They were too strong for him to fight. Too sly. Too entrenched.

"Only a bold leader can save you," Orliando said, "save your families, save us all."

Orliando Breckt was that leader! The thought exploded in Austin's head. He wanted to cheer in relief. He'd deluded himself into thinking he could be someone special. He was a dirty-faced nobody in ash-streaked clothes. The one standing before him, resplendent in white, was his champion, his hero!

Cabrill shouted. Arm looped around a rope on the lopsided raft, she clutched a band on her wrist. Austin heard her in stereo, through his ears and in his mind, but he couldn't decipher the words. Beside her, a dazed and startled Po seemed close to falling off the raft.

Austin stared at Orliando, who looked how Austin wanted

to look, who was how Austin wanted to be. They were allies against evil. Skylar and Cabrill crowded his mind. He pushed them aside. His own thoughts were muddled, but that was all right. He didn't have to think for himself, just follow his new friend who was so much smarter and braver than he could ever be.

Orliando gestured to the bridge. "Together we will complete this symbol of our common goal. The righteous people, the deserving people such as yourself, will prosper and will be safe from the others who want to destroy you and your way of life."

Austin clawed at the medallion under his jacket. Cabrill and Skylar screamed at him. This all seemed wrong. He could figure it out if only he could stop shaking with terror. He wanted to be safe. Safe from things he didn't know and didn't want to know. Safe from things that were different.

Skylar's voice came from far away. "Stab down. Stab the ramp."

Austin tried to think it through, but his brain was overflowing. He needed a minute to sort it out. He couldn't just act. He couldn't experiment without knowing from the start what the outcome would be. He'd already gone way over his quota for acting on impulse. He couldn't tolerate any more.

"*Stab, stab,*" exploded through his thoughts.

He wasn't like Skylar, running around on whim and instinct, perfectly at ease spinning in a circle on a cluster of stalactites sticking out of a gap in the air.

"*Stab, stab down,*" Skylar blasted at him.

He wasn't like his sister, but he trusted her, more than anyone or anything. Right now that had to be enough. It *was* enough.

Austin pressed his foil into the thickened sludge at his feet. A prickly shudder shook him as the charge ran through the ramp. His medallion quivered. He was instantly awake and alert, as if he'd shattered a glass cage. Orliando no longer invaded his mind. He looked to his sister.

Skylar's hand pressed the fabric covering her necklace. Her voice came jagged, as if she'd run a marathon. "Cabrill and I did it together. I couldn't break free of him on my own. She helped me. Then we helped you."

Austin's attention went back to the boy. Orliando spasmed and rubbed the silvery insignia on his white jacket. Ajrief, the same substance as the bridge and the medallions. When Austin had done the equipment check, jolting Skye's medallion had knocked her off her feet. A direct hit to Orliando's symbol should cripple him. Skylar realized it too. "Hey, space monkey brother, zap him in the icon."

Austin could feel Skylar backing away to give him room. He flicked his weapon to the side, clearing the tip of wet goo. Orliando's sword was more dangerous than the dull foil, even with a supercharge running through it. The sharp edges and lethal point could chop and dice Austin in a flash. He couldn't afford to take a single hit.

Orliando held his weapon ready. Jolting the bridge had disrupted his mind control efforts and given him a shock, but he appeared recovered. "I have seen my victory a hundred times in every kind of art. No one will prevent me from fulfilling my destiny. Not my timid mentors, and not you pretending to be me."

"Prediction is a slippery thing," Cabrill called from the platform.

Orliando did not glance toward her. He kept his eyes on Austin. "So my mentors tell me. Yet I am here and they are back in their barren cells."

Austin wiped gritty sweat from his forehead. It was not

comforting to hear Cabrill express uncertainty about artwork. "Barren cells. That doesn't sound like paradise."

Orliando struck. Austin countered. His foil bent a fraction and deflected the blow. They sparred along the confines of the lava ribbon. Narrower than a fencing strip but slightly wider than a wooden plank, it forced Austin to use his best form to stay balanced.

Facing the boy who looked like him, he advanced and retreated, advanced and retreated, along the linear space. It felt eerily like facing the practice dummy, only this opponent was more creative. He strained against his training, not going for easy hits away from the center of the chest. They would score points in competition but leave him open to serious slashing in this duel.

Orliando anticipated attacks to the vulnerable spot. He deflected Austin's blows with confidence but was cautious about moving in too close for strikes of his own. Agile, he handled his weapon well, but he shuffled his feet on the cramped slope, as if used to an open area where he could move in a full circle, as if the only swording he'd done had been nicks and jabs.

Austin made a feint to the right, as he often had on the plank, hoping to trick Orliando into a misstep; but his opponent held his line. With each block and each blow, he looked for a way to make a drive straight to the ornate emblem on Orliando's chest without getting skewered. *Take your time,* he told himself. But there was no time to spare.

A soft puddle under his back foot gave way. He slid onto a knee. Scalding heat pierced the tough fabric of his knickers. Orliando's blade sliced his cheek, leaving it damp and stinging. Austin blocked a second blow aimed at his head and struggled to his feet.

Orliando stepped back. "I know I'm going to win. I have

the pale hair and white clothing. I have the thin weapon, forged at great expense and effort, the only one of its kind. Far superior to your forgery." Austin swiped at the blood trickling from his wound, wanting to hit the shiny target more than anything.

Orliando attacked. Austin parried, deflecting the action then returning in a riposte. His duplicate blocked and managed a counter-riposte. Laser focused, Austin made a low lunge. A thought came from Skylar, *Drake.* His foil tip clanked against the mark of the Engineers Guild with clean precision. The charge surge through the two fencers, as if they were one.

Trembling, Orliando staggered. His brilliant braids darkened to the brown of ripe grain. Blue eyes flickered to a golden green. The rare weapon slipped from his hand into the soft metal at his feet.

Austin stared at a face suddenly longer, less angular and more mature than his own. Like the white uniform, the hair, eyes and features had been copied. The young man had transformed himself into the image in the art, thinking it would make him the champion in the prediction.

Sweat plastered a light brown braid in a curve around the stranger's face. He glared at Austin, quaking in disbelief. Suffocation gripped Austin as Orliando's thoughts flooded him with the smothering realization of failure. He had not captured this land. He had not siphoned its energy into his own world. His extraordinary efforts and the great risks he'd taken had gained him nothing. Ambition had lured him into this dangerous action and betrayed him. Revenge against superiors who laughed at him, against those who wronged him in so many ways, remained a dream. He was meant to rule planets. Now that future crumbled to dust.

Now that's the very *real stuff,* came a thought from Skylar with an echo from Cabrill.

Austin's mind swam in a chasm-deep sadness, the pain so strong he could barely move. Torment and darkness, bone freezing cold, stomach twisting hunger. Loneliness. He wouldn't, couldn't, force anyone to return to such misery. *Orliando,* he said, not knowing he spoke with his mind. *I'm closing the stiav. We're going to make sure it can't be opened again. When that happens, which side of it do you want to be on?*

"The dam is undone!" Po shouted.

Austin turned behind him to where Po pointed. A pool of lava had built up against Skylar's pile of decaying amphibians and seaweed. The pressure inched the barricade along the chute. Skylar slogged down the slope and blocked it with the tip of her sword. The clot broke apart into scaly skin, brittle bones and limp leaves that flowed around the wood. Released, the molten ajrief rolled faster down the trough, carrying remnants of the dam with it. Blue-gray syrup embedded with strands of seaweed dripped over the end in a long stretch. Cooling as it fell, it formed a thread for the rest of the stream to follow. Liquid metal crawled down the shaft, spread across the withered sedge carpeting the lakeshore and oozed into the earth.

CHAPTER 58

Cabrill clung to a rope on the tilted platform that swayed beside the strange bridge. She felt the soft land absorbed the ajrief. She felt the metal reach out to the thousand underground tendrils sent by Saffrian's gem to receive it. Energy surged through the silvery connection from world to world. The engines whispered to one another in a language from before the Separation.

She felt Orliando straighten with new breath and snatch up his fallen weapon. Lacey strands clung to it and rolled along the blade. He gave an angry shake to the side. Droplets fell into the lake like rain. "Our worlds are rejoined. And both are mine."

A revelation trembled through Cabrill, stronger than any quake she'd ever felt at Tarafalla. Austin could never defeat the invader. The weapon he held, which she had drawn over and over, for all its wonderful and strange properties, was not the right weapon. The brother would be defeated. And next would be the sister.

CHAPTER 59

The hearth keeper stood in the hall outside Mikol's door. Again she tried to coax him into unlatching it by described the wonderful meal she'd brought him.

Mikol heard her only as a distant whine. The ovals he'd drawn on his wall glowed with his artistry. As the earth quaked, he stretched his hands toward them. He leaned forward and pressed his palms against the gems, feeling them pulse in unison, feeling his heart match their beat.

CHAPTER 60

Grand Master Liaty Nobian called for wood and his tools. He'd carved nothing for months. Now the compulsion to create consumed him. Forliani thought his sudden inspiration was meant to annoy her. And it succeeded. She sent Cheche to the village with a wagon for a block of a certain size while she arranged the grand master's knives, gouges, and chisels, as if she were a mere apprentice.

This will change, she told herself. *When the gem in the round room strengthens and I wield its power, this will change.*

CHAPTER 61

Cheche pulled the little rumbly wagon to the wood smith's cottage. He knew rock better than wood; but since the chunk was for the Grand Master of the Artists Guild, he was sure the Master Smith would pick out a nice grain that carved well.

Along the way he snatched up a flat stone and tossed it into the slatted bed. Then he grabbed a pebble of just the perfect roundness. And there was another that seemed right. Right for what, he wasn't sure. He thought they could be, should be, must be, stacked and balanced in a certain way. He needed more stones. How good that he had a wagon to put them in.

CHAPTER 62

The tea chest sat open on the guild master's desk. Sadly, it was empty. Jomaray had not bothered to deliver the second-to-last compressed ball of pungent leaves to Cook himself but had sent it with Keep's youngest daughter.

What was left of the very last sphere, so like a miniature world, steeped in a large pot on the table beside him. Angling his favorite chair so it faced the open window, he inhaled the sharp fragrance, feeling the blissful properties of the tea. He refilled a tall, fluted cup depicting a great wave sinking a galleon, drowning all on board. Unfortunately, the ship was already at sea when the artist created it.

He sat and sipped, holding the liquid in his mouth until the bitterness mellowed. The calm seeped deep into him. He swallowed and sipped again. The window framed a plain courtyard that an abundance of potted plants had not improved. But now the paving stones, tiled benches and lacquered urns glowed with reflected scarlets and golds laced with blues and silvers, making it beautiful.

A flood of tea had been forced on the inhabitants of Tranquility House with little success. In a frenzy of creativity, the artists had organized a nude interpretive dance where they tossed about bright streamers like flames. Master Romielnsaokr had seen no harm in it. Then someone had decided that instead of paper the spectacle needed real fire. And so the building burned while its unclothed, former residents cavorting around it.

Jomaray was glad he didn't have a view of the actual flames. They would be harsh and angry. He simply couldn't tolerate harsh and angry. He would explain the situation to Grand Master Liaty Nobian in a letter in which he would also demand the return of the chamapl and the servant boy Cheche. Now that the lad had been stolen from him, Jomaray would never forget his name.

And he would demand a new colony to oversee. One in a city. At a lower elevation. With a warmer climate.

But that would be later. At the moment the glow from the fire was nice. And he still had half a pot of tea.

CHAPTER 63

Something happened. Skylar's medallion bounced around like a pet on a leash. Not that she'd every had a real pet, and she would never put it on a leash if she did. She stopped trying to coax the sludge sliding down the chute into a wall with the tip of her sword. Only closing the stiav could break the connection now. She looked for help to Po and Cabrill on the raft hanging from the rigging. Po swayed the platform back and forth, but couldn't reach the bridge.

Austin and Orliando blocked her path to the portal. Recovered from Austin's blow, Orliando seemed faster, more animated, as if the energy pulsing under his feet gave him new strength. Skylar felt the power too, but didn't know what to do with it. It was probably the same for Austin. Her brother was getting his butt kicked. She felt the sting of his bleeding cheek and the strain of fending off attack after attack from the brown-haired guy who no longer looked like his twin. He deflected each slashing, piercing strike but struggled to find an opening for his own attack. Ajrief stuck to his shoes, making his footwork sluggish.

Cabrill was trying not to broadcast her fear for Austin, but the artist might as well be blasting it from a satellite. Skylar wondered if she could at least erode Orliando's smugness and confidence. She thought hard, *Orly, you couldn't sneeze your way out of a nruken slug.*

Puzzlement bounced back at her. Their exchanged thoughts were more emotion than language, but Orliando needed more context to get her message. She sent him a gross image of the tissue-thin slug's interior dripping with boogers, and a cartoon Orliando letting loose a tiny sniff.

Angered, Orliando stabbed. Austin barely countered in time.

Okay. That didn't work. Wrong approach. Skylar pelted him with echoes from his own memories of the sparse, freezing cell he'd huddle in, alone and hungry. He shivered and struck out savagely.

Stop helping, Austin mentally yelled at her.

How could she not help? She tried to make her mind a blank. She'd never been thought-free in her life. Her head was always crammed full. How could she not think!

Orliando charged. Austin deflected the blow. Blade scraped across blade. They clenched together, face to face. Orliando gave a mighty shove with his muscle and his mind.

Skylar watched her brother soar to the side, arms and legs flailing. In a panic, she felt him grab at the energy amplified by his necklace, turning his wild thrashing into a slo-mo aerial ballet. He dropped from sight over the side of the bridge. Skylar cringed at the splush as he plunged into the shallow lake. "Austin?" she screamed along with Po and Cabrill. *Austin?*

I'm okay, he sent. But he wasn't. He hurt all over.

Skylar trudged up the ramp toward Orliando. He chuckled. "You are in none of the images."

"Predictions," Skylar said, "they don't always tell you what you need to know." So what if she wasn't in any of the art on his side of the gate. They weren't on that world. They were on Saffrian and she was in plenty of it here. But that didn't matter either. She was part of this, whether or not she was woven into a tapestry or spray painted on a barn. She clutched her wooden sword. The tip sparkled with a coating of ajrief that stuck to it from her efforts to repair the dam. If she could coat the whole thing—

Her opponent leveled his weapon at her. There was no time.

Po put his weight against the platform, swinging it closer to the rigging's support beam. Clutching a rope she might never be able to let go of, Cabrill closed her eyes to the swaying scenery. Mniadd surrounded her like vapor. It brushed against her skin and gripped her wrist. She inhaled it with every gasped breath, infusing it into her blood.

The boy, Austin, was defeated.

Orliando, follower of the old enemy the First Exile. Enslaver. Abuser. Selfish. Cruel. He would slay Skylar. In his mind he already celebrated his triumph.

Cabrill screamed at the image of her fierce friend defending herself with a wooden stick no more protective than the sword in Skylar's crude sketch tacked to the bucket on top of the spiked tower.

Cabrill pictured the lines and length of the blade that should be. Slightly broader. Edges keen. Point deadly. A warrior's weapon. A champion's weapon.

Cabrill fashioned the sword in her thoughts. Glittering and blue-gray, it formed in her mind as if it had always been there expecting her to call it forth.

ngines joined together. Two worlds united in power.

Orliando gloated. He would slice through this child, stride down the path he had built for himself, and take possession of this land. She was nothing. Less than nothing. Just a little girl in counterfeit braids not yet sword age.

Child? Skylar shot back at him. *Little girl!* "You don't have to work so hard at making me ultra-angry," she said using a mix of Lynawic and English. "I'm already riding that rocket."

She could hear Austin sloshing about in the lake of dead fish, fearfully calling her name. She didn't answer or take her eyes from her adversary. Orliando would carve her stick to toothpicks—they both knew it—but she could keep him busy.

She thought only about nruken slugs, not about Po behind Orliando, swinging ever closer to the bridge. She'd give him time, as much as possible. Maybe she could surprise arrogant Orly with a jab to the—

Ajrief suddenly swirled at her feet, forcing her a step backward. A thread rose up against gravity. The liquid climbed and lengthened into a spire, a spike, a stiletto. It flattened, forming crisp edges. The base thickened and rolled into a hilt.

A weapon hovered in the air, beckoning, a thing of deadly beauty.

Skylar didn't hesitate or question. She had come to Saffrian weaponless. She had borrowed a sword. She had stolen a sword.

With every cell in her being she knew that this one, fresh and pristine, was hers and hers alone.

She tossed aside the rough wooden stick and wrapped her gloved hand around the metal grip. It molded to her touch as if it had been waiting for her imprint.

Orliando scowled. "You have no skill with mniadd. How did you—?"

"It just came to me," Skylar said. She filled her mind with slugs, not the view in her peripheral vision of Po anchoring the platform to the rigging and jumping onto the bridge. Not Cabrill wanting to rush down the ramp and attack Orliando from behind. The heat would cripple her before she reached him.

Protect Po, Skylar sent softly to her friend. She kept it simple since Orliando received the thought too. Cabrill would understand the full message: Protect Po so he can close the portal.

Skylar circled the tip of her sword ever so slightly to keep Orliando's attention. Her sword, belonging to no other. Crafted just for her. Cabrill's essence wafted from it like perfume. The balance was perfect. She knew her enemy was about to attack. And she was ready.

CHAPTER 64

A chilling wind blew as if it always had and always would. Icy dust swirled across the terrain, bleaching the land and sky white. Po had expected to be on a high precipice overlooking the landscape, as on the Saffrian side of the stiav. Instead, he and Cabrill stood on a flat plain. Whether a vast tundra at sea level or a high mountain sheered into a mesa, he couldn't tell.

He and Cabrill had jumped from the wooden raft onto the ledge jutting out from the bridge. Po had wanted to charge down the ramp and attack Orliando so he would not harm Skylar. "Trust her," Cabrill had said. "She has a sword worthy of her." He'd nodded, not understanding but having faith in both Skylar and Cabrill. Something had passed among the two girls, Austin, and Orliando. Po was not sensitive to mniadd, as it seemed they were. In the time before the Separation, he would have been one of the many who became prey for predators who used the power only for themselves.

Cabrill held her sword ready, but no creatures confronted them in the bleak landscape. Po inhaled brittle air and took in the wonder of it. For the second time he'd taken a few short strides and suddenly been on another planet. He wished he had time to absorb the experience, but there was a task to be done quickly. And it was colder than cold.

Po pulled his sleeves over the knuckles of his freezing hands. "It appears no one has been here in all of eternity." But he knew that wasn't so. This was a brutal world that swept aside footprints. He wrapped his cape around him and began examining the portal.

It seemed stiavs could be in any form. On Callister they were made of stones. The one in the swamp was entwined trees. Po suspected the guardian hovering over the lake was invisible when inactive, like the gateway in the meadow. Otherwise, even deep in a forest, a cave entrance hanging in the sky would have been investigated. On this side the opening was outlined by thick frost studded with crystal bursts dulled with soot, fanning out from a portrait of the Saffrian forest.

Po probed the hills and valleys of the device. Ice stung his fingertips like angry insects. He found neither key nor the recess of the lock.

From the shelter of her hood, Cabrill scanned the frozen world. Attempting to shield herself from the energy that flooded through her was like trying to hold her breath, but she couldn't reject it anyway any more than she could stop breathing. She embraced it to stay connected to what was happening at the lake.

As if the emotions were her own, she knew Austin's torment as he searched for a way to reach his sister. She felt Skylar's delight in the sword, sensed the sweat dripping from her chin, witnessed the focus and resolve as she battled Orliando.

Cabrill didn't understand how she had shaped the blade for Skylar, but she knew the cuff that Mikol had clamped upon her wrist had helped her form it. The metal warmed her in this frigid landscape. It sang to the pulsing power around her. There had been no opportunity to examine it before. Now she saw it was not the bronze he had crafted himself. It was ajrief. And it felt old. Older than old, as Po might say. It curved comfortably against her skin, as if it belonged exactly where it was. How had impoverished Mikol come to own something so ancient and valuable? And what had compelled him to give it away?

Strange, if she hadn't been wearing a gift meant for another girl, she wouldn't have been able to add her will to Skylar's so they could break Orliando's hold on Austin.

Gripped her cold sword, she glanced at Po wiping soot from the stiav frame with his cape. Then she peered through the white on white landscape, hoping nothing nasty hid in the blowing folds. Although icy pellets polished the plain in serpentine streaks, this was not an unmarked landscape, as Po thought.

Rubble formed low mounds that cast subtle shadows. Depressions, scooped clean of rock and frost, formed pools that roiled with a thousand shades of grays and blues filtered pale by blowing snow. Cut channels joined the ponds. Strips flanking each one held oily remnants that once burned but now frothed with thick flakes. It must have taken a hoard of flame-things working constantly to keep the liquid flowing. Prone carcasses, some still gripping push-plows, edged the frozen grooves.

The arteries connecting the pools were already dusted white. Without the fires, the churning ponds would soon become rigid and covered by a snowy veil. The canal from the last pool snaked past Cabrill through the portal and into the forest. Ryster said ajrief, once formed, could not be melted or cut. The two worlds were locked together forever. Closing the stiav was the only way to break the link.

"I believe I've found it," Po shouted into the wind. He pointed at the frame, where he'd partially exposed a dark object encased in crystals. He pulled a short knife from his sleeve, stiff fingers fumbling to grip the handle. "This is not like the other keys." He dug into the jagged surface, chipping around the object and working the tip under it. The icy prison shattered. A thick disk popped into his hand.

The view of the Saffrian forest surrounded by the icy frame flickered. A warning shook Cabrill. She shoved Po through the opening then bolted after him.

CHAPTER 65

Skylar battled Orliando across the metal bridge that swept up over the lake to the cave in the sky. She deflected his blows and gritted her teeth as he countered her attacks. She wanted to send Cabrill a message to hurry, but that seemed whiny, like she didn't appreciate the gift in her hand.

Cabrill's imagined blade rested perfectly in her grip, but it behaved differently from the foil she'd left behind on Callister. She didn't have the right moves in her muscle memory and had to concentrate *hard* on every step and flick.

This was not nicks and jabs, not cat jabs, not swording for sport. The goal was not points, but a world. Skylar aimed for different body parts, very much wanting to hurt Orliando enough to make him give up. The trick was to strike while still shielding herself.

Orliando laughed at her naive strategy. His blows packed a mental sting, almost a physical push like the burst he'd used to launch Austin into the air. She assaulted him with images of humungous, squishy slugs so she wouldn't broadcast her strikes. She tried to use the mniadd, blocking an attack with an extra energy-twist. Although not as strong as she hoped, the effort shoved up Orliando's arm, startling him and giving her an unexpected opening. His weapon did not have a guard to protect the hand. She sliced at his exposed fist, willing him to drop his blade. It was a great move. Unarmed, he would have to surrender.

Her sword glanced off. No! Had he done that with mniadd mojo? She didn't think so. He must have a really great glove.

Orliando lashed out a chilling fear-vibe that she cushioned through her medallion. She sensed it was less an attack and more a distraction, like her slugs. She prepared to defend against a stabbing lunge at her soft, fleshy self. Instead, he smashed the sharp edge of his weapon against hers.

He was copying her! Trying to disarm her, as she'd tried to do to him.

Hey, get your own ideas.

She would never let anything dislodge the sword from her hand. She knew it. The sword knew it. Orliando knew it but wouldn't give in.

Again his blade flashed toward hers, the same silvery blue-gray as the bridge. She blocked the clumsy move. He'd done a lot of swording, but not with *that* sword. *So you've got a new weapon too.* Unfamiliar with its balance, he struggled to switch to the new strategy. "Your blade doesn't like you," Skylar taunted.

"It doesn't have to," Orliando said. "It just has to do what I want, when I want."

You're fighting two battles, she thought at him. *One against your weapon, and one against me.*

Her blade was a partner, an extension of herself. So different from Orliando's and yet it was the same, from sharp point to keen ajrief edges. She stepped back, suddenly understanding the change in his attack. He *was* trying to disarm her, but not by knocking the weapon from her hand.

Ajrief cuts ajrief. She practically shouted it. Orliando scowled and advanced. She met his sword with the edge of her blade—and failed. She needed to get the proper slant to slice through the other weapon.

She swung and slashed and swung again, seeking the perfect angle, blocking his attempts to do the same. Only the energy pulsing through her medallion and her sword kept her from giving in to exhaustion.

Past Orliando's shoulder the portal crackled and flashed. Po and Cabrill appeared and jumped to the ledge, shedding a flurry of snow. The bridge trembled and heaved in a great sigh. Skylar spread her arms, staggering for balance.

Orliando stumbled. Anger flamed across his face. He charged at Skylar with a great roar.

With all the strength left in her, she swept her blade upward against the sudden attack.

Metal on metal rang like a shattered bell. A glittering shaft soared free and tumbled through the air. Skylar watched it arc and dive into the shallow water, piercing the lakebed. The severed end showed above the surface like frozen lightning.

Drake.

Skylar pointed the lethal tip of her sword at the emblem on Orliando's costume, knowing she could cut through it if she chose. "This is where you surrender. Toss what's left of your weapon over the side."

Orliando stared at the useless stub he now held. Shock flooded his eyes. "I greatly regret that I am unable to do as you command." He turned his gloved hand to show her. "While sparring with your brother, I thoughtlessly grabbed my fallen sword from the stream of ajrief." Cold silver covered the hilt and spread over his glove, bulging between his fingers like frozen icing. "I am unable to release my grip. It appears I will carry this broken weapon forever." He gave a twisted smile. "Do not think this resolves the prediction." He turned to flee back to his home world. He stopped and stared at the empty sky. The portal had closed and vanished. There was nowhere for him to go.

CHAPTER 66

Master Artist Calbran Coriadler dangled against a cliff face from a frayed rope. Naked, except for pots of foul-smelling paint in various whites, blues, and smoky grays circling his waist, he held a scrap of his old shirt soaked in a silvery tone.

The same hue was scrubbed onto the stone in front of him. Far below, hopro and the rocks around them sparkled with drippings from his rag. The animals shook themselves and bleated in protest.

Calbran had a vague dream-memory of purposely putting himself in this startling and terrifying situation.

He had no idea how to get out of it.

CHAPTER 67

The room appeared to be used for nothing in particular, which meant it was decorated with cast-off items and was made available to troublesome guests. Narrow windows faced the forest. The angry dark cloud, once billowing like a shaken blanket, had dissipated into a streaked sky. Mikol wanted to take it as evidence that Cabrill and her friends, who apparently did not include him, had been successful. It could just as easily mean the opposite.

Behind him the door opened, bringing the fragrance of hot cider. Without looking, he knew the servant boy delivering it kept his eyes on the floor as he had been taught, while absorbing the atmosphere like a sponge. Forliani fussed over Cheche, as if he were special to her. Mikol had seen that act before. She would stab the child in the heart if she gained from it. She didn't sense the lad's eager intelligence weaving through the room, strong as the scent of cider, as Mikol did.

"Mikol," Forliani said when she was done praising Cheche for pouring her a cup without slopping over the rim, "Grand Master Liaty asked you to join us because he's very worried about Cabrill's welfare. He stopped work on an important new carving so we could meet."

"Yes, I'm very worried," Liaty said as if his thoughts were elsewhere. "Very worried."

"We both are," Forliani said, "and I'm sure you share our concern."

The invitation had been in Liaty's name, but Mikol knew it was actually a command from Forliani. The massive drawing that covered the walls of his room needed no more lines or color, but he ached to stay in its presence. Only possible news of Cabrill had pried him from his masterpiece. He needn't have been anxious about leaving it. Although rooms away, it stayed with him, pulsing through the manor house like music.

"It's obvious His Lordship cannot be persuaded to send more soldiers to protect her, so we must find an alternative," Forliani said.

Mikol guessed she and Liaty had been banished from the council room for insisting Kriken continue to chase the fugitives. Was she trying to get him to volunteer to go into the scary, dangerous forest? She didn't know he'd already been there.

His encounter with Cabrill had been a disaster. When he'd entered the clearing, he'd known it was the artist and not the girl. As he'd delivered the item from Shu, part of him had hoped to go with her, even though he understood he was not really part of this journey. Not in the same way as the others. But he hadn't expected her to treat him like an enemy.

Cabrill *must* survive whatever was in the forest. She must. It would crush him if she was gone—if that had been their final time together.

Cheche placed a small table beside him and set a cup on it. Mikol watched the sky and infused hope into the absence of the menacing cloud. *I never should have left her. I should have stayed.*

A quake traveled through him. He turned from the window. "Did you—"

Did you feel something? he wanted to ask. *Or rather, did you stop feeling something?*

Liaty blinked several times and looked around as if confused about where he was. Cheche raised startled eyes to the window then quickly lowered them.

"You have a suggestion?" Forliani asked as if she felt nothing unusual.

Mikol recovered and flashed a smile. "Did you notice the black cloud is gone?"

Forliani rushed to a window. Liaty and Cheche stayed still.

Mikol felt his masterpiece fall quiet. He was exhausted and suddenly starving. There was no food in the room. He reached for the cider Cheche had brought him and noticed three pebbles stacked next to the cup.

CHAPTER 68

A barrier rose in the empty sky at the severed bridge where the portal had been. Or rather where it still was, invisible. Cabrill hauled up another raft full of branches Po had collected and tied the rope to the rigging. Using the crook left by the once-flaming rodder, she hooked the off-center post, pulled the platform to the ledge, then secured it with a looped cord she'd set up.

Austin scraped sluggish metal up the slope with a plow retrieved from the rod-creature graveyard in the lake. He deposited the mushy pile at the top for Ryster to add to the slab he built over the unseen stiav. Cabrill tucked a bundle of wood into Austin's bent arm. He trudged down the bridge to a small blaze that kept the last of the metal syrupy.

The master smith worked the goo with improvised tools. Cabrill marveled at the agile way the large man went back and forth between the ledge on one side of the invisible opening and the cooled, flattened area on the other side, never stepping in the warm sludge. She handed him a stick. He stuck it in the growing barricade.

"And I wonder how a body would craft as fine a skiv as you created, Master Artist," Ryster said, referring to the ajrief sword. He seemed happy to be working the rare metal, even though he was just slapping up a free-standing partition braced with twigs. "Walk the length of Tarafalla naked to learn that trick."

"I'd tell you if I knew," Cabrill said. She remembered the thrill of pulling the elegant shape into the air as if she freed a sculpture from marble. In that moment her art had shifted from showing the future to being the present.

She craved more of the excitement and wonder of it, but it was gone, leaving her drained, as if nourishment had vanished from the air. At Po's prompting, she'd tried to raise the ajrief wall herself and failed. The energy was too weak now. No longer strong enough to fashion swords with her thoughts. As days passed it would evaporate until it was nothing. Although empty at its loss, she was glad to be released from a dangerous power she desired but did not want.

Skylar and Austin were still present in her mind. Without so much as a glance, she knew exactly where they were, but their thoughts had dimmed to vague impressions. She could no longer silently speak to them as before. That was good. The mind should stay a private place.

She'd been wrong, so very wrong, about what her art showed. Austin was not the singular hero she'd thought she saw in her work. True, he was brave and important, but his foreign weapon had not defeated Orliando. Created on Saffrian, the victorious blade had formed from her own vision, not to save a world but to save a friend.

What else, who else, had she been blind to in her own art? In her own life?

On shore tied to a half-dead tree, Orliando clutched the blunted shaft of the broken sword he could not release. He tried unsuccessfully to undo Po's specials knots one-handed. With what was left of his weapon, he poked at the ropes, but the blade was only a rough stub with no edge. Cabrill deflected the images of them setting him free and becoming his adoring followers that he blasted out with great effort.

"We're ignoring you," Skylar yelled at Orliando. She was on the other side of the bent tree, swinging her new sword at the thread of ajrief hanging from the chute to the ground. "Oooff!"

Clink.

"You're supposed to be guarding him, not messing around," Austin called from the bridge.

"I can break it," Skylar shouted.

"You don't have to," Austin yelled.

"Just in case," Skylar said.

"Just in case someone chisels their way through Ryster's thick, uncuttable wall?" Austin said.

"Not completely uncuttable," Skylar said. "Ahh-*ahh!*"

Clink.

"Needs a slanting blow," Ryster bellowed.

"I know that," Skylar yelled.

Clink.

"I looked to our friend's stump," Ryster said. "Not so much sliced as shattered, such as be done sometimes with sound. Don't see the like of it much with metal, but it be known. And I wonder if young Skylar be well skilled or kissed by luck."

"Some of both," Cabrill said.

Using a splinter from one of the plows he'd broken down to make tools, Ryster etched the symbol for the Smiths Guild followed by his own mark at the top of the vertical slab. He looked at the finished barrier and the bridge, shaking his head. "What I could do with the scrapes and scraps if I had my kit."

Cabrill lowered the raft then hauled it back up with Po on

it, so he could admire the smith's work. "Wonderful!" Po said. "A monument to stand forever."

"Forever be long," Ryster said. "Don't know if there be enough drippings to that unnatural island you think is under us to keep this rig stable. And there be quakes. Whole bridge could shift in a wink. A gale could blow. Too many birds could perch on my cloud-plaque here and tilt the whole of it like a board on a fulcrum."

"Let us hope none of that happens," Po said. He called to Austin, who tended the last of the fire. "My friend, could you manage to get me one last glob?" He turned to Ryster. "Might I impose on you for a small project?"

Cabrill hoped the fat disk Po had pried from the frame of the stiav in the frozen world was securely tucked away in a deep pocket. Po had confided in her that it was a mechanical device, not an original key but a counterfeit. Had Orliando built it or had someone else? Could that someone on the other side build another?

And where was the real key?

For Saffrian's sake, Ryster's wall had better last forever.

Austin pushed the last bit of pliable sludge up the ramp for the extra thing Po had Ryster working on. He didn't care if the barrier stood for a few days or centuries. It only had to hold until he and Skylar were gone. A selfish thought, but he was too worn out to think of anything but home.

Skylar danced and twirled with the new blade. She saluted the thin, silvery line stretching from the bridge to the ground. She circled her wrist in little flicking motions, preparing for her attack. The beautiful creature in her hand was, and always would be, hers.

CHAPTER 69

Tiny yellow blooms dotted the meadow, looking like specks of mirror reflecting warm sunlight. Po stood among the flowers examining the mechanism he'd recovered from the icy stiav. A little larger than his palm and three times as thick as a finger, the disk was filled with concentric circles inscribed with runes around a central mark. They seemed similar to the tumblers in the intricate locks on the Lian archives. He reasoned the symbols were set in a certain pattern to control the portal he'd gotten it from. All he had to do was change them to the unique combination for the stiav hidden here. Simple.

Alas, no. With so many runes, the variations were almost infinite. Finding the right pattern seemed impossible, yet he clung to the belief that he could do it. He shifted the outermost ring by one rune. He waved the device about and took a few steps. No doorway appeared.

He pulled a blue-gray wafer from one of his many pockets. and swept it over his head. Parchment thin, the twisted parallelogram of cut outs and bumps produced the same result. Nothing.

Alas, he was in a chasm of trouble and it was getting deeper. Lian Sunang Shu had summoned him to Astlia to tell him herself how angry she was that he'd renounced his family and shared Lian secrets. He was to bring Cabrill, the boy, and the girl, so they could be interrogated. She refused to accept his voluntary resignation from the clan and would instead punish him with expulsion.

The message didn't exactly say all that, but he knew his Gram, who wasn't his Gram anymore. She would never acknowledge the honor and necessity of his act. He'd cracked open the family vault and scattered its contents before those who were not blood. He could never beg for forgiveness. And Gram Shu would never grant it.

The idea rolled around in his head that he could negotiate his way back into Gram Shu's tolerance with the brilliant machine he struggled to decipher. Or he might use it to bargain for a position with his first-name family, the Ko clan. Even if it never controlled a stiav again, it brought the promise of knowledge. And knowledge always had value.

What would his life be as a disgraced member of the Lian clan? Or as an outcast begging for a position with the Ko?

Maybe he'd grown too independent to function within either of the rival families.

Being Po, and only Po, wasn't as frightening as it once would have been.

He moved the ring to the next rune. No stiav appeared. Alas. The excellent word made him even more heartbroken. He was incapable of planning anything beyond this field. His Azure Lady was leaving. Because it was her wish, he would make it happen for her if he could. But his life would never be as bright again.

Standing in the meadow where Skylar had fallen into her world and her life, Cabrill dreaded the sorrow that would eventually fill the emptiness. Her fury of the past years had burned away and left a hollow place.

No images compelled her to give them form. No creative frenzy gripped her. No color, line, shape, or shade drove the future, including her own. She closed her eyes and saw nothing. It was a strange freedom. When grief at the loss of her friend finally seeped in, she would not resist.

CHAPTER 70

Skylar and Austin sat in the grass on a gentle hill, watching Po stomp about. "Too far to the right," Skylar whispered. Austin dug into his sling bag, pretending to rearrange the gifts from their friends, Lord Kriken, and the Wasbiln villagers around his carefully wrapped foil. Most of the items were for Skylar, who insisted she couldn't carry another thing. Her pack was stuffed with her new sword encased in an extra thick sheath from Ryster, presents, things she insisted she couldn't leave behind, and pastries from a baker who wanted her to stay and marry his son.

His usually carefree baby sister was heart-heavy sad to leave. She wouldn't talk about it. She wouldn't talk about anything since their last exchange, which was almost a fight. He felt his medallion rolled up in his white fencing knickers. A patch of ajrief stuck to one of the knees from when he'd slipped while battling Orliando. He could try the mind link with Skylar, but he didn't want to share his head with anyone ever again. Telepathy was too close and immediate. Some thoughts should be only for yourself. He didn't know how Cabrill had mentally joined them. Must be a part of her artistic ability, like the flying drawings.

The ajrief connection probably wouldn't work anymore anyway. The engine hidden on Saffrian was alone again, unable to produce more than a whiff of mniadd. And they were far from the concentration of the bridge that now went to nowhere.

Skylar would be fine once she was back on Callister. Austin stood to get a better view of Po pacing with Cabrill following. There better be enough energy still floating around to operate the portal. Po seemed confident he could figure out the complicated gizmo.

Austin wasn't so sure. He wiped nervous sweat from his forehead and scratched at the welt on his cheek. The slash and the blistering on his knee had almost healed, thanks to the amazing Yeawoche salve left over from treating Skylar's burns.

They'd left Orliando in Kriken's care. How many years of labor in the quarry should the guy be sentenced to for trying to enslave all of Saffrian? Yeti Beard and the other fossils argued over ways to free the prisoner's ajrief-stiffened hand. Ryster had offered some thoughts, which were ignored. The advisors seemed more interested in discussing the problem than in finding a solution.

Ryster had smothered Austin and Skylar in great hugs when they'd said their good-byes. With Skylar's sculpture dismantled and the forest safe, the market for swords had fallen. "Wouldn't know how to be rich anyway," Ryster had bellowed. "Good friends be better than coin." He'd borrowed tools from Kriken's quarry and traveled back into the forest, hoping to chip Orliando's broken blade from the stone lakebed. He and Po had made some deal about its ownership. And something else had gone on between them. Po had allowed no one except himself to assist the master smith while he'd toiled at the special project on the bridge.

"What's that other thing Po's got?" Austin hoped that would pry a respond from his sullen sister.

"We're not supposed to know about it," Skylar said.

"It's hard to miss with him swinging it around like that." Austin watched the sun glide across the shape that was familiar yet different. "Po lied! He had the key the whole time."

"Laser brain," Skylar said. "Your thoughts only go in a straight line."

"I'm looking at the evidence," Austin insisted.

"What would I do," Skylar said quietly, "if I negotiated a tough deal to borrow a hyper-special object. And I have it in my hand. And it's super important, especially to a friend. And her brother. And it is absolutely the only one in existence. And I know I have to return it, and I'll never be able to touch it again, not in the lifespan of a star. Because I have to give it back, because I said I would. And a promise is super important too. What would I do?"

"Make a copy," Austin said. "It's sort of against the promise, but maybe you have to."

"I can't. I don't have the right material."

"I get it," Austin said. "You make a mold. And when you happen to come across a river of bluish goo, you ask your friend the metal smith for a favor."

"That's what I'd do," Skylar said. "Even though having the thing to make the thing could get me into latrine-level trouble."

"So now you own this illegal duplicate of the most important object to your dearest friend." Austin studied the sadness in his sister's face. "Or maybe it's only the most important thing to your dearest friend's brother."

Skylar flipped her braid over her shoulder. Having defeated

Saffrian enemy number one, she felt entitled to wear her trophies whenever she chose. "Jettison your angst, drama cadet. The copy won't work. It doesn't have the same guts as the original. Like Orliando. When he first showed up, he looked like you, but he wasn't you."

"Because we have different guts." Austin remembered seeing Cabrill at the fountain, so like Skylar yet not. He would never mistake anyone else for his sister again. He would know her in any form. If she suddenly became a giant gob-spitting beast, he would recognize her in a dozen ways—mostly by the accuracy of her gob spitting. "Cabrill didn't predict *two* guys in fencing whites."

Skylar dug in her pack under her ruined footgear. Encrusted with solidified ajrief that could never be removed, the unwearable shoes were now souvenirs. She pulled out a cylinder of parchment, unrolled it, and placed it in the soft green foliage.

Austin knelt beside her and looked at the drawing of the boy in a fencing uniform, tipping his sword in salute to an unseen adversary. It might have been him—or Orliando—or the fencing dummy—ready to perform motions programmed by the events on this world before he'd even arrived. Except it hadn't felt like pre-recorded destiny when he was going through it.

Skylar tapped the boy's face. "You can't blame Cabrill for thinking you were the designated hero. She didn't know she was getting blasted with a double dose—you and Orliando pretending to be you." She circled her finger around shapes of varying heights in the background. "Even if it's you, you're not alone."

Austin focused on marks that could have been trees or stones, no more than scenery to fill the page. Now he recognized them as Po, Ryster, Cabrill and Skylar. There was no single hero, but many champions.

A solitary slash flanked the other side of the fencer. Austin couldn't help himself. He stabbed at the smear. "I suppose that's Mikol, spying on us from the shadows like a predator."

The older guy had sent his little sister a present, an expensive-looking present, as if he were her *boyfriend*. Obviously Cabrill understood how inappropriate and creepy it was. She had pushed it at Skylar while Ryster and Po were busy on the bridge. Then she'd stalked away. Skylar had gone after her. There'd been a discussion with a lot of handwaving. Then suddenly it had morphed into a hug fest. With giggles.

Girls.

When Austin had quizzed Skye about it, she'd wrinkled up her nose, declaring the whole thing stupid, and Austin stupid, and Mikol slimy and stupid. That's when they almost had the fight. And they might almost have another one now.

"Mikol again!" Skylar said. "You are crazed by the guy."

"You kept the bracelet," Austin said.

"Cuff. It's a cuff. When the Yeawoche helped me, I thought Lawheleo said they had trouble finding me because I wasn't wearing the *didtl*, the cheese. He must have said I wasn't wearing the *dodtl*, the cuff. It didn't come from Mikol, you Urgorlia gnat. It came from the Yeawoche. Cabrill and I figured it out."

"So, Mikol was just delivery dude." Not a boyfriend. Austin's relief lasted only a moment. He suddenly realized his sister was being stalked by an entire community. One that had given her a strange tattoo and now a tracker. Good thing they would soon be on the other side of a portal.

"If slick, handsome, artist guy was going to give anyone a token of his affection," Skylar said, "it wouldn't be me."

Austin followed the tilt of her head to Cabrill, who stood in one spot while Po paced the meadow. Her art had prevented a catastrophe. Kriken had loudly praised her skill, forcing the Artists Guild to drape her with honors. She should be giddily dancing about; but she stared into the distance, as if she'd lost something precious. Po moved left, waggled the fake key, then fiddled with the round device. Maybe he was purposely delaying their departure, or maybe he couldn't see properly through his tears. He'd been sobbing almost non-stop since Austin declared they were leaving.

It appeared Skylar was right. The copied key was just a shell. And, as smart as Po was, he couldn't figure out the secret decoder ring. The meadow portal would never open. Austin thought through an alternate route. He was ready to slosh into the swamp, his sister slung over his shoulder if she wouldn't go on her own to the twisted-tree arch.

He'd trade the valuable ajrief sword for the key, even if he had to wrestle it away from Skylar. Or he'd challenge the leader of the mysterious subsurface creatures to a duel. What was fighting one water monster after he'd already defeated a bunch of flaming rods? At least there wasn't likely to be another mind-controlling, face-changing, power-mad egotist among the Droombians.

He took a deep breath and relayed a non-violent version of his plan to Skylar. She listened quietly. Then tears trickling down her cheeks. "I don't want to go home at all. I miss Mom and Dad and everything, but I really, truly, deep in my heart, don't want to go home."

Austin sat back on his heels, stunned and silent. Now that she'd said it out loud, he had to accept it as true. He should remind her their parents waited in agony. He should say they didn't belong here; it wasn't their world. He should tell her lies about their bright and exciting future on Callister. He should, but he couldn't.

Skylar rose, grabbed her pack, and tramped through the fragrant grass to her friends. She directed Po to a large cluster of flowers bursting from the fertile ground. A patch of air quivered and flashed with splintered light. The dusty arena on Callister shimmered like a frameless painting.

Austin snatched up his bag and rushed after his sister, feeling as if he'd been doing so most of his life. He hastily shook hands with Cabrill and Po. He'd taught them the custom, but they found it awkward. Cabrill, the extraordinary artist, wouldn't look at the face that had obsessed her for so very long. Po, his enthusiastic language teacher, could not speak. Austin was shocked he had to fight back his own tears. He straightened the strap of his sling bag and patted the bulk to feel his foil safely tucked inside.

Skylar had already hugged her friends and said good-bye a dozen times. Now she did so again. She grasped Cabrill as if she would never let go. Po held the round mechanism toward the portal in his cupped hand like a precious bird. He should be ecstatic that he'd gotten the incomprehensible device to work, but he looked as if his world was about to vanish. He tugged the older girl from Skylar's arms. Cabrill couldn't hold on to Skylar forever so she clung to Po.

Austin brushed away his tears. They had to go home. They had to. He gestured for Skylar to go first. She stooped to pluck a yellow blossom. With a sigh she tucked it into her dark braid.

The desert image sparked in a spiderweb of crackling light. Skylar stepped through the portal. Austin followed. Their voices, in unison, echoed back to the meadow.

"Drake."

ACKNOWLEDGMENTS

You can't understand the chaos and order of fencing tournaments unless you've been there. I'm not talking about a match between two fencers on a clean, formal, raised piste that you see during the Olympics. I mean a gymnasium crammed with simultaneous bouts on narrow rectangles marked off with tape and snaking with electrical cords.

You're surrounded by motion, with white-clad bodies propelling pointed metal. You're in a hurricane of sound punctuated by uncoordinated buzzes from scoring boxes as weapons connect with their targets. Sometimes a blade snaps and tumbles through the air. "Heads up!" But it's too late to protect yourself if the shaft happens to be plummeting toward you.

My thanks to Matt Clausen and Aaron Clausen for introducing me to the fencing world and for providing expertise. I would also like to thank the Missoula Fencing Association for keeping my inspiration fresh.

MEET THE AUTHOR

DANITH McPHERSON writes science fiction, fantasy, and mysteries. In keeping with her Scottish heritage, she is a kilt maker and proudly wears McPherson tartan.

Her fantasy novels include *Monarch of Lightning*.

Her mystery novels feature sleuth Cassie Windom solving murders in Minnesota lake country.

Her short stories have appeared in *Asimov's Science Fiction Magazine, Amazing Stories,* and other places. You can find some of them in *Roar at the Universe*. The collection includes "Roar at the Heart of the World," which was selected for *The Year's Best Fantasy and Horror, Seventh Annual Collection*.

amazon.com/author/danith

goodreads.com/danith

facebook.com/DanithMcPherson

LEAVE A REVIEW

If you enjoyed *Blade of Mad Vision*, please leave a review on Goodreads and Amazon through the links below. Like most authors, I depend on reviews to help readers find my stories. Thank you for reading!

At Goodreads scroll down to "Write a review."

At Amazon scroll down to "Review this product."

AVERTED VISION

A Cassie Windom Mystery

Sometimes you have to look away to see murder clearly.

After a frightening tornado, a figure floats on the surface of Beauty Lake. Cassie swims out, desperately hoping the person is still alive.

If not, well, this isn't her first dead body.

Haunted by the vicious murder of her best friend by an abusive lover, Cassie Windom abandons her career in Los Angeles and flees back home to Minnesota.

She hopes to leave behind the guilt of a gruesome secret and to reshape her life. But escape is not as easy as changing geography, and a quirky small town is not the quiet retreat she expected.

Buy *Averted Vision* from Amazon

Buy *Averted Vision* from Barnes and Noble